LIVE A LITTLE

Live a Little

Howard Jacobson

JONATHAN CAPE
LONDON

1 3 5 7 9 10 8 6 4 2

Jonathan Cape, an imprint of Vintage Publishing,
20 Vauxhall Bridge Road,
London SW1V 2SA

Jonathan Cape is part of the Penguin Random House group of companies
whose addresses can be found at global.penguinrandomhouse.com

Penguin
Random House
UK

First published in the United Kingdom by Jonathan Cape in 2019

penguin.co.uk/vintage

A CIP catalogue record for this book is available from the British Library

ISBN (hardback) 9781787331433
ISBN (trade paperback) 9781787331440

Typeset in 12.25/15.25 pt Bembo Book MT Std by Jouve (UK), Milton Keynes
Printed and bound in Great Britain by Clays Ltd, Elcograf S.p.A.

Penguin Random House is committed to a sustainable future for our business,
our readers and our planet. This book is made from Forest Stewardship
Council® certified paper.

MIX
Paper from
responsible sources
FSC® C018179

For Mitnik, naturally

BOOK ONE

I

'Words fail me,' the Princess tells her son. She isn't sure which one.

'Why, Mother, what's happened?'

'Nothing's happened. Words fail me, that's all.'

'Is that what you rang to say?'

'I think you'll find,' she says, 'that it was you who rang me.'

She grips the corded telephone receiver as though she means to squeeze the breath from it. She has never touched anything gently in her life.

'No, that's not the case, Mother.' He too is a strangler, a cost-cutter by profession, and chokes a yawn, wanting her to hear the sleep in his voice. 'I would never have called you at two in the morning.'

'Don't exaggerate. It isn't two in the morning.'

'It feels like two in the morning. And I didn't ring you. Perhaps I should have, but I didn't. Anyway—'

'Anyway what?'

'What did you ring to say?'

'Stop showing your vest on television.'

'That must be Pen you're talking about. And I think he'd tell you it isn't a vest, it's a T-shirt.'

'Whatever it's called you should do your shirt up.'

'Tell Pen that, not me.'

'Who's Pen?'

'Your son.'

'You're my son.'

'You have more than one.'

'So which is he?'

'The parsonical one.'

'Then which are you?'

'The prodigal one.'

He knows she knows.

'Well I didn't bring any of you up to wear a vest on television,' she says.

'You didn't bring any of us up to be anarcho-syndicalists. My dear brother is making an ideological statement that is entirely his own.'

'By wearing a vest?'

'It's a T-shirt. The disaffected young are excited by the sight of an aged politician in a T-shirt.'

'Yes, now you come to mention it, I remember I was. Pen's father – it must have been his father, mustn't it? – had a whole wardrobe of vests. I called it his vestiary. He would throw his old ones on the bed and wait for me to wash them. Pen was conceived on a bed of vests, so I suppose I shouldn't be surprised.'

'Mother!'

'There's no reason for you to be squeamish. You were conceived in the back of a Rolls.'

'I am putting the phone down now if that's all you rang to say.'

'Don't *you* think vests are slovenly?'

'No, I think they're worse than slovenly, I think they're artful. They seduce the gullible. They did the trick with you, after all.'

'That's no way to talk to your mother. If that's all you rang to say . . .'

'I didn't ring you to say anything. You rang me.'

'I don't think so.'

But in truth the Princess doesn't choose to remember who rang whom.

★

She isn't a real princess. That's just a bit of fun she's having with herself.

The Princess Schweppessodawasser. Her real name – the name she

4

was born with – is Beryl Dusinbery. It never suited her to change it for a man. Princess Schweppessodawasser is, she says, her *nom d'oubli*, after the heroine of *One Thousand and One Nights*, whose actual name keeps sliding from her memory. *Schhh . . . you know who*. She had thought the reference might amuse her children – they are old enough to remember the 1960s advertising campaign – but nothing amuses her children. They blame her for that. 'You never permitted gaiety to enter our lives,' they remind her. 'It's a bit rich you thinking you can play with us now. Frankly, it's embarrassing. You are the least playful mother who ever lived.'

'I?'

'*I!* There you go. Any other mother would say "me".'

'In an age of derelictions I brought you up to express yourself correctly. You should be thankful you were born to a teacher and not a scullery maid.'

'What's a scullery maid?'

The Princess commends herself for not saying 'You married one'.

'Your ignorance vindicates my system,' she says instead. 'As I instructed my pupils in the higher things, so I instructed you.'

'We weren't your pupils, Mother . . .'

'I haven't finished speaking.'

'Is that you being playful again?'

'I never pretended to be playful. It's in the nature of fathers to look after that side of things.'

'Our fathers were never there.'

'That too is in the nature of fathers. But satisfy an old woman's curiosity. You say I was the least playful mother who ever lived. How many other mothers have you been brought up by?'

'It's a safe bet no other mother refused to read her children bedtime stories because she found them jejune. You actually used that word – *jejune*, for Christ's sake!'

'There you are – I gave you a word you still remember . . .'

'But can't use.'

'Then try moving in more educated circles.'

'I sit in the House of Lords, Mother.'

'You make my point for me.'

'Life isn't just words . . .'

'Yes it is. Life is only words.'

'It is also feelings.'

'Feelings! And what are feelings without the words to express them. You grunt until you have the word that tells you what you are grunting about. That's why pigs don't experience *Weltschmerz* or *nostalgie de la boue*.'

'How do you know they don't?'

'Because they never mention it.'

'When you grunt out of fear you know you are afraid. We never mentioned we were afraid. But we were.'

'Afraid because you were threatened or afraid because you were naturally timorous?'

'We never had the chance to find out. You put the fear of God in us from the moment we were born. You read us the Brothers Grimm and Struwwelpeter before we went to sleep – in German.'

'*Ich?*'

'*Dich!* I still wake screaming in the night because the Great Tall Tailor's coming to snip, snap, snip my thumbs off.'

'It was necessary to remind you of the dangers the Germans posed. I lost your father to them, remember.'

'That wasn't my father.'

'They were confusing times.'

'So are these. And you make them even more confusing when you decide suddenly to be light-hearted. You brought us up with a heavy hand and we'd prefer you to stay that way. It doesn't suit you to be coming over all girly suddenly.'

'Words fail me,' she said.

This isn't the record of an actual conversation with an actual child but the sum of many. Afterwards, her children regretted their harsh words. Mothers leave an oil slick of blame and guilt behind them. Even this mother. Yes, she had much to answer for – the absence in them of anything approaching a sense of the ridiculous, for one; the absence in their lives of anything approaching a father, for another:

the lack of an affectionate interest in one another's welfare; maybe even their steely drive originated in her. But she *was* ninety-something. You can't go on blaming your mother. And maybe if they had shown a little more affection to her – hard to imagine how that would have worked, but still . . .

She can tell when her children are having second thoughts. She senses the retraction coming and puts up a ringed hand to stop it. Snip, snap, snip. The next they'll be wanting to kiss her. The rings on her fingers, denoting all the hearts she'd stolen and never given back, act as a deterrent. '*Ne vous embêtez*,' she'll say, knowing how much her finishing-school French exasperates them.

That woman!

Well, can she blame them?

Can I blame them?

She/I. The Princess fears slippage. Then/now. Today/tomorrow. Me/her. Slip sliding away. Slip, slap, slip.

But she retains her unsmiling sense of the absurd. *Girly!* I have been called many things, but girly!

She wonders if she should take it as a compliment. Standing before a full-length mirror, she lets her hair down. The oldest girl in London.

Preposterous. Why, though, does she still have long hair?

Once she wore it in the style of Cleopatra. Her favourite character in all literature, when her favourite character in all literature isn't Medea. Cleopatra, Queen of the Nile, a woman too smart for any of the men who came calling on her. Which Medea wasn't quite. Medea let love for Jason emasculate her. *Emasculate?* Yes, emasculate.

The imputation that she might be seeking her children's favour is not something Beryl Dusinbery can take lying down. She has made mistakes but never the mistake of thinking she can beguile her way into her children's hearts. She knows her limits.

She pins her hair up again.

I know my limits.

★

7

Of limits themselves, she is coming to realise, there is no end. Who would have thought there were so many things to run out of? When she runs out of sugar there is a carer to get more for her. When she runs out of energy or gets lost in her own apartment there is a carer to help her navigate her way around it. But there is no one to help her when she runs out of words. Mislaying would be a better way of expressing it. One minute she has a word, then she hasn't. Where does it go? Rolled under the bed like the biscuits her day carer Euphoria brings her, balanced foolishly on the saucer of her tea cup? Or flown out of the bedroom window in her sleep? Because she definitely had the word before she closed her eyes.

She has slept with her window open ever since she came to London she doesn't know how long ago. Some time after the children – that'll do. After she didn't need a playroom for them. 'Them' meaning husbands as well as children. At first she opened it to listen to the hum of the city. She had lived in small unexciting towns in the company of small unexciting men for too long. She should have made the move earlier. The noise of the streets corresponded to the noise in her head. She had a city brain. But now her hearing has deteriorated it isn't the urban roar she hears. It's a lower, less purposeful end-of-summer drone, as of bees sipping their last, flies falling, the heat draining out of the day. I can hear the roses dying, she thinks, though she has only ever enjoyed tangential relations with flowers. *Tangential* – that's another moth of a word that fluttered out through her open window the minute she shut her eyes. Where to? All the way back to Tangiers?

So why doesn't she close the window? It's a good question. There's a word for why but she's mislaid it.

Names have been going for years. She would lose a person's name before she knew it. Couldn't listen to an introduction. Why not? Conservation, she thought. Sparing her brain for better things. But now the better things have gone too. The ideas she once entertained – all that's left of those is the immoderacy with which she entertained them. She can remember the inside of her anger. It lies like clothes spilled from a suitcase. But the suitcase itself is gone. As is the destination for which she packed it.

After people, things. What's that biscuit called? What was that place? Remembering Tangiers delighted her. But what was it a memory of? And then suddenly a word returns, for no other reason than that she can see the shape of it. *Otiosity* has just popped into her mind. The condition of being perfunctory. *Otiosity* she can play with on her tongue. Is it that, rather than its meaning – the condition of being perfunctory – that reminds her of someone to whose face she cannot put a name? And if he was perfunctory – he was definitely a he – why remember even this much about him? Will the otiose stick in the cobwebbed cellars of her mind longer than the important-to-her? Faces are hanging around longer. She wishes it were the other way around. At a pinch she could manage without faces. But names she needs. Sounds have always been more suggestive to her than sights. Names are the key to her past, and therefore to her continuance. Names root her. No names and there's just her spinning in space, seeing faces she doesn't want to see, a blurry gallery of the otiose. And what happens when her own name goes? Does she become otiose to herself?

What *is* she called, the Princess who has to go on talking to save her life? *Sch . . . Schh . . . Schhh . . . you know who.* Some days she does know who, some days she doesn't. And there is nothing cute about that. She too has to go on talking to save her life. To her, a word gone is a day gone. And the more I misplace, the more use I have to make of those I can still lay hands on.

O my oblivion is a very Antony and I am all forgot . . . *that* she remembers.

So she fills filing cards left over from the days she kept one for each of her pupils and telephone pads stolen from hotel rooms she can't recall ever having stayed in. She writes letters to friends when she

remembers which of them is still alive, though letters to the dead will
do as well. She rings her sons, though she doesn't at all care for her
sons. She talks to herself. She unscrolls her old school photographs
to see how many faces she can recognise and how many names she
can give to those she does. Some days she scores highly, some days
she doesn't. Now it's her best friend's name that's escaped her, now
she can't pick out the headmistress, now she can't find herself. But she
works at it. Tomorrow she will recognise the whole school again.

And she needleworks – not flowers or birds, not cottages or sunsets,
but words, silken letters, one at a time, with vindictive deliberation,
slower than the silkworm expends his yellow labours . . .

```
        he died in great pain but turned his eyes to God
           and never once complained. I will see you,
                he told his wife, on the other side.
          She didn't have the heart to contradict him
```

Funny, the difference stitching can make to letters. A mythical garden worked in finest threads, lovers with purple pouting lips in
golden robes, twined hearts incarnadined, signed in dancing nursery letters – Beryl Dusinbery – and people don't notice what
cruelty you're stitching. That was how I got my husbands. It didn't
matter what I said, my good looks distracted them, my breathtakingly blue eyes turned my poison words to love.

(She is not a woman it is wise to contradict, but as a point of fact
her eyes aren't and never were as breathtakingly blue as she fancies;
what distracted men was the cruel, angular cubism of her face, the
impression she gave of both listening intently and turning away, an
engrossed aloofness which, in conjunction with her wide, protuber-
ant cheekbones, suggested a bored, predatory intent.)

I never set out to find a husband, using the word husband loosely.
The way Cleopatra used it. 'Husband I come.' *Dead* husband, I come.

Just as I never set out to have children or *carers* – a word I despise
when I remember it. What's wrong with staff or retinue? My maimed
retinue of dimwits who sit around the gas oven to keep warm and

bring me precariously balanced biscuits, waiting to catch me when I fall. Sometimes I fall just to give them something to do. Oops a daisy, I shout, sliding out of my chair. I see it as a favour. It increases their job statisfaction. 'Coming, Mrs Beryl, coming,' Euphoria calls, waddling in from the kitchen. I'd be dead if I really had fallen and had to rely on her to raise me. To attract the attention of Nastier I have to shout even louder. She is permanently wired up to a Romanian music station and wouldn't notice if her clothes were on fire. Let the flames roar around her – what matter, so long as the music keeps playing? It must affect her balance. It's only a matter of time before she falls over her cables and strangles herself in them. They find me back in my chair, anyway, by the time they get in here. 'Anything I can do for you?' I ask, barely bothering to look up from my frame.

I was more of a man than any of my men were and I don't doubt I will prove to be more of a carer than my carers.

It's already happening. Euphoria is a devout and fleshy black woman from Uganda. I tell her she'd be advised to wear more comfortable shoes and skirts that have more room in them. She finds it difficult to walk and more difficult still to bend down. You aren't here to be a mannequin, I tell her. She has never heard that word before. With a 'q' not a 'k', I say, but she is none the wiser. Still, it is better to be a mannequin, I think to myself, than the Russian whore my night carer from Moldova aspires to be. It's like a cathouse here, in the hour they change the guard. Who are they hoping is going to see them? My doctor? My chiropodist? My sons? The window cleaner? Or is it enough for them to display their voluptuousness to an old woman? One of these days I will show them photographs of myself when I was their age. You think *you* can light a fire in men's hearts. Look on this face and imagine the damage I did.

I'm toughening the black one up emotionally as well as physically. She has a heart like molasses. She stands by my bed while I'm working on the antique mahogany stretching frame my dear boys clubbed together to buy me (and keep me bed-bound, though I walk perfectly well), and gasps in untutored admiration. 'That's beautiful, Mrs Beryl,' she says. 'Is it a true story?'

'It's the truest story you will ever read,' I tell her. 'I wrote it.'

'It's very happy,' she says. 'It makes me smile.'

'It shouldn't. It should make you weep.'

'No, it's so happy.' She claps her hands. 'I imagine his excitement waiting for his wife to join him.'

'She won't be.'

Euphoria shakes her head vigorously. 'Oh, she will.'

'It's my story. And I tell you she won't be.'

But Euphoria is a modernist, a post-something or other, when it comes to narratives: she believes she is the author of what she reads and knows better than any mere narrator. She retires to the kitchen, still shaking her head, and brews more tea. I hear her tutting over me. 'Lordy, lordy,' I imagine her saying, and there's no point in my castigating my imagination. It is of another time.

Eventually I'll be making tea for her, I know I will. She'll be in this bed talking gobbledegook and I'll be taking her temperature. It's the fittest who survive and I'm far stronger than her, despite my years.

Nastya from Moldova – *Nastier* I have started to pronounce her – also comments on the sampler. 'How it means that wife didn't have heart?' she asks.

I wave her away. I haven't reached my age to be explaining basic English usage to a Moldovan tart. But that's a mistake. I am a fool to my own impatience. My stock of words is dwindling and I need to be giving constant employment to those I have left. It doesn't matter who understands what. I'll speak to the air if I have to.

How it means that *I* didn't have heart, she lies in bed and wonders. It's a question she has only recently started to ponder. Or at least she thinks she's only recently started to ponder it. She can't remember when recently started. But she does remember one thing about herself: she has been a horrible woman all her life. And this is why her husbands, lovers, passing fancies – who knows what the name for them should be? – went missing, drifted away, passed on, and why her children don't invite her to stay with them.

That's two things about herself.

In the morning, before the sun comes up over North London and the end-of-summer drone recommences, she starts another of her death samplers.

```
he was born without fuss and died without
       fuss, slipping out of life like
    an oyster down an open throat.
   'That wasn't so difficult,' he said,
            and expired.
       No one was listening
```

2

Shimi Carmelli, erect, unsmiling, deals the cards as though strewing flowers on the grave of an enemy.

A red silk handkerchief spills like a splash of blood from his top pocket.

The Widow Ostrapova suppresses a shudder. Such scrubbed, stern, well-manicured fingers he has. She lowers her head to smell their perfume. She is past the age of shame. As he, she imagines, is past the age of embarrassment. But she is wrong about that. In his ninety-first year, Shimi Carmelli retains the bashfulness of a boy. A man untroubled by memories of childhood, assuredly venerable, confident in his own body and at ease in the proximity of women's, would not dress as finically as Shimi does.

'Oil of spikenard,' Ostrapova guesses, closing her eyes.

He shakes his head deliberately. All his actions are deliberate. At ninety nothing is to be left to chance.

The Widow is not to be deterred. This time she brings his fingers to her face like flowers. 'Essence of calamus?'

A bundle of myrrh is my wellbeloved unto me; he shall lie all night betwixt my breasts . . .

'Soap,' Shimi says prosaically. But doesn't mention where he imports his soap from.

'You are such a flirt, Anastasia,' the Widow Saffron remarks.

'Always has been,' agrees the Widow Schoolman.

Anastasia Ostrapova, unafraid to show her turtle throat, comely with chains of gold, throws her head back and laughs. 'I will be dead when I'm not.'

Shimi Carmelli attempts to withdraw his hand from the Widow Ostrapova's grasp. 'If I am to read your cards . . .'

In the mock struggle that ensues the cards are sent flying from the table. Shimi Carmelli stoops to retrieve them. It is a bold action for a man his age. The care with which he lifts his trousers at the knees before he bends is not lost on the Widows. It is not agility they admire these days. It is aforethought.

The Widow Ostrapova worries that in re-dealing the cards he will adversely affect her destiny.

'They are back exactly where they were,' he assures her.

'You can remember?'

'I remember everything.'

He isn't speaking figuratively. He truly does remember everything. What he would give not to.

There are five Widows present, self-arranged more with a view to appearance than comfort, at a large round table from which every-thing, including the Lazy Susan that fifteen minutes ago held skinny ribs, steamed vegetables and pots of Chinese tea, has been removed. This is to give Shimi Carmelli, the restaurant's resident cartomancer, maximum room to spread out the cards.

'Such authority,' the Widow Wolfsheim whispers to her nearest companion.

This is not her first visit to the Fing Ho Chinese Banquet Restaurant on the Finchley Road. She wouldn't want it to be thought she comes only to have her cards read by Mr Carmelli, but it is a happy coincidence that on the nights she does come he is here.

He remembers her from each of her visits – where she sits, what she wears, and how she removes her legs from under the table and crosses them with the slow deliberation of a cabaret artist. The Widow Wolfsheim is famous for her legs.

She should cross and uncross them to music, Carmelli thinks. Borodin.

This isn't favouritism. He isn't sweet on Wanda Wolfsheim. In point of fact, he remembers all the Widows from previous encounters. When the Widow Schoolman suddenly and with worrying inconsequence interrupts his interpretation of the cards to say he is strangely familiar to her, he tells her that he sold her sunglasses on the eve of her honeymoon more than fifty years ago. 'You haven't changed a bit,' he says gallantly. The Widow Schoolman shows her astonishment to each of her fellow diners in turn. Her face is famous for the expressions of wonderment it can command, but already it is in danger of expending them all. 'Can you believe this?'

'I can even tell you where you bought them,' Shimi goes on. 'Stanmore High Street.'

'Next you'll tell me you remember the name of the shop.'

'I do. Shimi's of Stanmore.'

Now something stirs in her memory. Could it be catching? 'Was that the one with all the heads?'

'Correct.'

'You worked at Shimi's of Stanmore?'

'I *was* Shimi of Stanmore.'

The Widows gasp. In another age Shimi's of Stanmore was a shop of renown. Or at least they think it was.

Only the Widow Marks, originally from Leeds, is in the dark. 'How do you mean the one with all the heads?' she asks.

'Originally I opened the shop to sell phrenology busts,' Shimi explains, as though this is not a matter for vagueness. 'They're the porcelain skulls that map our faculties. You must have seen them in bric-a-brac shops. There was a craze for them once. I displayed sunglasses and Panama hats on them as a joke. But by then the craze had died down and more people wanted the glasses and the hats than wanted the busts. I sold your husband a hat on that same visit,' he reminds the Widow Schoolman. 'Did you enjoy Juan-les-Pins?'

The Widow Schoolman puts her hand to her mouth in astonishment.

'What a memory!' the Widow Wolfsheim says. 'What a gift you have.'

She crosses her legs again. Her legs are famous, too, for the sound they make when she crosses them. Something between a hiss and a rattle, reminiscent of the serpent snaking through the Garden on a sultry afternoon.

So maybe Debussy, rather than Borodin.

'I have selective morbid hyperthymesia,' he tells her. 'It's more a curse than a gift. '

'Because it's selective?'

'Because it's morbid. There are things I'd like to forget.'

'There are things we'd all like to forget, Mr Carmelli.'

'But you, I imagine, are able to forget some of them.'

'My memory,' the Widow Wolfsheim wants it to be absolutely clear, 'is generally good.' Unlike the Widow Schoolman's.

'Do you remember the day you were born?' Carmelli asks her.

'Of course I don't. No one remembers the day they were born.'

'I do. Like yesterday. A sweltering afternoon in July, my mother bathed in sweat, a tarantula scampering over the bedclothes, and the midwife chasing it. How could I forget?'

Wanda Wolfsheim makes as if to slap his wrist. 'A tarantula! Where was this? The Amazon rainforest?'

'Whitechapel.'

This time she does slap his wrist. 'You are teasing us,' she says. Though funnily enough, she can see that tarantula running across the baby Shimi's feet.

He gives a concessionary shrug. 'All right. I may have made up the part about the midwife.'

Is he flirting with her?

Whatever he is doing, it is beginning to irritate the Widow Ostrapova, who raps the table.

He straightens his back and adjusts his floppy-eared bow tie. 'Yes, let's return to the cards,' he says. It could be that after the tarantula the Widows will not trust the futures he sees for them. But who can resist mysterious strangers and journeys to faraway places?

The Widow Schoolman grows tearful remembering Juan-les-Pins. The Widow Wolfsheim wonders if there's a place Mr Carmelli might like to visit.

There *is* a place Mr Carmelli would like to visit. The conveniences.

He wishes he were able to make light of the necessity and with suave facetiousness beg the Widows' leave to pay a visit. But he has never been able to make light of anything. For some sins – he means sins of the body; maybe he even means the sin of *having* a body – there is to be no remission.

When he leaves the restaurant he finds Ruthie Schoolman's black BMW parked outside. She is sitting in the back seat and when she sees him she orders her driver to lower her window.

This is not the first time a Widow has beckoned to him from the back seat of a BMW. Among the Widows of North London, Shimi Carmelli is whispered about as the last of the eligible bachelors – by which they mean the last man able to do up his own buttons, walk without the aid of a frame and speak without spitting. He knows this is not really about him. He has been in the retail business and understands the law of supply and demand. And the importance of location. The demand is greater up here. More emotionally charged, too. On account of the air of catastrophic masculinity with which, when he is out and about, he carries himself – his high shoulders, his drooping eyes, his slightly crazed, insurrectionary stare, and the Cossack hats he favours – he reminds many of the Widows of the fathers and grandfathers they left behind in their old countries or know only from faded photographs. So he is under no illusion: they wouldn't be opening the windows of their BMWs to talk to him on the streets of Canterbury or Wells.

'I want to thank you personally,' the Widow Schoolman says, extending a hand. Shimi is touched to see she wears false fingernails.

After a certain age, hands are history. Not mine, Ruthie Schoolman's hands declare.

'As long as I gave satisfaction,' Shimi says with a barely perceptible bow. 'I hope the cards won't disturb your sleep.'

'Mr Carmelli, everything disturbs my sleep. But in especial I worry about the first card you dealt me—'

'The seven of hearts . . .'

'The seven of hearts, yes, which you called the Card of Dubiety. I don't need dubiety. I need certainty.'

'I also dealt you the four of spades, which is the Card of Consolation. You have to balance these things. Interpretation is the key.'

'Mr Carmelli, tell me – is there anything in any of this or is it just a parlour game?'

'Well that's for you to decide. It certainly isn't a science. But people have always turned to augurers—'

'Is that how you see yourself? As an augurer?'

'I try not to see myself.'

Ruthie Schoolman sighs deeply. 'There is so much more I have to ask you,' she says. 'Can I offer you a lift somewhere?'

He detects concern in her voice. It is late for an old man to be out. He declines her offer with another of his barely perceptible bows. It is a fine evening so he is going to walk a little, he tells her. He likes walking at night. Maybe they can talk more about the cards when they next meet.

'In another fifty years, you mean,' the Widow Schoolman says bitterly, ordering her driver to close the window.

No sooner is she driven away in her BMW than the Widow Wolfsheim drives up in hers. She winds down her own window.

'You are in demand,' she says.

'There is always more that people want to hear after a reading.'

She laughs her joshing laugh. 'And is there more you want to say?'

'Sometimes. Not tonight.'

'I'm disappointed. Why don't you think of something while I drive you home. I'm a good driver and haven't drunk a thing. I'll have you back in Stanmore before you know it.'

He no longer lives in Stanmore but is reluctant to say that he is already home. It will take from his scoured aloofness to admit he lives above the Chinese restaurant. 'I'm not going directly home,' he says. 'I like moonlight and am of a mind to sit and think a little somewhere quiet.'

'You could do that in my garden. Though I can't promise you tarantulas.'

She can see he doesn't want to do that in her garden. 'I'll tell you what,' she says. 'I know just the place. Hop in. I won't bite.'

He obeys. He can't refuse every Widow in North London.

She drives in silence but for the shushing of her legs when she brakes. She stops when they reach Hampstead Pond. 'Quiet enough for you here?' she asks.

They sit on a bench together. She promises to be silent but does, after five minutes, introduce the subject nearest to her heart. 'I would so like it,' she says, 'if you'd consider reading cards for one of the charities I help run. Would you? Please?'

'What charities are they?'

'Well, the one I'm thinking of in particular is a care home in Kilburn—'

'For the elderly?' Shimi Carmelli does what he rarely does and touches another person on the arm. 'Have you forgotten what I do? I introduce people to their futures.'

'And you think the elderly don't have futures? Let me tell you that's not what they think. And they love it when the performer – forgive me – is closer to their age than the usual acts we hire. It increases their optimism coefficient a hundredfold. We had Tony Bennett along last year. He is a good friend of our Chairman. The minute he left, half our residents were out of their beds singing "The Way You Look Tonight".'

'I don't have it in me to increase anyone's optimism coefficient to that degree,' Shimi says.

'That you know of . . . Can you be sure Anastasia isn't singing in her bathroom right this minute?'

It crosses his mind to say, 'And you? Will you be singing when you get home?'

But he shouldn't. Or rather, he can't.

3

Beryl Dusinbery, despising indistinctness, stitches with a merciless precision whatever her fingers want to stitch, though the only thing her fingers want to stitch is death.

Fear is not what drives her. It is more exhilaration. A sort of glee.

She forgets herself when she is at her frame. She could be any age. She is a true artist, no matter that her subject matter is limited. When she stitches, her soul leaves her body. Intention flees her mind. It's her fingers that call the tune.

She is not so free when she writes. She is more, then, the person she means to be. More the woman, less the artist. Though even when she's filling out the old school filing cards she is not circumscribed by mere actuality. These are meant to tell the true story of her life, but she is only in possession of the truth she can retrieve. Who the hell cares, anyway, she thinks. It's true if I say it is. It's true if I recall it that way.

She must have said something of that sort out loud because Euphoria comes running in from the kitchen. 'Is everything all right, Mrs Beryl?'

'In the world or with me?'

'I heard you shout. Did something frighten you?' Euphoria hitches her tight floral skirt and steals a quick look under the bed. Nastya had reported seeing a mouse there. Mice are everywhere in these North London mansion blocks. Generations have lived in them since the beginning of the last century. They have brought up families here. Generations of proud mansion block mice. As long as they aren't rats, no one has ever minded. 'The English are filthy,' Nastya says.

Beryl Dusinbery peers over her smudged spectacles at Euphoria, who is chancing a second look under the bed. Afraid she might encounter a mouse peering back at her, Euphoria tries to bend her back and keep it straight at the same time. It's not just her clothes, the poor girl has bad posture, Beryl Dusinbery notices. But then, don't they all in Africa? It's what comes of eating lizards and carrying baskets of bananas on their heads. She'll be in traction before she knows it and I'll be running in and out to see how she is. 'It would appear that it is I who should be asking,' she says, 'if something has frightened *you*. What on earth are you looking for under there?'

Euphoria shrugs her shoulders. Something else that isn't good for posture. *Stand up straight, girls*, Miss Dusinbery can hear herself say.

If she had a ruler handy she'd strike Euphoria's shoulders with it. *Straight!*

'Boo!' she booms instead.

Euphoria jumps.

'Your nerves are clearly very bad,' Beryl Dusinbery says triumphantly. 'You need to see a . . .' But she can't remember the name for the person Euphoria needs to see.

'Yes, Mrs Beryl.'

'What have I told you a thousand times? If there's any fear in this room it's yours. Nothing frightens me.'

'No, Mrs Beryl.'

'Except forgetting what the name for you is.'

'I'm Euphoria.'

'No, the name for what you do.'

'I care for you, Mrs Beryl.'

'Ha! Is that what it is? Did anyone ask you to?'

'Yes, your son, Mr Sandy.'

'I have a son?'

'You have three, Mrs Beryl.'

'Do I really? Are they all called Mr Sandy?'

'No, Mrs Beryl. There's Mr Pen, and—'

'All right, all right, let's not run through them all. And please stop calling me "Mrs". It makes me sound provincial. I am the Princess Sch . . . Schh . . . Schhh . . . you know who.'

She has forgotten who herself. The Princess Scherbatsky is it? Why does she recall that name? The Princess Shostakovich? Schnitzler? Schrecklichkeit? Schumann? *Struwwelpeter*?

The she remembers. 'I am the Princess Schicklgruber.'

Euphoria can't help with any of that. 'Yes, Mrs Beryl.'

The Princess sits up in bed and pulls her bedjacket tighter around her shoulders. It is embroidered with the words life is a tale told by an idiot. There is a blood-red pansy with a smiley face between each letter. 'As I was saying to you,' she goes on, 'I am not an easily frightened woman and don't at all dread my own decease – when I go, I go – but I do fear being dead while I'm still alive, opening my mouth to speak and nothing coming out of it. My life is how I describe it and I haven't finished describing it yet. So' – she points to a chocolate box on her bedside table – 'everything is going down on the cards I keep in there. I tell you this in case I omit to mention something important later. If I do, you will find it on one of these. Just don't ask me which.'

'I love your stories, Mrs Beryl.'

'You won't love these, and they aren't stories. I don't want you making that mistake. What this box contains are annals. Don't look so alarmed. I said annals, not animals. The chronicles of each year of my life, though I will certainly have confused one year with another. That doesn't matter. Chronology is for the little people. I care only for eternal truth and eternal truth isn't ordered in time. And it isn't even true. I am Mother of the Century – did you know that? I have a medal to prove it – that's also in the box. I am Mother of the Century so it's important I keep a record of what the century's been doing. It's all in here. The men I married, the men I divorced, the children I had, the children I didn't. The century's story, not mine. It is essential to your understanding, not only of me but of the times you live in, that you read it.'

Euphoria shakes her head. She couldn't do that. She has been brought up never to read personal correspondence.

'I give you permission. There are things in here you need to know, in case someone tries to tell you otherwise. Lists, dates. Husbands and lovers alphabetically arranged – sometimes, that is, when the fancy takes me and I can remember the alphabet – when and where they died, what shocks or diseases they died of, and the manner in which they failed as men. Read them carefully, Nastya, you are to be my witness, it's your job to report me and my causes—'

'It's Euphoria, ma'am.'

'It is. You are right. Though I'm not sure that's a good enough reason to interrupt me. Attend to me more carefully, Euphoria, yes. Read what I have written and you won't make the mistakes I have. Unless you want to be Mother of the Century after I'm gone.'

Euphoria shakes her head again.

'A wise decision. It's a big responsibility, having the century's children. And they will only ever disappoint you. To give birth to a child, to sharpen its wits and teach it all you know, and then to watch it join the Labour Party – better you never come to know how that feels.'

'No, Mrs Beryl.'

'So read. We will discuss it from time to time. You can be my sounding board and tell me if you find anything incomprehensible or outré, but only when I ask you to. It will give us something to talk about other than cups of tea and tablets. Stand up straight, Euphoria. That's better. All I request in return is that you don't make the error of expecting happy endings. I don't want to hear you snivelling about the place. I can tell you now that none of my husbands or inamoratos made me happy and they all died in great pain and misery. That's men for you.'

Though she knows she's been dismissed, Euphoria seems unable to tell her legs to move. It is as though compunction has made her heavy.

'Mrs Beryl,' she says at last.

The Princess, turned vacant, is surprised to discover she is still there. 'Yes, Nastier.'

'Euphoria, ma'am.'

'Whoever. Go on, go on.'

'Why is it so terrible to join the Labour Party?'

'Who said it was?'

'You did, Mrs Beryl.'

'Did I? And did that upset you? Are you a Labour voter?'

'I don't think I should say, Mrs Beryl.'

'Quite right. We don't want politics here.'

Euphoria is pleased with that, but not pleased enough to resume her kitchen duties.

The Princess thinks she understands the problem.

'It's not because he joined the Labour Party that he broke my heart,' she says. 'I felt the same about the other one when he joined the Conservative Party. You don't bring your children up to think along the same lines as other children. Or along the same lines as their fathers, which is worse. You bring your children up to defy their genetic disadvantages and to honour their . . .'

There is a word for what she's brought her children up to be but it's flown out of the window.

'You have brought your children up very well, Mrs Beryl,' Euphoria says.

The Princess snorts.

She can't remember bringing up children at all.

4

When it's mild the Princess likes to walk in the little park that was once the burial ground for St John's Wood Church. Euphoria, who accompanies her on these walks, keeps suggesting they cross the road and go to Regent's Park, where there is more to see.

'More to see of what?' the Princess wants to know.

By way of reply, Euphoria describes a circle with her hands. The globe. The universe. Creation.

'If this is meant to be a charade,' the Princess says, 'you'll have to tell me how many syllables and what it sounds like.'

'I could take you boating on the lake, Mrs Beryl.'

'You! On a lake! Why would I trust you on a lake? You don't have water in your country, do you?'

Euphoria has learnt that there are some questions she isn't bound to answer.

'Or we could feed the ducks.'

'Ducks!'

Euphoria wonders if Mrs Beryl might have forgotten what ducks are. 'Birds,' she says helpfully.

'If I want to feed birds I can hang a bird box outside my window.'

So it's the little park. The one drawback of which is its play area, but the Princess has worked out that she can avoid the sight and sound of children if she walks when they are in school. Euphoria loves children and is always disappointed not to find any on the swings or climbing frames when they get there. 'We are out of luck again, Mrs Beryl,' she says.

'Such a shame,' the Princess says. 'Maybe we'll time it better when we come again.'

What primarily draws the Princess to the park are the gravestones. She likes the disorder in which they seem to shoot up wild under the trees, like toadstools. Push a branch aside and you enter a gothic mystery. Some of the stones are lined up against the walls, like paintings surplus to requirement, others moulder under moss, never having seen the light all century. 'It's like *The Mysteries of Udolpho* in there,' she tells Euphoria, pointing to a crow disappearing into the gloomy undergrowth.

'Yes, Mrs Beryl.'

'Are you frightened of ghosts?'

'I have never seen one. I might be.'

'Then don't go in there.'

The Princess, who has a taste for oracles and sibyls, likes to pause to read the writing on the headstone of Joanna Southcott, the eighteenth-century prophetess.

'The future is always brought to us through the voices of women,' she tells Euphoria. 'Men are moribund. They only listen to the past.'

Euphoria, who isn't sure whether this is true, does what the Princess tells her and reads aloud the words on Joanna Southcott's headstone. *Behold, the time shall come, that these TOKENS which I have told THEE shall come to pass, and the BRIDE shall APPEAR . . .*

'With more feeling, Emporium.'

'It's Euphoria, Mrs Beryl.'

'That shouldn't stop you putting feeling into it. Try to make the bride resplendent, child. Imagine it's you getting married with a pineapple on your head.'

Euphoria asks who the bride refers to and whether she has appeared yet.

'The bride refers to me,' the Princess tells her. 'So yes, she has appeared. Several times, as it happens.'

'You must have been a beautiful bride,' Euphoria says.

'It was said of me that I beggared belief. It isn't for me to confirm that or deny it. But I can tell you that the second man to marry me fainted when he saw me coming towards him in my wedding gown and tiara. It took half an hour to bring him round. I had to speak his vows for him. Unless that was the third man I married.'

'What about the first, ma'am?'

'He was killed, but not by me. By Italians, if what's left of my memory serves me right. It would have been a kindness had I shot him before they did. But you don't always know these things at the time. By my fourth and fifth marriage I could no longer see the point of putting in the effort. That didn't always stop them fainting, mind you.'

She throws Euphoria a knowing, sideways look. Woman to woman. What caused them to faint, she wants the girl to understand, was not the spectacle of her in her gown but anticipation of her out of it.

Euphoria looks back at her blankly. The Moldovan slut would understand me better, the Princess thinks.

'How many times were you a bride, Mrs Beryl?' Euphoria asks.

The Princess doesn't want to say she's forgotten. She lifts up her left hand and then her right. 'I don't have enough fingers to count them,' she says.

She likes asking Euphoria to read what's written on gravestones from which all inscriptions have been worn away, and then, when Euphoria has stared her eyes out and discovered nothing, telling her what they say.

'Here lieth the body of Abigail Mills,' she pretends to read, 'a woman who gave everything to a man who deserved nothing and now enjoys eternal rest while he lies rotting, his body gnawed by worms as his conscience was never gnawed by misgivings.'

'I love the way you describe things, Mrs Beryl,' Euphoria says. 'But how can you see those words when you aren't even wearing your glasses?'

'They come to me,' the Princess tells her. 'I feel them through my fingers. Here, feel these with me.'

She takes Euphoria's index finger and guides it over one of the smoothest of the standing headstones. 'In memory of Elizabeth Sturridge – can you feel? – wife, mother, philanthropist and head teacher who, after years of faithful but thankless service to her community, had sex with the devil and went to hell with a smile on her face.'

Euphoria snatches her hand away. 'I am surprised such a woman is buried in a Christian graveyard,' she says angrily.

'My suspicion is she wasn't. The devil must have moved her here in the dead of night. We could come back after midnight and see if he returns to visit her. He might bring her flowers.'

Later Euphoria will ask Nastya what she thinks of this story. 'Poppycocks,' Nastya tells her. 'Mrs Beryl is having one over you.'

'Why would she do that?'

'She thinks you're ignorant colonial person who believes in black magic. My advice would be to look for job somewhere else.'

The Princess sits awhile on one of the benches opposite the empty playground. For some reason the sight of unused ropes and swings soothes her.

'So quiet here,' she says to Euphoria.

Euphoria is about to reply but the Princess puts a hand on her arm. So quiet, so let's keep it that way.

On a nearby bench an elderly man in a fur hat is sitting forward with his head almost between his knees. He doesn't appear to be praying or weeping. He could be breathing in the earth's deepest smells. Smelling out the dead. He too seems to be relishing the silence of the park, the sound of traffic muffled by the trees, and not a plane in the sky.

A squirrel, taking his posture to imply a willingness to communicate or dispense bounty, approaches his leg. Without malice, the man shoos it away with his foot. You stay in your world, the Princess takes his action to be implying, and I'll stay in mine. A sentiment that strikes a chord with her. Parks are wonderful places – especially for connecting to the spirits of the long-gone – but among the living there is too much mingling of species.

'So what else did you do in park beside talk about devil?' Nastya asks Euphoria when she gets back.

Unable to think of anything else, Euphoria mentions the squirrels.

'Those are rats,' Nastya says.

5

At some remote period in the history of humankind, anthropologists say, a terrible crime was committed. One brother fatally struck another. We gave up gardening for hunting. We ate a god. We sent a goat into the desert. We killed our father.

Shimi Carmelli tried on his mother's underwear.

He was eleven. About the age Homo sapiens was when it discovered the joy of murder.

Out of humankind's great originating transgression – however it's defined – religion, morality, and, eventually, neurosis evolved. We became less carefree. We came to know guilt and shame. The fun went out of us.

This is exactly what happened to Shimi Carmelli.

He climbed into his mother's bloomers and tumbled into hell.

There is more than one sort of hell. There is man-hell – a fiery ocean in which fratricides and god-eaters hang upside down for eternity. Or there is boy-hell – the Cave of All Humiliations where bedwetters and fledgling masturbators sit with their heads in their hands while grinning devils in caps and bells roar ridicule in their ears. Torment for torment there is not much to choose between them. Shimi tumbled into boy-hell.

★

Narcissus saw his own self-reflection and died of self-love. Lucky Narcissus. Aghast in his mother's rayon bloomers, little Shimi saw his reflection in the bathroom mirror, and waited for the earth to open up and swallow him.

Did it have to be like that? Couldn't he have struck a pose and laughed off what he'd done? Couldn't he have pulled his trousers back on and chalked it down to experience? Assuredly, if he'd been someone else.

'Don't look at me as though you want me dead,' his doctor, Bernie Dauber, tells him. 'It's my job to give you the lowdown on the drugs I'm prescribing you.'

Dauber likes having Shimi Carmelli as a patient. At least he gets here under his own steam. Otherwise the elderly are spilled out onto his surgery floor like sackfuls of stray cats. For their sakes, Dauber wishes he had the freedom a vet enjoys and could lethally inject them all. First the Telazol and ketamine to knock them out, then the overdose of barbiturates administered intracardially. Goodnight little pussies.

Keeping them alive does them no favours. It's institutionalised sadism. But he is in private practice in the dead heart of Care County so he understands the economics of keeping the old alive. Without the old to care for in Belsize Park the caregivers' own families would go to bed hungry in Velingrad and Tbilisi.

'You could describe what the pills are going to do to me with less brutality,' Shimi says.

'Where's the brutality in warning you that Tamsulosin might result in retrograde ejaculation?'

He has one of those deep American, inflexionless, testicular voices that proclaim inexpugnable manhood.

'What's brutal is that such a thing exists,' Shimi says.

'Tamsulosin?'

'Its side effect.'

'Well, had I thought you were planning a family . . .'

'There you go again. That's brutal.'

'It's you that wants the pills. I've told you – stay in when the urge to pee is too great. And if you have to go out make sure you're never far from a park. You can always piss against a tree. Give me the prescription back if you don't want it.'

Shimi covers his ears. He likes playing Squeamish from Little Stanmore to his doctor's Ballsy from Brooklyn. Not that Shimi's pretending. He really is Squeamish from Little Stanmore.

'It's the last of my dignity I'm trying to protect,' he tells Dauber. 'You as a doctor should understand that.'

'As a doctor,' Dauber says, 'I have some words of advice for you – you can keep your dignity or you can stay alive.'

'You're telling me it's dry ejaculate or die?'

'That's about the size of it.'

All very well, but Shimi can't leave his flat without refreshing his mental map of every public urinal in North London. He has been accustomed to taking an abstracted two- or three-mile walk most days, not always knowing where his feet will lead him; now he has to plot routes and calculate distances.

An incident in the park has upset him. A diminutive elderly lady, still taking trouble with her eye make-up and lipstick, though supported on either side by a carer, has mistaken him for someone else. 'Oh,' she says, stopping in front of him. It's almost a chirrup. 'Oh, my word.' He can't be certain it's Horowitz, who died in 1989, she's taken him for, but it won't be the first time, and she does say how much she treasures, above all musical memories, his performance of Schumann's *Kinderszenen* at the Royal Festival Hall she can't now remember when. Shimi removes his hat and bows to her. He would like to tell her he is not who she thinks he is, but that the Schumann was one of his mother's favourite records – indeed, at the mere mention of it he can picture her listening to it in that sad, half-absent way of hers – so perhaps there is some strange musical serendipity at work here, which makes this meeting a particular pleasure. But the old lady is quicker in her movements than he is in his speech. Releasing herself from her minders, she moves intrepidly upon him – like a tiny bird flying to the uppermost branch of an old bare tree, is how it strikes him – and takes his hands between hers. This is the second time in a week that a woman has taken Shimi's hand. Is it a sign of something, he wonders. He's the oracle; he should know. Maybe they can detect he's taking pills that turn emission back the way it came. 'Such sensitivity,' she says, putting his hands to her ears, as though like sea shells they must bear the memory of all that's washed through them. Whether it's the shock of the contact that causes him to lose control of his bladder, he doesn't know. But it happens, anyway, the thing he's been dreading ever since he became aware of that unfamiliar pricking in his urinary tract, and he has no recourse but to cover himself quickly with his hat, bow one more time, and disappear into the bushes.

It is some consolation to think that, should this incident ever be talked about, the person it will reflect badly on is Horowitz.

He stumbles back out of the bushes, plucking twigs from his coat. He has always taken trouble with his appearance. He has all his hair. He has a straight back. He wears glasses only for reading small print and hears perfectly well. He has no clothes that could be called casual. The old lady did not go far wrong in mistaking him for Vladimir Horowitz. He has deliberately cultivated the great pianist's air of elegant, international desolation. To match every jacket he owns he has a shimmering silk handkerchief that drips like a Japanese waterfall from his top pocket. (That there's now a dripping joke to be made, he knows, but dripping is another of the brutal words he shies away from.) Without a woman to advise him or check him over, he has taken great pride in his freedom from the usual marks of dilapidation in men his age: the nostril hairs, the razor cuts, the shirts escaping the belt and falling open at the navel, the jackets that have grown too long, the trousers that have grown too short, the scuffed shoes, those give-away stains and, saddest of all – because they bespeak awareness and desperation – such conscious signs of urinary-tract embarrassment as a buttoned jacket on a warm day, or excessive abrasion on the fly-front.

And now he is on the point of becoming one of these men himself.

He finds a park bench, close to a public lavatory, and lets his head drop between his knees. A rudeness has been forced upon him. Not just to the birdlike old lady who can still remember a Schumann concert of long ago, but to his mother. He would have liked to stay longer discussing her and the music she loved. Better to remember her for that than the cheap underwear he stole from her.

A squirrel mistakes his abstraction for loving kindness to living things. Shimi puts out a foot. So far and no further.

There's a horrible shapeliness in the morning's encounter and all it's made him recall. A lifetime ago he smelt urine on his mother's bloomers. Today he smells urine on himself.

Is this the slow stew of retribution?

Does sin contaminate? Had he picked up some infection from that garment of his mother's whereof he dares not speak or think other than in language – *Aghast in my mother's bloomers* – that belongs in a treasury of Celtic Twilight verse? Not a psychological infection but an actual infection, a nodus of viruses and bacteria that has been gestating vengefully for eighty years, waiting for the perfect time to strike? That this is a terrible calumny of his mother he accepts. So his sighs are expiatory. It is for her too, his poor dear violated mother – once moved to tears by Schumann but now a mere assemblage of dry bones and dust – that he exhales them.

Dry, too, the irony of it all. For no one has tried harder than he has over the last eighty years to remove the stain of common humanity from his person, and in that way expunge it from his soul. His bathroom, which he is in the habit of locking though he lives alone, is at once a fortress and a decontamination chamber, the cupboards stocked with sufficient amounts of bleach and hydrogen peroxide to wash away the sins of an entire London suburb – failing which, to blow it up. The soaps with which he washes his hands a hundred times a day are handcrafted, lightly scented with oud perfume to

35

disguise the industrial smell of ammonia. He chooses his nail and bath brushes from a catalogue sent to him every quarter by a perfumery on Madison Avenue. Though it is part of their service to initial all his brushes *SC*, it is for the resilience of their bristles that he buys them. But nothing is more important to him than the Hanebisho toilet paper, made from Canadian wood fibre pulp washed in the clear waters of the Niyodo River, which he imports directly from Tokyo. Preciosity is not his motivation in this. Certainty is. He wants to be sure he isn't buying toilet paper that has been recycled. The thought of something with a previous functional life touching his person *there* is what a desecration of the host would have been to a holy person of the Middle Ages. For what lies behind his scrupulous attention to cleanliness is a religious veneration of the body not incompatible with a horror of its functions.

6

Beryl Dusinbery's *journal d'amour* is arranged, as she had told Euphoria, roughly but just as often forgetfully alphabetically, and is written in a conversational style consistent with her years as Head of English at some of the best girls' schools in some of the best parts of the country. 'Nothing too grand, girls,' she would exhort those to whom she taught composition. 'You aren't Churchill making a stand against the odious apparatus of Nazi rule, but the occasional flourish will grab the attention of readers and make them continue. It will also scare off the hoi polloi, which is never a bad thing.'

> *So I start, as start I must, with Albert, or Albear as he insisted it be pronounced, Frenchly. 'Je t'aime, Albear,' I had to whisper in his good ear before it too furred over, by which time I could as safely and more truly have whispered 'Je t'haine, Albear' — he, the cowardly preacher of free everything, screamed without a hint of French for what seemed like an eternity when he discovered how little of eternity was left to him. True, at forty-eight he was on the young side to be fatally struck down, but he made no effort to rearrange his affairs or his thoughts, whether in accordance with the teachings of the church, the stoics or the scepticism by which he'd lived. And where's the point of living by anything if you can't die by it?*
>
> *He was a junior don at a junior Cambridge college and the editor of a thin rationalist journal printed on smudgy paper like a comic —* The Disbeliever *— secretly funded by the successful children's writer Algie*

Camborne (*I have falsified that name to protect the guilty*) – *successful by the standards of the 1950s – who, though he couldn't say so in his books, took the very notion of a god as a personal affront. Algie was more a man of now than of then, a short-tempered, public, literary festival atheist before there were literary festivals, which untimeliness might have been what irked him into disbelief. That and an all-round unwhole-someness of person – flaky skin, dirty fingernails, thin hair, foul breath – for which he had to blame somebody. Albear, who was a sort of protégé, mesmerised by Algie's grubbiness and bulk, forced his students to buy* The Disbeliever *at a discount price, otherwise I'd be surprised if he ever sold a copy. He wasn't in it for the circulation. It was enough for him to think himself a thorn in the side of the god in whom he disbelieved and to enthral every woman he encountered with the fact of his being an editor and the spectacle of his eschatological fearlessness. It's a miracle I remem-ber that word and to be honest with myself I don't. I have it written down in my Albear scrapbook. Alongside psittacosis. He didn't actually have parrot disease – as far as I knew, anyway, though he could easily have caught it off Algie Camborne – but he did attack himself in the way of parrots who have been caged too long. He would walk around my little Cambridge kitchen while I cooked him coq au vin and pull his beard out hair by hair. 'I'm a free spirit,' he used to say. 'I can't stand being cooped up.' 'So leave,' I told him. 'Who's cooping you?' 'I will, after supper,' he'd say. But after supper he was unconscious on the couch. In his editor-ials Albear scoffed at people who feared the afterlife. 'What's to be frightened of?' he'd say to me, as though I were the embodiment of all human fear. 'I know where I'm going when I die . . .' It pleased me to say nothing. It was a battle of wills. How long before I'd ask him where it was he knew he was going to. But my will was stronger than his. In the end he'd finish his own sentence. 'Nowhere, that's where. The great black nowhere.' Once the question of his going became something other than hypothetical (eschatological, psittacosis, hypothetical – it's so important to write words down) he made the doctor promise he would not sedate him. Why? What did he want to remain conscious to see, if he was going nowhere? 'My own dissolution. I want to be there when my light goes out,' he told me.*

We weren't in love by then. We'd disappointed each other. I'd proved too rational for him. And he was not the inspiration I'd hoped he'd be when I'd moved to Cambridge to be with him. Nor the rock. And if a man isn't an inspiration or a rock what use is he? He also brought back small-time sexual infections to our bed. Many of my friends who were living with or married to philosophers reported the same thing. As though pubic lice were a condition of speculative thought. But I didn't say 'What light, Bert?' On some nights the screaming was so terrible, as though his throat had claws and was tearing at him, paying him back for all the stupid words and strumpets' bacilli he'd caused to pass through it, that I had to run out of the house, actually run, round and round the block, trying to drive out the sound of him with my own breathing, hoping that when I got back it would be over. I ran so blindly I could have been over before he was. Once I collided with E. M. Forrester, Foster, Fister, Funster — what was his name? — the little Edwardian novelist whom everybody assumed had died decades before but who was still pedalling around Cambridge like a ghost in cycle clips. He stared at me in shock, barely higher than his handlebars, and apologised, though I was the one at fault.

Did we end up going back to his room and having sex? If we did, nothing of the experience remains. For me, at least.

And still, when I returned home, it wasn't over with Albear. He dragged on. Never over. Until it was, it wasn't. Always there when I got back. Until it is, it won't be.

Cruel to leave him, yes, but he didn't want to be watched over, he just wanted to be heard by someone, and that someone wasn't me. 'Where is it?' he cried once, in a quieter moment. 'Where's it gone?'

'Where's what gone, Albear?'

'Not you! I'm not asking you. What do you know!'

He didn't even look tired when there was no more scream left in him. Just mystified.

I couldn't bring myself to shut his eyes for fear he would look no less mystified with them closed.

7

Among the several words Euphoria finds it necessary to look up in a dictionary – 'Don't be ashamed, you weren't a teacher of Senior English to superior young women as I was,' Beryl Dusinbery consoles her – is psittacosis. It baffles her that poor Mr Albert died of a disease that afflicts budgerigars and macaws. She wonders if he'd ever travelled to Africa and contracted the disease there, though Nastya says there's no illness you can't pick up in England. 'So why are you here?' Euphoria asks her. 'To find man with title,' Nastya says. 'And what about the filth?' Euphoria asks. 'It doesn't matter if you have title,' Nastya says. 'No one notices it then.'

Euphoria believes Nastya is wasting her time if she has her eye on one of Mrs Dusinbery's sons or grandsons. She has seen the way Mrs Dusinbery looks at Nastya. If Nastya thinks the English are dirty, Mrs Dusinbery evidently feels the same way about Moldovans.

Without doubt, Mrs Beryl is, and must always have been, a difficult woman to please, a fact that makes her feel sorry for Mr Albert, who would have found a more accommodating or at least more understanding companion in Kampala, and might eventually have done so had psittacosis not brought him down. Mind you, his godlessness would not have won him any more friends there than in Cambridge.

Mrs Beryl, too, strikes her as unfortunate. Not just to have lost her heart to a man with parrot's disease, but to have no family support to fall back on when remembrances pain her. Yes, there are sons, but they show a strange sort of love to their mother and she shows a strange sort of love to them. No embracing, no kissing, no laughing in one another's company. If Nastya is right and the English *are* filthy, that might explain the distance they keep from one another. But Nastya is wrong about a lot of things. She is wrong if she thinks she can snare Mr Sandy or Mr Pen. And she says the English have no soul and understand nothing of love, but Euphoria has cared for other elderly English women and in her experience the country is awash with love. They sing songs about it, queue up to buy tickets for musicals about it, exchange birthday and Valentine's Day cards that speak of nothing else. 'Love you,' she has heard them say when they finish their phone calls to relatives living at the furthest ends of the country. True, the fact that English family members choose to live so far apart argues against their being devoted, but she's been told it's employment that makes that necessary, not indifference. That and the cost of housing. Nastya says that Mrs Beryl's flat is worth more than the entire gross national income of Moldova, so it's not surprising that her children can't afford to live on the Finchley Road but have to squeeze into cramped politicians' accommodation in Westminster and Pimlico. But she has also seen Mr Sandy on television claiming that thanks to all the new affordable house-building schemes the government has embarked upon those sons and daughters who once had to move out of London will be able to move back into it and enjoy living close to their families again. The great migration out of the capital will soon be over, he promised. But Nastya says the only reason children are moving back into their parents' houses in London is that there are no jobs for them anywhere else in the country because Syrian immigrants are taking them all. Soon London will be like a Delhi slum with a hundred people packed into a single room and having to sleep standing up. Euphoria is not dismayed by these forecasts. She knew crowded conditions in her own country, and crowded conditions, in her estimation of the matter, bind family members to one another. She lives in a very small flat with her husband in Uxbridge and though they get in each other's way and one has to sit in the bath while the other prepares the evening meal they would rather have closeness than distance. Half the day she is at Mrs Beryl's, but when she goes home she wants to enjoy the proximity of the man she married. He tells her he feels the same way. They even sleep wrapped around each other, now with her face in his hair, now with his in hers. Because of that she carries the smell of him around with her all day. Disgusting, Nastya calls this when they discuss personal matters in their crossover hour. A wife should not be so dependent on her husband. It isn't dependence, Euphoria insists. It is affection. And anyway, what does it matter if her husband is equally dependent on her. Nastya tells her she should be more of a feminist. What, like Mrs Beryl, Euphoria asks. 'No, like me when I have title,' Nastya says with a laugh. And that is usually the end of the conversation.

It is Euphoria's impression that Mrs Beryl's children and grandchildren all have important jobs in the City and Westminster and houses in the country they need to go to to rest in at the weekend, and so won't be hurrying back to the Finchley Road any time soon, whatever the upturn in the economy. But she is sorry in her heart for Mrs Beryl and half-hopes that her children and their children lose those jobs and have to live with their mother again. She only half-hopes this because that would be the end of her job too and she enjoys working here no matter that kind words are seldom expressed and no one says I love you before putting the phone down. She would miss plumping the cushions and polishing the silver and shining the crystal and hoovering the curtains and feather-dusting the chandeliers – none of which falls within her job description as originally outlined, but the Spanish maid whose responsibilities these are is often ill and takes advantage of Mrs Beryl's poor eyesight by never finishing, and half the time never starting. 'This setting bad precedent,' Nastya tells her, but Euphoria doesn't mind if it is. Polishing the silver beats sitting on a stool in the kitchen waiting for death, the way every other carer on the Finchley Road does. This is why carers are all overweight. A doughty fatness is the price they pay for their unspoken unionisation: their refusal to let care cross over into cleaning. Besides, she enjoys keeping busy. And she wants to stay in Mrs Beryl's favours so she can go on looking at her beautiful samplers and reading the lovely stories she embroiders, which surely prove that Mrs Beryl has a good heart filled with sweet memories, however much she pretends otherwise. She would also miss conversations about the English with Nastya. But her personal happiness isn't the issue. An old lady is nearing the end of her life and the old, in Euphoria's eyes, are to be revered. There cannot, in her world view, be such a thing as an old person who isn't redeemed by love of children, longevity and the coming closeness to Jesus, no matter how much they've offended against him in the past.

'All old ladies are sweet,' she says. Then she adds, '*Ipso facto*,' which the Princess has taught her means by the very nature of them.

'She isn't what I call sweet old lady,' Nastya remarks in the kitchen. 'Not by long chalks.'

8

Manolo Carmelli – from whom Shimi must have inherited his smarting memory – never forgot where his wife was when he first saw her, how she struck him, what he said to her, how he felt when he went home that night.

He did not get round to asking her what she thought when she first saw him. So this might be where Shimi got his second life weakness from: not vanity, more other-blindness. Which is a cruel thing to say about Manolo, given that he saw only her – Sonya Jilinik with her yellow hair and slanting lynx eyes, Sonya Jilinik standing alone, twisting an embroidered handkerchief between her fingers, trying not to be noticed, Sonya almost insane, it seemed to Manolo, with shyness. But he desired what he saw, and desire is deemed to be proprietorial.

He hadn't gone to the dance in Shoreditch Town Hall to fall in love. He'd gone for a hot night out. Then he saw her. 'Be careful, she's a Hebrew,' a friend told him as he was gathering his courage to go over. 'Is that a problem?' 'It might be when she discovers you aren't.' 'I'm not marrying her.' 'You soon might be.'

The friend was right. 'You don't have to reply immediately but I'm in love with you,' he told her on their second date. She didn't so much blush as curdle, all her yellowness rushing to her cheeks. She flickered and smelt bad, like a candle going out. She was as different from him as it was possible for a person from the same planet to be. Her face was twice the length of his. When she was overtly sad,

44

such as when he told her that for all the darkness of his complexion he wasn't a Hebrew, he thought her face would never finish. He gave off light, she stole it. His eyes danced, hers slid sideways as though ashamed of what they saw. She seemed a person of secrets, he was candour personified. She looked lonely, he had never been lonely in his life. 'When I first saw you I thought you'd just come down from the mountains,' he told her. 'Which mountains?' 'I don't know. Are there mountains where your family comes from?' 'The Carpathians.' 'What are they like?' 'I've never been there but my grandmother used to say she'd lie awake at night in fear, listening to the lonely howling of wolves and wildcats.' 'That's exactly what I heard when I spoke to you the first time.' 'I'm afraid there's nothing wild about me,' she told him. He thought about it – no, not wild, but there was something unkempt and creased about her, not shabby but ill-cared for, as though she'd been badly folded away in a drawer, her skirts rumpled, her blouses perhaps worn for the second or third time, the straps from her slip never properly in place and rarely spotless. She wore too much powder and cologne. And sometimes smelt of moth balls. For Manolo, all this added to her drooping appeal. He wanted to shake her out. She was poor, he realised. She lived in a small house with a big family. She was having to make do. Well, he would make it all right for her. He was earning a bit of money as a mechanic. He had done an apprenticeship in Bologna for Maserati. His people were Maltese pretending to be Italian, but they had done all right. Restaurants, ice cream parlours, tailors. His father worked as a cutter in Savile Row and had eminent clients who asked only for him. On the door of the cutting room was a picture of him with a piece of chalk in his mouth measuring Rudolph Valentino for a suit in which to go hunting with the Royal Family. Manolo liked the idea that he was well-connected enough to do things for the girl, help her off the mountain, take her somewhere nice, spruce her up – yes, give her an engine overhaul.

He didn't know if she'd been waiting for him, but he'd been waiting for her.

The Hebrew thing turned out not to be a problem. 'Every Hymie

I've ever cut a suit for could pass as an Italian,' his father said, 'at least when I've finished dressing them. But you, you have to find a Slav with a horse's face. Still, if you tell me you're happy . . .'

Sonya's family put up no resistance either. Manolo looked more Semitic than they did. When he came to visit, bearing gifts and telling jokes, it was they who felt Gentile. And they were glad to have her off their hands. She was the oldest of seven sisters. Six more to go. They'd have greeted six more Manolos with open arms.

The couple had two boys – Shimi and Ephraim. Barely a year separated them. Their quick succession made Sonya's spirits droop. She didn't do anything easily or bravely. Fear knew where to find her. She was always seeing vermin or insects, moths, giant bees, armies of ants, at the edges of her sloping eyes. Manolo had moved them out to Little Stanmore where he'd been offered a job fixing cars for bigwigs. He found them the lower floor of a worker's cottage, the bottom half of which was built below the level of the road so they could see nothing from the windows but the feet of passers-by. It was hardly rural England but Sonya even managed to see a snake there. On the path. There! There! For a week she wouldn't leave the house. 'Kill it, kill it!' she would shout when anything moved in their little garden, and the two small boys had to go after a slug or an earthworm with their plastic spades.

So this might be where Shimi got it from. Not faintheartedness, exactly. But a nameless dissatisfaction, a sort of disillusionment that formed before he'd even had time to be illusioned.

No wonder his father didn't like him.

★

He was sitting at the kitchen table reading, pretending to be a normal boy, when the first blow struck. He knew what it was for. There was almost relief in it after three days of waiting for the earth to open. It was more a swipe than a blow. A contemptuous crack with the back of the hand as his father was passing. Shimi kept his head lowered. He didn't want to turn and see the scorn in his father's eyes.

This, he realised, amounted to a confession of his guilt.

The second blow was crueller. To land this his father had to summon resolution, return to the room, mean murder. The first swipe had been with the open hand, the indiscriminate sort that teachers give while walking up and down an aisle of badly behaved pupils. This time his father made a fist. Shimi felt the knuckles crack against the bone above his cheek. His eyes watered. He didn't think he was crying; it was more as though the jolt had burst whatever reservoir held his tears. Still he didn't turn, but shrank his head into his shoulders. Was another strike in the offing?

He thought his father said, 'You are no son of mine,' as the punch landed. Or was that his own voice?

If his father had spoken, he said nothing more.

There was a frightful ominousness in his silence. Some transgressions use up all the language going.

His mother was upstairs in her bed. Another of her migraines. Was that what his father had been waiting three days for – the chance to beat the boy without his wife seeing him? Another and more terrible thought crossed Shimi's battered mind. Was his mother in bed because she knew too? Was he the cause of her migraine?

There was no explaining how anybody knew. He had made sure the house was empty before raiding his mother's dirty laundry basket. It was the very emptiness of the house that had given him the idea. That was one of the great lessons of all this that would always stay with him: never leave a boy alone in an empty house.

So who had witnessed what he'd done?

It couldn't have been his mother. She'd have fainted.

And it couldn't have been his father. He'd have struck Shimi there and then.

Leaving only Ephraim. Ephraim creeping about the house, looking to do mischief, steal something of Shimi's or deposit something disgusting in Shimi's wardrobe.

Ephraim onto whom, had Shimi not admitted his guilt by acquiescing in the punishment, he might have tried to shift some blame.

No matter that Ephraim was ten months Shimi's junior, everyone knew he was the stronger character. The family clown. No one would have doubted Shimi had he accused his brother of suggesting the escapade. Ephraim up to his tricks again. 'Come on, Shim, let's do it while no one's home.' Ephraim had an infectious laugh, a round face, wide mouth and white teeth. He could have been an Arab urchin. He had hot sand between his toes. You'd smile if he ran off with your wallet. And you'd smile if you saw him posing in women's underwear. Everyone loves a scallywag. But Shimi on his own, Shimi with his lugubrious eyes and drooping mouth, Shimi made a dismal felony out of what in Ephraim would have been an exuberance.

That was why his father struck him. Because he wasn't a scallywag.

It was Ephraim, then, looking for trouble and finding it, who'd told on him. That would explain the three-day delay. Three days was how long it took Ephraim to laugh himself silly, then tell.

Shames swarmed around Shimi like hornets. The deed, the knowledge of the deed, the punishment of the deed. Years later, Shimi would dream that he was his mother and that his father was lying on top of him. He remembers that in the dream his mouth was soft and open.

For the moment things went no further than the beating. But there was a prefiguring of a sort of submissiveness.

He didn't feel a man in the presence of his father.

9

'Now that,' the Princess tells Euphoria, 'suits you very well. I'm not sure about its appropriateness for helping me to the bathroom, but you could certainly go to the opening of Parliament or meet the Queen in it.'

Euphoria practises a curtsy. 'That's what I bought it for, Mrs Beryl.'

'And where are you anticipating meeting the Queen? Underneath my bed?'

The Princess's sarcasm is lost on Euphoria. 'No, Mrs Beryl, in her house.'

'Has she offered you a job?'

'No, no, I am very happy working for you. I am only going for tea.' Having said which, she draws from her drawstring floral handbag an official invitation to one of the Queen's summer garden parties.

'Is that from Primark?' the Princess asks.

Euphoria looks with consternation at the invitation.

'Not that,' the Princess continues, 'I mean the bag. Anyway, show me.'

Euphoria shows the Princess her bag.

'No, not that, the invitation.'

In her confusion, Euphoria drops the invitation and has difficulty retrieving it, so tight is her skirt.

'You'd better not drop anything in front of Prince Philip,' the Princess says.

She scrutinises the invitation from the Lord Chamberlain to a Garden Party at Buckingham Palace with a degree of annoyance. She has herself been invited to Buckingham Palace only four times, and that, given her venerable age and connections, is a paltry number compared to Euphoria's once, allowing that Euphoria has neither venerable age nor connections.

'And what public service have you performed that explains this invitation?' she asks.

Euphoria shines with pride. 'My husband is a fireman.'

'Is this a garden party for firemen?'

'He risked his life rescuing a baby. Twice.'

The Princess wrinkles her nose at the first baby, and turns her face away at the mention of a second.

'So now explain to me why you have come here wearing the dress you mean to see the Queen in? Are you planning to go there after work? It will be a little late for a garden party.'

'I was hoping for your advice, Mrs Beryl. Nastya says that when it comes to royal protocol you are the one to ask.'

'Are you telling me that you and that Moldovan trollop sit in my kitchen discussing royal protocol?'

Euphoria covers her face with the invitation from the Lord Chamberlain. 'Not all the time, Mrs Beryl.'

'And what are you wanting my advice about? The suitability of your dress?'

'Is it too colourful?'

'I do think it's too colourful, yes, but from what I know of the Queen I'd say she'd enjoy seeing you in it. She's been around the Commonwealth many times and finds ethnic costume much to her liking. The Prince, too, is given to admiring dusky ladies in bright frocks. I'd recommend a turban if you have one. If you don't I could make you one out of a tablecloth. But you mustn't be too disappointed if you don't get to shake either of their hands. There will be thousands of people there. Not all of them firemen's wives.'

Euphoria rebuts this with a vigorous movement of her head. It would seem she knows a bit about royal protocol herself. 'I have an invitation requesting the pleasure of my company,' she says. 'So I will be shaking her hand. Do you have a message I can give her.'

The Princess thinks about it. 'I had one but I've forgotten it,' she says.

Nastya has been listening in to the above conversation from the kitchen.

'Well *I* think you look smart enough to meet Queen,' she says, the moment she has a chance to talk to Euphoria on her own.

'So does Mrs Beryl.'

'No. Mrs Beryl patronises you. You are cheap adventure for her eyes. You are package holiday. That's how the English see black people.'

'She said my dress was beautiful.'

'Yes, for black person.'

'Well I am a black person.'

'Not in way you're black person for Mrs Beryl. I have boy-friend reading book about western people looking down on culture of eastern people by admiring it. Appreciating us is new form of imperialism.'

'I'm not eastern.'

'We are all eastern people to western people.'

'Well, I'm still wearing this dress for the Garden Party.'

'You should. But don't let Queen insult you by saying you look nice. You tell her she looks nice first.'

'Do you have a message for her?'

Nastya thinks about it. 'Tell her days of culture appropriation over.'

Euphoria nods, though secretly decides she won't be telling the Queen that.

'And ask her,' Nastya continues, 'if she has spare prince I can marry.'

★

In order to prove her point about Mrs Beryl's condescension to the exotic, Nastya turns up to work the following week in Moldovan national dress. Mrs Beryl is going to rave about it, she tells Euphoria.

'How I look?' she asks her employer with a twirl.

'Like shit,' the Princess replies.

IO

So that, Dear Diary, is Dear Albear, but before I get onto the *B*s – in point of fact there were no *B*s unless we count Baldwin, who kissed my hand when I was a young girl and Blair, who kissed my cheek when I was an old woman – I must record my determination not to go out perplexed and petrified as Albear did. You get everything in some sort of order if you don't want to end up howling. Keep a record of where it all is. Just in case. Stop it all slithering away.

What they call dementia, she has decided, is nothing but a failure to maintain a comprehensive filing system. And what they call losing your mind is forgetting to use it.

The more names desert me, the more I make up. Soon, like God, I will know no one except by the names I've given them. Dementievna I've conferred as a female patronymic on the Moldovan harlot who is paid to sit up all night in case I fall out of bed but is almost certainly performing sexual activities on her mobile phone the minute I turn out my light. It wouldn't surprise me if Pen and Sandy turned out to be among her clients. 'Now I taking off my girdle . . .'

That would excite my boys, given the frigid bitches they've married.

Nastier Dementievna . . .

So plausible I mightn't have made her up after all. Either I've seen her business card lying about or she's a Russian tennis player I've caught a frilly glimpse of on the floor-to-ceiling television Pen bought me for watching Wimbledon – anything to keep the old hag quiet.

(A 52-inch television for every person over seventy in the country was his avowed ambition when he was Shadow Minister for Work and Pensions. No pension, just a television. Unless that was Sandy.)

Albear would have fallen for the slut. 'Where is it, Dementievna darling? Where's it gone?' And I don't doubt she'd have shown him. I was never the right woman for him. But then he wasn't the right man for me, if a right man for me existed. Someone who was rarely there is the closest I can get. Company only for the hours or minutes I needed it.

Everyone stays too long. A couple of great-grandchildren have just been to see me. Hoping to be remembered in my will I must presume, since they can't be coming for the affection. Pen's children's children they must have been. Pen whom, if you believe me, I named after Pentheus, eaten alive by his mother. Sandy, as must be no less obvious, being short for Tisander who was murdered by Medea. These mothers! I belong to a long and proud line of filicides. If only I'd been born two thousand years earlier, which I very nearly was.

'Hello, Great-grandmama.'

Pen's they must have been. I am no more a marvelling great-grandmama than I was a doting granny or caring (there's a word I'd like to forget) mother, and would rather look away from any child than at it, but I took in enough of this pair through the back of my head to recognise that don't-see/don't-want-to-see expression in their eyes, the blind stare of the baby-righteous, looking down their noses at their deluded great-grandmama already, using their eyelids to bat away unpleasing visual information. Pen's eyes to a T, and before him his father's – the marooned Marxist Leninist whose plebeian vestiary it fell to me, as Hand Maiden of the Revolution, to launder. Funny, you never see a portrait of Marx in a vest. Your true revolutionary dresses like a dandy and is too vain of his appearance, as a rule, to turn his face from you, as Pen's dad did, in the hope that when he looked again you'd be gone.

A tender lover notwithstanding, Pen's dad, which wasn't half a surprise. Deposited a baby in me sweetly, left it there as though by happy accident, and even helped, when he could get his union chums round to observe, with the associated chores. Eyes averted the whole time for fear of offence – receiving it, not giving it – but help's still help in whatever form it comes.

Conservatively, no – Freudian slip – *conversely*, the father of Sandy, my High Tory Boy, stared his eyeballs out at as he fired me into pregnancy, like a pilot looking down to see where his bomb had landed. Otherwise, now I come to think of it, he rarely took me in. Never saw what I was wearing. Never saw what I wasn't wearing, come to that. He used his eyes for two activities only: driving and fornication. The rest of the time he might as well have been blind. So maybe I'm wrong about whose grandchildren have just visited me. The grandchildren of men – let's leave it at that. Heirs to the alarms that shook their fathers and their grandfathers out of bed at night and made them run from everything with their eyes lowered.

Has this last hundred years been the worst ever for men? Too smug or too scared to look at anything, the lot of them, and I'm not sure even that distinction is worth making. Pen senior – what *was* his name? – could not stomach a contrary view on any subject, could not bear a person to so much as *look* as though he held a contrary view, but wasn't that because he feared what anything contrary might reveal to him about himself? Terror. Terror is the only word for it. Terror of something else. And in woman, if they look at her, they know they're going to meet the ultimate, finally unanswerable something else.

So it's eyes down and plough on.

How old am I? I have authority, whatever my age. So don't doubt me when I assert that there isn't a man out there who can candidly and fearlessly meet a woman's gaze, whether in the bedroom or out of it. Will I be up to it? they're all thinking. Will I make it through? Will I be man enough? War, lovemaking, career – each one another test. Can I do this?

It would have been a kindness in every case to tell them No. It needn't matter – I have absolutely no expectation of you – but No, you can't.

I've heard it said that the Great War put paid to men.
It did.

My first son was conceived on the day Britain declared war on Germany. I suspect many children were conceived that day. 'I have to tell you now that no such undertaking has been received,' we listened to the undertaker who was our Prime Minister say, and went immediately back to bed. It was like jumping off a cliff and taking out a life insurance policy at the same time.

'If it's boy we'll call it Neville,' my husband Harris said, mopping his brow.

'And if it's a girl?'

'Nellie. But let's hope to God it's not a girl.'

'Why?'

'It's too cruel a world for a girl.'

He was a sentimental man, Harris. 'Soppy,' his mother had warned me. 'You'll have to wear the trousers.'

Harris was the headmaster of a primary school in Salford where I helped out sorting the children's toys. We were only home that day because it was September 3 — you can't fault my long-term memory — and the school holidays weren't over yet. 'I don't know how I'm going to explain this to the children,' he said.

'Our going back to bed?'

'Our going to war with Hitler.'

'Tell them we're opposing evil with good,' I said.

He shook his head. 'We'll be killing people who aren't all evil,' he told me.

As I say, a sentimental man. He was always buying me coats and scarves and wellingtons to protect me from the weather. 'You're so young and so fragile,' he said. 'Sometimes I think of you as more of a daughter than a wife.' Yes, well. I was still a teenager. Like Hamlet's father with Gertrude he would not beteem the winds of heaven visit my face too roughly. Does that mean I would go on to have an affair with his brother? We'll come to that, if I remember to. If not, don't despair. I'll concoct something comparably méchant.

It was a boy and we did call him Neville. He looked a Neville from the off. You could imagine him in a morning suit similar to the one Chamberlain wore to broadcast the solemn news to the nation. The same moustache as well. And now my offspring talk to the nation in vests. God help us all if we have to go to war with them in charge.

Harris and Neville – my little world of men. In truth, though I was a chit of a girl, I was guardian to them both. Harris might have protected me from the weather but I protected him from everything else. When he went off to fight I did up his shirt, straightened his tie, put a pen in his pocket to write newsy letters to me with and held him by the ears. 'Be strong,' I said.

Tears shot from his eyes as though from two water pistols.

It was then that I realised for the first time how cruel it was for a man to have to be a man. There seemed to be nothing inside him. Just a liquid flow of feelings. The wrong sex had been chosen for the job.

I held him in my arms. 'I'm not afraid for me,' he said, 'I'm afraid for you and little Neville.'

He couldn't imagine how we would get on without him though he'd never been much of a protector. I had to kill the rats and the spiders. I had to get out of bed carrying a shoe and shouting like a gang of navvies when a floorboard creaked in the night. He wasn't much of a provider either. The little he earnt he didn't know how to spend wisely. How many pairs of wellingtons did I need? How many cash books and ledgers into which he religiously wrote his name, his address and the year, and then ignored? He kept a record of every stamp we bought but had no idea how much our rent was. The children at his school loved him because he was one of them – he had the same irresponsible meticulousness, biting his pencil over a problem and then running out to play. 'Boys and girls,' was how he began each day's assembly, and when he returned home he addressed me and the baby Neville in the same way. 'Boys and girls . . .'

He was killed within a week of his arriving in Libya, unless it was the Lebanon, though he fancied he'd be safe there, fighting Italians rather than Germans. I think he thought it would be more of a singsong, an exchange of arias from popular operas rather than gunfire. But I knew in my heart he'd never survive wherever he was sent. They'd have been better sending Neville. I imagined him charging at the enemy, waving his rifle like a piece of chalk and shouting 'Boys and girls, settle down.'

I can see him vividly now, more vividly than I see men for whom I had far stronger feelings, but he slipped out of my life with a terrible facility at the time. Just as memories of this morning do now. It was as though I'd been held upside down and he just fell out of the pockets of the trousers I'd worn for us both.

Harris. Was he thinking of Neville and me when he fell in battle? If so, what sense does it make that we have had so much life entirely unknown to him? Was he thinking that himself — that in time he would be as no one to either of us? Was he thinking his tears were just a waste of grief? Or was he thinking nothing, as I'll be thinking nothing when the plates finally disconnect and fly off randomly into orbit? In which case, is oblivion a condition to be welcomed?

Lest we forget,
best we forget . . .

II

1939. Bloomers year. Incidentally, the outbreak of the Second World War. There is a point to war. It can put personal problems in perspective. For Shimi Carmelli it was the frozen snapshot of himself in his mother's underwear that put the war in perspective.

It was Ephraim's war, not Shimi's. As soon as the reality of it dawned – a column of armoured vehicles passing through Stanmore and an old man with a Union Jack leaning out of his bedroom window to cheer them on – Ephraim enlisted. He made a wooden rifle out of an old broom handle and ran out onto Little Stanmore Common, pointing it at anything in the sky that could be taken for an enemy aircraft. His parents ordered him to stay inside, especially when smoke could be seen rising from the City to the south, and sirens warned of danger closer to home, but he was always able to find a way of getting out of the house, wearing his gas mask to frighten invaders, and spraying the night with anti-aircraft fire. Little Stanmore itself wasn't an object of particular interest to the Luftwaffe but Hendon aerodrome, where Polish pilots trained, was worth taking a pop at, and when a German plane was reported as having come down in the vicinity of Hendon, Ephraim claimed responsibility and cut a notch in the lapel of his school blazer. 'That's another one,' he told his brother, who shrugged and walked away.

They argued about patriotism. Ephraim thought Shimi wasn't doing enough for his country.

'Like you with your wooden rifle,' Shimi said. 'Do me a favour.'

'At least I'm cheering the country up. When people see your face they think it might be better to lose.'

Was losing so terrible? Shimi wished no harm to other members of his family but for himself the idea of a German pilot singling out their house had much to recommend it. Fall, bombs, and destroy my shames.

'We'll never survive this war,' Sonya told her husband. 'I know how these things end.'

She feared the boys would be evacuated, but they weren't. She feared Manolo would be called up, but he wasn't.'Little Stanmore is as safe as Derbyshire,' Manolo insisted. 'That's why I brought you here.'

She nodded, as she always did at whatever Manolo told her. His words had magical properties. They reassured his wife so long as she could see them coming out of his mouth. But the moment he left her his words left her too. Derbyshire? How safe was Derbyshire?

Manolo would not be conscripted because the work he was doing was considered too important to the war effort. He had told her he was fixing motor cars for bigwigs but he hadn't mentioned that the big-wigs were senior members of Fighter Command, which had set up its headquarters in Bentley Priory just a few miles away on Stanmore Common. He knew what she would say to that. If a bomb was going to fall up here, it would fall on Fighter Command, wouldn't it? Yes, if you took the gloomy view. No, if you were Manolo Carmelli.

When the local school closed, first because of teacher shortage, then because Anderson shelters had to be built in the playground, then because no one remembered to reopen it, Sonya undertook to teach her boys herself, but she didn't get beyond borrowing textbooks, opening them on the kitchen table, and leaving them there. The family ate their supper around them. So it was an education of sorts – dining within the purlieus of knowledge. Otherwise, she would sit for hours on the straw sofa, by the window from which nothing could be seen, with her knees drawn up to her chin, enshrouded in a nest of antique babushka shawls and quilts, holding an embroidered folk-art hand-kerchief to her mouth, pretending to read, but in reality listening out for bombers. With Manolo fixing cars for Bomber Command and Ephraim busy shooting down planes, she had only Shimi for company. They could hear each other breathe. Another mother might have shooed the morose boy out to help the war effort like his younger brother, but Shimi's silent presence suited her lowness of spirits. 'He's my fault,' she sometimes mused, but like him she was too lonely to think about what wasn't her for long.

So they sat, in a crossfire of mutual guilt, he on the floor, supported by his elbows, engrossed in the markings on a ceramic phrenology bust which his father's brother Raffi, an extrovert with a Pashtun's complexion and an English wing commander's moustache, had given him for his birthday. This he would compare with his own head by taking constant measurements of them both. When he thought his mother wasn't looking at him he would stop what he was doing and look at her. Who was she? Yes, yes, his mother, but what did that mean? He had inherited her drooping horse face, with those great blank spaces beneath the eyes, but he couldn't trace himself back to her or see anything about her to which he could feel bonded or attached.

He was sure she didn't know what he'd done. His father hadn't told her. He began to wish she did know. He could have said sorry and she could have said he had nothing to be sorry for. All secrecy did was breed more guilt.

As it was, he winced in her embrace, uncertain whether the smell that overpowered him with its powdery sweetness was her, the mouldering Russian fabrics, the peasant scarves and crocheted shawls she wore, or the mouldering thing that was him.

He'd invaded her – that was his sin. He'd invaded the sacred priv-acy of her marriage, and his punishment was to know more about her than it was right for him to know. There are some places a son should never go.

And never expect to return from? That was the big question he wanted an answer to.

Tell me I'm wrong, Ma. Tell me it was nothing.

But she didn't know what he'd done or what he was going through. Yes, his nature was sullen and defeated. But so was hers.

No wonder his father couldn't look at him. One flinching person in his life was enough. Thank God for Ephraim.

Uncle Raffi's gift turned out to be a brainwave. Shimi borrowed books on phrenology from the local library and fingered his own head a hundred times a day, intent on discovering where secretiveness or mimicry or hope were to be found, or whether some abnormality in the size of his brain, detectable on the uneven surface of his skull, might account for the deviancies of his personality.

Soon he began to make crayon portraits of the cranium. Anyone not knowing what he was doing might have taken them to be maps of Africa, the neural pathways like great rivers dividing the continent, the cranial sinuses flowing beyond the confines of the skull like jungle vegetation gone mad.

These interconnecting rivers were not based on science. Phrenology didn't look inside the brain, but assumed that whatever it was up to showed in the configuration of the cranium. Shimi's crayon portraits were similarly externalisations of inner workings. It was art, not science. What the skull denoted confirmed what he knew to be true of those terrible caverns below the skull. So why did he go on feeling for bumps and craters? Was it a wild hope that in the act of exploration he would discover a pathway to another, better him? Somewhere, between the selfish propensities and the moral sentiments, the great cleansing river of expiation?

The only time he left the house was to descend with the rest of the family into the air-raid shelter under the village hall. He pleaded with his parents to let him stay home and take his chance. 'So what if I get blown up?' he said. 'You'd still have Ephraim.' But down into the shelter they led him. The crowdedness was hell. The closer he got to people, the more he felt they knew about him. Who'd told them? Ephraim? His father? Or did his own face betray him?

If the war largely passed him by, so did the peace. Ephraim danced in the streets, Shimi stayed resolutely within doors, progressing from crayoning atlases of the cranium to making plasticine models of it which he would sit on the mantelpiece in his bedroom, like African skulls dug up after a massacre.

Sonya's sudden death less than twelve months after the war ended was an altogether bigger event for Shimi than the war itself and ought, he thought, to have been the death of him. She had not been a vivid woman except in her proneness to sadness, terror and fatigue. But she hadn't been expected to slide out of life before she was forty-five. Was it his fault? Could he have *thought* her into dying? Had he, to alleviate his crime, disowned her in his soul until she couldn't tell his repudiation of her from her own repudiation of herself? Feeling the bumps on his head didn't provide an answer. What he really needed was a porcelain model of the human heart . . .

He left her, in his own heart, the moment she became ill. He tried to tap into the sources of sympathy and sorrow but couldn't find them. Her illness became his inadequacy. He woke each morning not wondering how she was but how he would get through the day. What would be required of him? What would he have to look at? There was so much he couldn't bear to see. Not just her physical deterioration but the hardware of infirmity: first the walking sticks and frames and wheelchairs, then the foreign objects that suddenly appeared by her bed and in the bathroom – the bins and buckets, the commode chairs, the bedpans, the aids to he-didn't-want-to-know what, the bags of waste matter. And then the smell of a body that no longer functioned. Shimi thought he would go mad with his own revulsion. This is my mother, he told himself. I must not be appalled. I must love her the more.

His father and Ephraim worked together as men, tending her, turning her, bringing her whatever she needed. He wondered if they excluded him on principle – not wanting him around them, or around her for that matter, believing he would only make things worse; or were they, out of something like kindly consideration, sparing him responsibilities they knew he couldn't shoulder? Either way, he moved about the house like a ghost – his mother's ghost, was he? – not belonging, not noticing, and not noticed.

And when, in her final feebleness, she called for him – but that's another story.

He didn't become any less ghostly in the months following her death. He performed badly at school for the brief time he was there when it reopened. His teachers, seeing him looking out the window, threw chalk and blackboard dusters at him. Sometimes he didn't even notice he'd been hit. Actuality and event passed him by. In another age he might have become a mystic. 'Shimi lacks concentration,' his school report said, but he had no mother now to talk to him about this, and his father had started to become abstracted himself. Manolo was lost without his wife. He had loved looking at her sad face from the moment he'd first seen it, and now he missed not only her but the purpose she'd gifted him. He'd been her protector. She'd called to him plangently from the mountains, whereupon the aim of his life had been to help her down, sustain her and cheer her. Save her from whatever she was afraid of. The more afraid she was the better. The more of a man, in protecting her, that made him. But he had failed.

Though he'd thought of himself as a family man, only Sonya had truly mattered to him. The boys were appurtenant to her. When she left him, they left him.

And Shimi he had given up on years before, anyway.

He had never interested himself much in his wife's religion. It had been a picturesque shawl she wore, that was all. A woven hiding place. But he arranged for her to be buried in a Jewish cemetery and found a synagogue where they were willing to teach him the prayer for the dead. He recited it conscientiously for a year, not missing a morning.

He didn't take his sons along with him.

Unless, as Shimi suspected, he sometimes secretly took Ephraim.

64

12

To assist her carers in the smooth running of operational matters, the Princess has produced what she calls a maintenance manual, though what it is designed to assist her carers in is not so much the maintenance of her or her apartment, but the personal maintenance of themselves.

She has embroidered the cover with purple smiling pansies in order that it shouldn't be too off-putting. It is short and titled, briefly, *A Guide for Young Serving Women of Foreign Extraction in the Lower and Middle Ranks of Life*.

It is divided into five sections:

Hygiene
Respect
Discretion
Gratitude
Language

and is to be kept on top of the fifteen-bottle wine cooler in the kitchen, a place which, by the Princess's calculations, must present maximum temptation, to Nastya if not to Euphoria, but then Nastya is more in need of behaviour guidance than Euphoria who, if anything, suffers from having received too much.

The Princess prides herself on the accessible, conversational English in which her manual is written, and the soundness of the advice it dispenses. Where her carers might have expected strictures, they find indulgence; where they might have feared condescension, they find only understanding.

That's Euphoria's view anyway. Nastya is in two minds.

'Why I have to brush under my fingernails?' she asks Euphoria. 'I am not peasant woman.'

'Well you are always saying the British are filthy,' Euphoria replies. 'Perhaps Mrs Beryl agrees with you.'

'Then why doesn't she clean under own fingernails?'

'I'm sure she does.'

'Have you seen?'

'Have I seen her doing it? No. But if you are asking if I have seen her nails, yes.'

'And?'

'And they are clean.'

'For old woman they are clean. And why must I wear hairnet in shower when I stay at night?'

'To stop your hair getting wet.'

'That's shower *cap*. Hairnet different. Hairnet is to stop hair going down plug.'

Euphoria shrugs. That seems a wise enough precaution. It's always her that has to fish the hair out.

'*My* hair,' Nastya goes on. 'I'm the only one who has hair in this house. You have wire, Mrs Dusinbery bald.'

'She is *not* bald. She has beautiful hair.'

'Thin.'

'Your hair will be thin when you're a hundred.'

'When I'm a hundred I won't need hair, I'll have throne.'

In the matter of respect the Princess has sweetened her advice with a pull-out embroidered sampler of a Persian proverb.

she who wants a rose
must respect
the thorn

66

Nastya tells Euphoria that Persia is the country we now call Iran and that Iran is the world's foremost sponsor of international terrorism. Euphoria wonders how Nastya knows such things. Nastya taps her forehead. 'I have brain,' she says. Euphoria says she would prefer some harder evidence than Nastya's brain if she is to believe this. 'And I read newspaper,' Nastya says. Euphoria has never seen Nastya so much as look at a newspaper. 'When I go out,' Nastya says. 'When you go out where?' Euphoria asks. As far as she knows Nastya goes to health food shops when it's light and nightclubs when it's dark. 'My itinerary is my business,' Nastya declares. 'Anyway, I have American boyfriend who tell me.' Euphoria warns her that you can't always trust the political views of Americans, especially those you meet in clubs. 'I meet him in health food shop,' Nastya says.

Euphoria asks the Princess whether Iran was once called Persia and whether it's true that it is the world's foremost sponsor of international terrorism.

'I am gratified to see you taking an interest in world affairs,' the Princess says. 'It shows my maintenance manual is bearing fruit already. In answer to your question, it depends what you mean by terrorism. It is said by some that one man's terrorist is another man's freedom fighter.'

(Euphoria will repeat these words to Nastya later that day. 'Typical soft liberal hogwashes,' Nastya will reply.)

But Euphoria isn't herself entirely certain where the Princess is coming from on this.

'I am being even-handed,' the Princess explains, 'in deference to my sons. To one, a terrorist is a terrorist. To the other he is a freedom fighter. Do you see my difficulty?'

'What about your other sons, Mrs Beryl?'

The Princess doesn't know what Euphoria is talking about. Aren't two sons enough? 'And now that will do for world affairs for one day,' she says. 'It's time for my lunch. I'd like a lightly boiled egg. With soldiers.'

Euphoria considers making a joke. 'Will those be freedom fighters, Mrs Beryl?' But she has a feeling the maintenance manual warns against making jokes.

Persia might be settled, but the proverb itself goes on causing controversy. This time it's Nastya who would like clarification. 'What means to want rose?' she asks the Princess.

'To long for something beautiful.'

'What if you don't like rose?'

'Then you can substitute another flower. I am presuming that you haven't seen many growing things in your life, given the climate of Bulgaria. I could suggest a geranium, a gaudy proletarian flower I suspect would appeal to you, though it would not work in this instance because it lacks a thorn—'

'I like water lily.'

'There again there is a thorn problem. But I could adapt the saying to *She who wants a water lily must respect the water.*'

Nastya shakes her head. 'I like idea of thorn better than drowning,' she says.

'So do I.'

'I'm guessing you must be thorn.'

'You are guessing right.'

'Then are you rose too?'

'I am everything beautiful and dangerous, yes. Or I was.'

She waits for Nastya to say, 'You still are, Mrs Beryl,' but then remembers it's Terpsichore or whatever her name is who says that.

This one is altogether more self-centred. 'My boyfriend tells me I am beautiful and dangerous, ma'am.'

'I am pleased for you but I hope you have no intention of bringing him here. Under *Discretion* I stipulate no boyfriends.'

'I thought that was under *Hygiene*, ma'am.'

'Quite possibly, child. But there is no reason why one stipulation shouldn't appear twice. Or three times. Under *Gratitude* for example. As a way of showing your gratitude to me you leave your boyfriend at home.'

'My home or his home?'

'Either will satisfy me.'

'His home is America ma'am.'

'Ah. Then as a way of showing gratitude to this country you

should have left him there and found an English boyfriend. Which would have the advantage of helping you when it comes to category five – *Language*. See how wonderfully everything is interleaved?'

Nastya assures the Princess her American boyfriend speaks like perfectly good English.

'Did you just say "*like* perfectly good English"?'

Nastya smiles. 'He teach me.'

'Then you'd better find someone else to teach you pronto – and by that I don't mean a Mexican. We tolerate no "likes" in this establishment. And I hope you're wearing your hair net in the shower.'

'And I scrubbing under nails.'

'Don't cheek me, child, unless you want to bleed. I am the thorn, remember.'

'But not rose,' Nastya mutters under her breath as she repairs to the kitchen.

★

The Princess tries to remember if she has ever slept with an American. She did once meet Ronald Reagan at a ball at the American Embassy but she cannot picture herself in his arms. Bill Clinton, too, who held her hand longer than was necessary when he came upon her in a receiving line. He told her she had beautiful nails. Later she learnt that he held every woman's hand longer than was necessary and told them all they had beautiful nails. Yes, that took from the compliment marginally but she wasn't a girl of twenty when she received it. She was eighty. And to have beautiful nails at eighty is no small achievement.

'I'm having an affair with President Clinton,' she told her son on the phone. 'He has lovely hands. He puts them on me.'

'Don't be disgusting, Mother,' Sandy said.

It had to be Sandy. She routinely mixed up her sons but took pains, in this instance, to be ringing the right one. It had to be the Tory she told about Clinton. Just as it had to be the Socialist she lied to about sleeping with Reagan.

Unless she did sleep with Reagan.

13

In his final year at school Shimi's class read *King Lear* aloud. The play suited the national mood. *We that are young / Shall never see so much, nor live so long.* Shimi, with his air of imminent catastrophe, was chosen to read the old King.

But it was Perkin 'Peanut' Padgett, a foul-mouth with dandruff and unsavoury skin, who stole the show. 'Pray you undo this button,' Shimi read without much feeling, relieved the ordeal was almost over. 'And I'll show you my peanuts,' Padgett whispered, loud enough for everyone, including Brendon Venvers the English teacher, to hear. Perkin Padgett's ambition was to introduce a hidden part of the body – but in particular this part of the body – into every lesson, not crudely, by just blurting it out, but subtly, unexpectedly and even seriously, as though motivated by a selfless linguistic and anthropological scholarliness to reveal the sexuality lying just below the surface of things. 'Peanut' was his favourite cover word. He could pronounce it halfway to 'Penis' and then deny all salacious intent should any teacher pick him up on it.

It happens among boys that there will be always one who undertakes the sexual education of the others. Perkin 'Peanut' Padgett looked after Shimi's class but in addition offered Shimi private remedial tuition.

Did Shimi need it? In his own estimation he had, the very year war broke out, descended into the sewer of his nature and discovered things which many a grown man would never come to know about.

Yet in other regards he was inexperienced and naive. He had never kissed a girl. He had never held a girl's hand.

Observing his shyness, Perkin Padgett offered to teach him words he would need, if not now then in later life. Words for women's underclothes for example. Shimi put his hands to his ears. He didn't want to hear words for men's underclothes either, he made clear when Perkin had exhausted his list of women's.

'What, not even jockstrap?'

'Above all, not that.'

'Why? It's not rude.'

'It's facetious.'

'Now you're introducing another criterion.'

'No, I'm not. Facetiousness is vulgarity's first cousin. It trivialises serious things.'

'What's serious about your peanut?'

'Everything.'

'What about codpiece? You know what a codpiece is?'

Shimi was determined to get in first. 'Of course I know what a codpiece is. A pouch to keep your peanut in.'

It was a mystery to Shimi why Padgett bothered with him. He wouldn't swear with him or go to football matches with him or hitch a lift with him into Stanmore on a Saturday night to go looking for what Padgett called dolls. But Padgett hung on to him as a friend. Once, when Shimi invited him home, he went straight to a photograph of Sonya as a bride, stared Shimi boldly in the eyes, rubbed the bridge of his nose, shook out a little dandruff, and said, 'Now I get it.'

'Now you get what?'

'What a doll! Now I get why you were in love with her.'

And then one sticky autumn afternoon, after they'd bunked off from a cross-country run and lay in a corner of the common smoking a Player's and swigging sherry from Padgett's hip flask, Padgett propped himself up on one elbow, leaned across Shimi, and said, 'I wasn't being rude about your mother the other week, you know.'

'I know you weren't. I'd rather not talk about her, that's all.'

'I understand. I get it.'

'Get what? There isn't anything to get.'

'We all have secrets. I'm not saying anything other than that.'

Shimi looked up at the sky. Normally he didn't bother with skies. A sky's a sky. This sky, though, was of the lightest blue, dotted with cotton-wool clouds like the backs of sheep. A nursery-rhyme sky waiting for 'Peanut' to defile it.

Shimi took another swig of sherry and wiped his mouth. To hell with it. Whatever Padgett knew he knew. 'Come on,' he said. 'Everyone else will be in the showers now. Let's get back.'

But he felt a hand tugging at the waistband of his shorts and when he looked down it was to see 'Peanut' Padgett sliding his hand inside. For all his horror, Shimi tried one of his sepulchral jokes. 'Shame I forgot to wear a jockstrap.'

'Don't worry,' 'Peanut' was saying in a voice Shimi had never heard before. A voice of the purest wheedling sweetness. A voice as corrupt as the smell that had filled Shimi's house in the months his mother was dying in it. 'Relax. I know exactly what I'm doing. You're safe with me. This is nothing.'

But nothing was nothing for Shimi Carmelli.

'Have it your way,' Manolo Carmelli had conceded when his wife said she saw nothing wrong in Shimi's sitting on the floor by her feet measuring his head with a tape measure. But what he said and what he believed were two different matters. There was something not right with the boy. There had always been something not right with the boy. He confiscated the tape measure when he next saw it lying about and would have done the same with the ceramic phrenology bust had he not paused long enough to see an elegance in the object. Shimi clearly loved the bust with its weird markings, dividing the brain's capacities to think from the brain's capacities to feel;

and there could be no doubt that some of the crayon pictures and plasticine replicas he was making had a peculiar beauty.

'What you should be doing, if you're so concerned,' his wife had told him, 'is getting him to take an interest in something else.'

'Like what?'

'Cars, maybe.'

'Cars! Him!'

Manolo's brother was an importer of toys and games and even during rationing was somehow able to lay his hands on things you couldn't any longer find in the shops. Having learnt of Manolo's worries about Shimi, he bought the boy a globe of the world which Shimi spun once and never touched again, a chemistry set which Shimi couldn't be bothered to experiment with, and finally a compendium of magic. AMAZE YOUR FRIENDS it said on the box. Shimi had never amazed anyone. He didn't get the chance to do so this time either. Ephraim, muscling in on everything as he always did, mastered the tricks before Shimi got round to reading the instructions, making a silver ball dance under his chin, holding glasses of water upside down without the liquid spilling. 'Abracadabra,' he liked saying, poking a little wooden wand into Shimi's chest. Shimi walked away. This wasn't magic. Magic changed the world. Magic made you not have tried on your mother's bloomers. Maybe even made you love your brother. This stuff was mere footling illusion. If it had been a compendium of necromancy that taught how to change the composition of your own heart or erase an event from the book of life, not just dispel it from your memory but make it not have happened, he'd have shown some interest. He mentioned this to Uncle Raffi, who stared at him hard, walked out of the room without saying anything, and came back weeks later with a book on cartomancy. 'This is the nearest I can get to what you asked for,' he said, ruffling Shimi's hair. 'It will teach you the art of divination by playing cards. Have fun with it.'

And Shimi did. Divination struck him as a version of phrenology, in that it discovered the springs of human action outside individual decision making. What happens happens, whether you want it to or not. It is all decided before you come along – and yet, maybe, maybe, you can change the course of consequences. Take Ephraim, who stole attention, stole the light, stole all the cheek and brazenness going. Did he choose Ephraim? No. Why would he ever have chosen a brother who blotted him out? Ephraim was simply one more external instrument of unhappiness. But did Shimi have to remain in thrall for ever to such instrumentality?

Cartomancy turned out to suit Shimi's temperament and he soon became adept in it. Thanks to his extraordinary memory and strong powers of concentration he was able to call up quickly the astrological import of every card he fanned out in the course of a divination – as, for example, that an eight of hearts presaged an unexpected visit from someone you loved, the five of clubs an offer that couldn't be refused, the six of diamonds a tumultuous falling-out. Few people are able to resist hearing about their future when it consists of unexpected visits and offers they'd be foolish to refuse. So, within their little circle word spread about his powers. All Sonya's sisters heard about it, invited him down to Spitalfields, and showered him with praise. Uncle Raffi had a card printed for him.

Avoid calamity! Let Shimi the
Great tell you about your life
before it happens.

But time soon showed that Uncle Raffi had it wrong. Divination wasn't a warning; it was a harsh light shed in advance upon a fait accompli.

His mother died and that was that. Shimi might have been to blame but that didn't mean he could have saved her. He kept up the cartomancy but with a diminished sense of his powers. That seemed to be the recurring story of his life so far: diminished powers, apart from the power to remember.

And then his father vanished into the night. Shimi had been expecting it, but again could not have done anything to stop it. He had been expecting it because of the way his father had been looking at his two boys in the years since their mother died. It wasn't, Shimi thought, that he held them responsible. But they were flesh of their mother's flesh and hers was rotting away in the dark while theirs was flagrantly alive. In such circumstances he didn't doubt that he would have vanished into the night himself. He had no idea where his father fled to. Perhaps to a neighbouring suburb where he was living in disguise. With another woman, perhaps. Or *as* a woman. Who knew? Perhaps he too had once tried on his mother's underwear.

Uncle Raffi was unable to provide information as to his whereabouts. He shrugged his shoulders. 'My brother!' he said, which could have meant anything. He began to take less interest in Shimi too. It ran in the family. One minute you were interested, the next you weren't.

Shimi wondered if he were made of similar stuff. Out of sight, out of mind. 'That leaves just us, then,' he said to Ephraim.

'No, it leaves just you,' Ephraim replied.

'Why, where are you going?'

'To find him.'

The thought had not even occurred to Shimi.

But, for the time being at least, Ephraim did not go anywhere. It had been enough just to say he was a more conscientious son than Shimi, and threaten to leave him in the lurch.

14

She was once voted Mother of the Year, but let her tell it. She needs the practice. She does memory-enhancing puzzles on an iPad her boys bought her for her last birthday, but no puzzle exercises your memory so well as the puzzle of your life.

She gets Euphoria to test her.

'Ask me who I am.'

'Who are you, Mrs Beryl?'

'I'm not sure you've grasped the principle of this, Dementievna.'

'I'm Euphoria, ma'am.'

'Are you now? In that case, Euphoria, since you know who you are, will you ask me who I am?'

'I know who you are, Mrs Beryl.'

'But I don't.'

'You are—'

'No, stop! I have to remember by myself. Do you see that certificate on the mantelpiece, between the photograph of two children I don't recognise and the framed letter from the Lord Chamberlain inviting me to Sandy's investiture – a word it is a miracle I remember and would be an even greater miracle if you understood—'

'Shall I bring it to you, Mrs Beryl?'

'No, just read it to me.'

'It says "I hereby certify that Beryl Dusinbery has satisfied the examiners . . ."'

'Are you sure that's what it says?'

'Yes, Mrs Beryl.'

'Has satisfied the examiners in what?'

' "In the programme in Moral Science. And is hereby awarded . . ." '

'All right. That's not it then. You'll just have to take my word. I was Mother of the Year.'

'I am not surprised, Mrs Beryl.'

'There is no reason to be sarcastic, Euphoria.'

Euphoria is horrified by the imputation. 'I am speaking my heart, ma'am. I am always telling Nastya what a good mother you are.'

'And she, I wouldn't be surprised to hear, doesn't believe you.'

'She doesn't see what I see, Mrs Beryl.'

'And what's that?'

'How proud you are of your sons and their families.'

'Evidently the Mothers' Union saw what you saw, Euphoria. I am grateful to you all.'

So what did the Mothers' Union see?

Let her tell it.

I don't know why I asked the stupid girl to look for a certificate. It was a medal. Still is a medal, presumably, if I knew where to find it. Some floozy from daytime television made a speech saying I was an example.

An example to or an example of, I wondered.

Given in recognition, the citation read, of the extraordinary contribution, thanks to my mothering, my sons had made, and their sons and daughters, in so far as I knew them, were still making, to the political, financial and cultural wellbeing of the country. So I suppose you could say it was really a medal to them. Or to my womb from which had sprung, taking the long view, more ministers than there were ministries, more parliamentary advisers than there were parliamentary parties, more CEOs of government-friendly FTSE 100 companies than the FTSE could accommodate, more greasers than there were palms to grease, one announcer on independent radio and two television critics.

I exaggerate but only to revive the dying art of hyperbole. On which subject – greasing, that is, not hyperbole – it was Blair who presented me with the medal. Hung it round my neck as though he were garlanding me with a wreath made of butter and kissed my cheek. 'Something very American about this,' he laughed. 'That should please you then,' I retorted. He smiled from ear to ear. Never believe it when you hear that expression. No one can smile from ear to ear. But Blair could. I didn't hate the man the way my boys did. No cause or person had ever united them before. Only Blair. That alone was reason to fall in love with him, or at least reserve judgement. Then he prosecuted what my youngest son Tahan, the possibly gay human rights lawyer, called an illegal war and on the grounds that Tahan had never yet been right about anything, though I much preferred him to his brothers, I became a Blair supporter. I think the phrase is Blair Babe, though at seventy-seven I was a touch old for that. 'He has warm lips,' I told his detractors.

'He's deranged,' they said.

'Every man is deranged once he kisses me,' was my reply.

Do I believe that? I only believe things while I'm saying them. Believe any longer than that and you stray into fanaticism.

What I don't believe is anything a human rights lawyer, in particular Tahan – no matter that I care for him – has to say. *Illegal war!* As opposed to?

My sons didn't just disparage Blair, they disparaged the medal he hung around my neck. They objected to my being rewarded for their success or, which amounted to the same thing, their success being traced back to me. What they'd achieved they'd achieved in spite of, not thanks to. They had a point, but in spite of, I reminded them, is also a debt. If you make something of yourself to escape your mother it's your mother who gave you the head start. All I ever wanted for my children, I lied in my acceptance speech, was for them to be healthy and happy. Success never mattered. I held my breath for them every hour they were out of my sight. I worried about house fires, road accidents, terrorism, war – legal or illegal – disease, head lice. Nothing mattered to me except getting them through. The mere fact of survival was enough. Dear God, just let them live. And then you pray even harder for their children because there are more of them now to be devastated by any mishap. So the 'caring' never finishes . . . My eyes glistened.

What do you think? Worth a medal in itself.

If you think, as my boys clearly did, that the Mothers' Union should have forged a few more for the army of au pairs and nursery maids and baby-changers and nannies that actually brought them up, I'd ask you not to forget that it wasn't the mere fact of being looked after and kept alive that made my family what it is; it was the stern intellectual example I set them when I was there, and the spiritual stimulus they received from me even when I wasn't. However much they chafed against the little maternal Sparta I made for them, they would have fared nothing like so well in Arcadia.

And now a message to their children's children: Say 'Hello, Great-grandma' and then beat it. My time is precious. I need to listen to the sound the plates of my brain make as they sidle past each other like ships that piss, excuse me, in the night. I had a husband, or he might have been a lover aspiring to be a husband, who thought it was funny to call a possibility a pissabolity. An Australian, naturally. Quite pissably he's alive somewhere still, one of the pending, in a leaky old home in Queensland trying to remember – now that he can't pass water without yelling out in agony – what it was about piss he found so funny.

What's so funny, girls?

Nothing, miss.

Nothing will come of nothing . . .

My teaching trajectory was spectacular, though I say so myself. I began as an assistant in a northern village primary, handing out crayons, and reached the dizzy heights of Head of Just About Everything in a Hampshire school that numbered foreign royalty among its pupils. Nothing will come of nothing, Your Royal Highnesses. *Rien de rien. Nada de nada.* I was wrong there. For them, everything came from nothing. Neither moral nor intellectual nothingness stood in their way. But that's a tedious thought. When did it ever?

That was a long time ago. Half of them will be dead now. Maybe all of them. Long lined up like ice mints in their frosty little coffins.

How good a job did they make of it? I wonder. How many died, as they say, like a man?

There's a joke – dying like a man. I should sooner teach the world to die like a woman. The women, in my experience, don't go out screaming, ravaged by failure, having to revisit the site of every botched opportunity one more time before they can accept that life has not delivered. One more time, one last laceration. Being less grandiose – I don't say less grand – women are less disappointed. Expect not that much and you lose not that much. For me, it's not the looking back on loss and underachievement I fear. I have that in my cabinets. The one thing I can't file away is the habit of self-communing. I've known myself so long I will miss me. Miss my company. Miss the talk.

That's the unimaginable part – me not talking to me. Or should that be *I* not talking to me? The rules of grammar, too, are going.

Me talking to I?

★

I talked, grammatically, to Arnold – Arnold Fini I liked to call him – for three whole days before realising he was dead.

Never mind who he was. A passer-through. Think of me as a holy place, and you won't have difficulty thinking of him as a pilgrim. A tourist of sorts, anyway, with his Michelin Green Guide in his pocket. Word gets around. If you happen to be in the vicinity, Princess Schh . . . is worth a detour. Women get passed on by men, like a foul rumour.

Hence Arnold Fini knocking at my door. I don't remember how long he stayed with me alive. But dead he stayed three days.

Three days! Couldn't I tell? Was I unable to distinguish between flesh and blood and a cadaver? Not that straightforward, as it happens, with men of Arnie's calibre.

What about the one-sidedness of the conversation? What about the rigor mortis? What about the stench?

So who are you to ask — the police?

The answer I gave them, I give you. I have always been a soliloquiser — audience enough for my words, accustomed to the half-company of men lacking the acuity or the patience to keep up. Were I to have waited for them to respond, I'd have lost my thread. So I talked and talked and left it to them whether or not they wanted to follow me.

Three days conversing to a dead man?

I know how it sounds.

But I have to tell you — Arnie was a very good listener.

A very good dissembler, too, though I suppose that amounts to the same thing.

He'd been — where had he been? Basel. Somewhere like that. Switzerland. He'd asked me along, to hold his Michelin guide, while he scrutinised Holbein's dead Jesus, but I'd said no fear. Basel? Cuckoo clocks?

So he went on his own and took in what greater men than him had been taking in for centuries. Christ on his back with his mouth open, fresh off the cross, as dead as meat.

'Why that in particular?' I'd asked him before he left.

'Pivotal painting,' he told me.

'What's turning on it?'

'Modernity.'

I kissed his cheek without pleasure or affection and off he went carrying a copy of Fyodor Dostoevsky's The Idiot.

'Why that?' I thought of asking him, but knew the answer. Because dear deranged Fyodor rolled the Holbein out of art history and into modern madness science first by nearly fainting in front of it — thank the God who doesn't exist that wifey was standing by with the smelling salts — and then by having that idiot/saint Prince Munchkin or whatever his name is describe the painting as sufficient to make a man lose his faith. Arnie wasn't sure whether he had faith or not — I didn't only go for atheists, let it be noted — but what he did have was art. He was art crazed, always on the point of fainting in front of some work or other himself.

I didn't dare walk him past the Royal Academy in case the odour of pictorial genius leaked out and knocked him over. Otherwise he had a strange way of showing his passion. He was a Dadaist after his time and a conceptualist before it. He didn't paint – couldn't paint, I suspect – but when he saw something that moved him he 'became' it. Sat for hours on end with his hands folded low between his thighs in a blue dress borrowed from me in imitation of Cézanne's portrait of his wife. He became an Ingres nude, a Matisse odalisque, a classical athlete and, serially, Géricault's inmates of the asylum, all reason fled from their sad faces and, subsequently, his own. He had a soft spot for idiots and cadavers. Get to know what it's like to be the subject, he believed, and you get to know the artist.

'Why do you want to know the artist?' I asked him. 'I've known several. They are invariably a disappointment.'

'Not know in that way,' he said. 'I mean know the mystery of creation that burns inside them.'

He had – poor Arnie – no mystery of his own. So, he did what aesthetes commonly do and endeavoured to acquire an aura through theft. On the morning I kissed him on his way I could see the intention in his stare. A day's absorption in morbidity in Basel and he'd come back Holbein, Dostoevsky and Jesus rolled into one. What he hadn't calculated was that he'd come back Death as well.

I gave him supper on his return, after which, Inspector, he put himself into the bath – the nearest he could get to a marble coffin – and laid himself out with only a pillowcase tied round his loins. Then he threw back his head and opened his mouth. It was the hideous open mouth, in his view, that convinced Munchkin of the painting's power to make men lose their faith, there being nothing less suggestive of spirituality let alone regeneration than an open mouth. In that I agreed with all of them. He looked very convincingly like the end of religion to me, one claw-like hand hanging over the bath – did I mention he'd been David's Marat the month before? – and the head pointing to the ceiling beyond which a merciful Father was not. I went in and out of the bathroom, discoursing on this and that, not expecting him to break the transfixed state into which he'd willed himself. I respected his wishes. Knowledge of another was what he sought and I did not begrudge it him. Had the washing machine not broken and I not needed to do some laundry in the bath the whole thing might have gone on another three days.

'Arnold Fini! . . . Arnie! . . . Arnie! You'll catch a chill in there.' I thought he must have fallen asleep with his mouth open.

But he had fallen into something deeper.

I know the charge to be laid against me. If I had paused long enough to close my mouth I might have thought to close his.

Easy to be wise.

Cardiac arrest, apparently. You can try too hard to escape the confines of yourself.

They were surprised I hadn't been able to tell from the colour of him but I explained I put that down to his search for artistic verisimilitude.

Anyway, the good thing is that he died doing what he loved doing.

And at least he didn't go out screaming.

The Holbein made a good embroidery. Life size, worked in shroud-white silk with hints of putrescent green. For surrealist effect I had flies buzzing in and out of Christ's open mouth. And beneath, in black, the legend:

Beelzebub pays the Lord a visit

She has forgotten where it's stored. In the junk room somewhere. But Euphoria will find it and faint, just as Dostoevsky nearly did.

15

Something has gone missing from the fridge. Nastya's pomegranate seeds. 'Gone missing' is a nice way of putting it. Nastya believes that Euphoria, as the only person who can have stolen them, *is* the person who has stolen them. Nastya has been buying pomegranate seeds ever since she read in a magazine that they can reduce arthritis and joint pain. Her mother is confined to bed with arthritis and Nastya doesn't want to suffer the agonies she does. So she buys the seeds in sealed plastic bags from a health food store on the Finchley Road and adds them to the tomato, cucumber and pepper salad whose recipe has been in her family ever since Michael the Brave won the battle of Bacau in 1600 and gifted sole ownership of it to Nastya's ancestor Maxim Eminescu, the Prince's private secretary. Euphoria believes Nastya has made this story up to impress her with her aristocratic connections. I also come from good family she'll tell her English duke when she finds him. Any seeds left over after adding to the salad she reseals in the plastic bag and puts on the second shelf of the refrigerator with the rest of her private foodstuffs.

'Why are you telling me the history of pomegranate seeds?' Euphoria asks.

'This show you aren't listening. I am describing history of Moldovan salad.'

'Then why are you telling me that?'

'To prove historical importance.'

'Of you or the salad?'

'Of both.'

'Do you think the historical importance of Moldovan salad is the reason I have stolen your seeds?'

'You tell me.'

'I haven't stolen your seeds. I don't know what pomegranate seeds look like.'

'This is big lie. I have seen you eat pomegranate sandwich.'

'I have never eaten a pomegranate sandwich.'

'Yesterday you eat. Here in this kitchen.'

'That was a cranberry sandwich.'

'This is another big lie. Who eat cranberry sandwich?'

'Who would eat pomegranate sandwich?'

'African woman.'

Though Euphoria and Nastya rub along well enough for carers, their alienness to one another does from time to time sour the atmosphere of Beryl Dusinbery's kitchen. This sourness is reported in most households where an elderly person is cared for by an Eastern European and an African. But there aren't enough carers in the world for a better selection process to operate.

Euphoria is cowed by Nastya's confident opinionatedness in the matter of human rights and entitlements but she wouldn't say she liked or trusted her. She suspects Nastya of running a sort of secret service in their employer's kitchen, steaming open mail and listening in to private conversations. She believes, too, that Nastya occasionally steals her phone to send emails to Moldova, though she has yet to find proof of this. Nastya, for her part, thinks that Euphoria is idle. 'Lazy African woman,' she repeats, though she knows this will either make Euphoria very angry or reduce her to tears.

Today it reduces her to tears.

'Crying won't make big lie go away,' Nastya says.

'And insulting African people won't bring back your pomegranate seeds.'

'Who insulting African people? I'm insulting you.'

'What would you say if I accused Moldovan people of lying?'

'I'd say that's another fake news.'

'I am going to tell Mrs Beryl what you called African people.'

'In Moldova we call this being cry-baby.'

'In Africa we call you slut. Even Mrs Beryl calls you slut.'

'Mrs Beryl is allowed to call me slut. She pay my wages. What do you do except steal my pomegranate seeds?'

'I braid your hair.'

'And make me look like slave in cotton fields.'

'I don't tell Mrs Beryl when you come in late or throw teabags down the toilet.'

'And I don't tell Mrs Beryl that you take home biscuit.'

'Only stale biscuits.'

'Like my stale pomegranate seeds . . .'

By now, wind of this altercation has reached the Princess. She calls them into the living room and makes them sit on upright chairs while she walks up and down in front of them. They are to imagine they are being court-martialled. 'I'm not having race wars in here,' she says. 'This is a harmonious, colour-blind establishment. Now, who's going to tell me what's going on?'

They both try to tell her at once.

'Hush,' she says. 'Hush or I will fire you both. I don't need either of you, anyway. I only employ you out of charity. So, what's your version of events, Euphoria.'

'Why you not ask me?' Nastya wants to know.

'I'm doing it alphabetically. Euphoria?'

'Does that mean she get final words?' Euphoria asks.

'Only I get the final word. Now. Spit it out. Take deep breaths. Not from your chest, from your abdomen. That's not what we call an abdomen in this country. Lower down. One, two, three, breathe. Now, tell me, why have you been crying?'

'Because she crybaby,' Nastya says.

'Who asked you to speak?'

'I thought this free country.'

'It might be a free country but this isn't a free house. Now, who's done what to whom?'

'She has stolen my pomegranate seeds, ma'am.'

'Why would she do that?'

'To put on sandwich.'

'A pomegranate seed sandwich? She'd have to be insane.'

'She is insane.'

'Not that insane.'

'Thank you, Mrs Beryl,' Euphoria says.

'Don't thank me yet. You still stand accused of stealing this one's bread . . .'

'No, ma'am,' Nastya puts in. 'My pomegranate seeds.'

'Whatever, whatever. The details aren't important. Now then, Euphoria – once and for all, did you steal anything from Miss Moldova?'

'No, Mrs Beryl.'

'There you are, matter settled. Now both of you kiss and make up.'

'This is unfair justice,' Nastya says.

'All justice is unfair. That's an important lesson for you to learn. I've had jewels stolen. I've had watches stolen. I've had husbands stolen. Had anyone been able to find my heart they'd have stolen that. Own something valuable and people steal it. This is the law of the jungle. And you dare disturb the peace of my apartment for some useless seeds!

'They are important for health, ma'am.'

'Why, what do they do?'

'You sprinkle on salad to stop arthritis.'

'Do you have arthritis?'

No, ma'am.'

'Then how do you know they've stopped it?'

'They stop it starting.'

'That's called prevention. It's always good to use the right word if you can remember it.'

'They prevent losing memory too.'

The Princess pauses. 'So why hasn't either of you thought of recommending them to me?'

'Because she too lazy,' Nastya says.

'So what about you? What's your excuse?'

'I'm not in charge of diet.'

'That's not how we do things here. In my entourage the staff multitask or face the sack.'

'So am I now in charge of diet?'

'Who said anything about "in charge"? I warned my sons not to hire carers from any country east of Paris. They're all still commissars there, I told them. Try to remember you're living in a democracy here.'

'So if I in charge of diet, what she in charge of?'

'I'm in charge of making things nice here,' Euphoria proclaims. 'Like cleaning the carpet and rearranging the cushions – everything you think you are too superior to do because you come from Chiswick.'

'I am not maid. And I don't come from Chiswick, I come from Chisinau.'

The Princess raises a hand. 'That's it. Enough. No one is in charge of anything except me. Get back to work. I don't want to hear another sound. I have a diary to write and I haven't got to 1947 yet.'

She calls them back before they leave her presence. 'If either of you is wondering where the cranberries went,' she said, 'I ate them in a sandwich. Disgusting. Don't buy them for me again.'

16

Manolo Carmelli didn't vanish without making provision for his sons. The cottage, or at least the bottom, sunken half of it in which their mother had cowered the war away, was theirs. They could live in it, rent it, or sell it. Whatever they chose to do, money would be sent to them, so long as there was any, until they reached their eighteenth birthdays. After that they were on their own. If they wanted help running the house in the meantime, Aunty Iona, their dear, late mother's youngest sister, had agreed to help.

A quaking hand made a grab for Shimi's heart. No. Not another sad-eyed Jilinik woman who left underwear in the washing basket. Ephraim, too, didn't feel they needed to be looked after. He'd won the war. He could do his own shopping.

Shimi left school with no qualifications to speak of. Had the war not interfered with his schooling he would probably have left earlier, with fewer qualifications still. 'Peanut' Padgett proposed their going into business together selling second-hand books on Stanmore Market. They'd get the books from the houses of people who'd just died. Free. No one wanted dead men's books. Asked for his advice on this, Uncle Raffi stroked his moustache, shook his head, and suggested that Shimi come to work for him in his toy and games warehouse on Seven Sisters Road instead. Shimi was told to acquaint himself with the stock, given a clipboard and a Micky Mouse pen, and shown how to go round with the wholesale customers and take their orders. After about six or seven weeks Uncle Raffi called him into his office. 'This isn't going well, Shimi,' he said. 'I'm impressed by how well you know the stock – but you aren't good with people.'

By knowing how well he knew the stock, Uncle Raffi meant how much time he spent playing with it. Puzzles, in particular sliding puzzles, fascinated him. He loved pushing the tiles around to make words or pictures, loved the principle of moving one tile up or down into the empty square to free another. The board was his domain, the empty square his control centre. He was a wizard at solitaire. Ten seconds was all it took him to clear the board and end up with the last marble in the centre. Once he did it in eight. Uncle Raffi thought of issuing a challenge to his customers: beat Shimi's time and you'll get a discount. But solitaire wasn't called solitaire for nothing. The minute Shimi was on show his fingers froze.

'Can't I do it where they can't see me?' he asked.

'Then there'd be no point,' Uncle Raffi told him. 'But never mind. How would you like to be my stock controller instead?'

'What would that involve?'

'Everything that you're doing now but without the people.'

Shimi could hardly say no to without the people. But enthusiasm wasn't in his nature.

'If you think I can do it.'

'I *know* you can do it. But how do *you* feel about taking it on?'

Shimi shrugged. 'OK.'

There the problem was. Just as Manolo had said. The boy lacked – what was the word? Boyness.

He controlled the stock well. Not that hard, given how little was being imported so soon after the war, but what there was to do he did.

It was while he was clambering around the warehouse, familiarising himself with every room and cupboard, that he discovered the building had a cellar. Since it was empty he asked Raffi if he could have that as his office and studio. Raffi was pleased the boy had finally expressed a wish. And he was no less pleased when Shimi explained that he wanted a studio so he could make phrenology busts like the one Uncle Raffi had bought him, experiment with materials and glazes, maybe even go into business selling them. Raffi knew his brother had not liked his son and he wanted to make amends. He didn't think installing a kiln in the cellar would please the fire authorities, but there was a small derelict garden at the back of the building and he saw no reason why Shimi shouldn't 'cook' his heads out there. And then, maybe – he was making no promises, but maybe – they could try wholesaling them to their more upmarket customers. Some shops had horology sections and they would fit in there. Or just sell them as curios. Art objects. Things that were pleasing to look at in their own right. Talking points.

Ephraim visited him in the cellar just once. 'You're like a Nibelung down here,' he said.

'I want to be a Nibelung.'

Ephraim shrugged. 'You always were the peculiar one in the family.'

'Which family?'

'That's what I mean. Well I hope you'll end up happy down here if that's what you want.'

'And you?' Shimi asked. 'Where do you intend to end up?'

'I don't intend to *end up*. I'm going travelling.'

'Where?'

'Somewhere spacious, somewhere sunny. Somewhere I can grow up straight.'

Shimi was to remember those words.

For himself he wanted neither space nor sun. He didn't intend to be happy underground, or even fulfilled. He meant to vanish, that was all. Down, down into the lonely dark.

And he was content enough, in his discontented way. He did the work he was paid to do, read books on cartomancy and phrenology, fired ceramic busts, struggled with the free-will-versus-predestination argument, and took a strange satisfaction in the single life. When people asked him what he did he said he was an importer of games from around the world. How interesting – that must mean he travelled a lot. He nodded. From Stanmore to Haringey on the Seven Sisters Road and back. He became sardonic and as he turned into a man found a look that concealed the person he feared he was. Somewhere between Vladimir Horowitz and Ivan the Terrible.

There was to be no wife, no children, few friends. He didn't go without the experience of loving or being loved entirely. But it generally turned out that his body wouldn't function without the cooperation of his head and as an amateur phrenologist he didn't think it fair to wish the contents of his head on another living person. In the end, bought love turned out to be preferable to the real thing. If he was bound to recall the creepy slither of alien rayon on his skin every time he undressed in front of a woman, or hear Ephraim's mockery, or shrink from his father's infuriated violence, a basement flat in Baron's Court was the place to do it all. You were meant to be demeaned by what you paid for. It was part of the service. They would probably let him play out the entire pantomime if he paid them enough.

After Raffi retired, Shimi opened Shimi's of Stanmore: Items of Interest. Raffi had not enjoyed success selling phrenology busts and neither did he. But he made a little with the Panamas and sunglasses that started out as shopfittings, and that, together with the small sum Raffi settled on him when he sold the business, kept him in silk handkerchiefs and expensive soaps.

He tried his hand at other things – teaching craniometry part-time to day-release hairdressers at Stanmore Polytechnic before it became the University of North West London, performing table cartomancy at Rotary Club dinners and golden weddings, exhibiting his more outré phrenology busts in arts and crafts fairs up and down the country. He even briefly wondered if he oughtn't to put his air of mannered torment to good use and become an artist full-time. As far as he could see it was just a matter of picking up the jargon and thinking up smart titles. One of his phrenology busts, constructed out of odd Meccano parts, Lego bricks, jigsaw pieces, scraps of women's underwear and titled *A Toy Importer Ponders The Aetiology of Bloomers* came close to being accepted for the Sensation show at the Royal Academy.

'Another near miss,' he thought. 'The story of my life.'

But you should never suppose you know the story of your life until it's over.

17

Beryl Dusinbery, laid low with one of those UTIs to which elderly ladies are routinely susceptible, watches bendy men climbing the mansion block on the other side of the Finchley Road. Two have made it to the top of the drainpipe and are throwing babies into the street, while a third is trying to smash his way through a window with the silver soup ladle she was given as a wedding present, but don't ask her by whom. She doesn't care much about the babies but she is concerned for the safety of the ladle.

'Quick, Anastasia, help me,' she calls. But because there is no one called Anastasia in attendance it is a while before help comes.

Finally it is Nastya who turns up carrying a sliced peach on a side plate. Sitting up in bed, the Princess beckons Nastya to her then kicks the plate from her grasp. 'When I call you, you come,' she says.

'I am Nastya, not Anastasia, ma'm.'

'Get the police,' the Princess says. 'Hand yourself in.'

'Is it something I do?'

'It is something you don't do.'

Nastya, in a skirt tighter even than Euphoria's, bends to pick up the slices of peach.

'Eat them,' the Princess orders her.

'They've been on floor, ma'am.'

'And who put them there? Eat them, I want to be sure they're not poisoned.'

'I will wash.'

'No, eat now. Quick. And tell them I want my ladle.'

'Which ladle?'

'There, there! That ladle, there! They're stealing it and poisoning my peach. Do what I tell you or you'll regret it for the rest of your life.'

Nastya opens the window wider and calls out to the bendy men she can't see, 'Bring back cradle now. Mrs Dusinbery want.'

'Not cradle, you cretin. Ladle, ladle. Who gets a cradle for a wedding present unless they're a slut like you.' The Princess kicks out at her again. 'Get out,' she says, 'before I disfigure you.'

From the kitchen Nastya rings Euphoria. 'Come round now,' she whispers into the phone. 'Mrs Dusinbery lose brain.'

An hour later she's being wheeled out into an ambulance. 'How do I know you're real?' she asks the ambulance men.

'I can vouch for him,' one of them says.

'And I can vouch for *him*,' says the other.

'But what if you're both fakes?'

'Well I know I'm not.'

'And I know I'm not.'

The Princess laughs wildly. 'Well I know I am.'

Four days later she's back home, restored to calm normality. She looks out of the window. No flying babies, no bendy men attacking one another with her silver ladle. Until the next infection.

Meanwhile she's recovered the ladle's emotional provenance. The novelist Howie 'Houdini' Somebody had given it to her as a tortuous way of saying sorry – he was always finding tortuous ways of saying sorry – for the creative tantrum he'd thrown when she'd dared to question a sentence he'd written. 'I don't just ladle this stuff out, you know,' he'd shouted. 'It's not fucking soup.'

To keep the wolf from the door and the harpies from his sentences, he worked as a bus conductor in Bournemouth, conspicuously reading his proofs on the running board when he should have been punching tickets. It was a way of seeing the real world, he said, though when the Princess asked him what he'd seen today he could only describe inane editorial comment.

He didn't have looks. He had what we called in those days personality. He walked into a room and didn't work it — he talked it. That's when he didn't have a novel on the go. You could always tell: he'd been loosed from his desk so he assumed no one else had anything particular to do. He'd propose a topic, no matter that there was already conversation underway. Or rather he'd propose two unrelated topics and display his genius by getting us to consider all the unexpected ways in which they were not only related but actually the same. The release of the James Bond film Dr No earlier that year prepared us, didn't we think, for Crick and Watson winning the Nobel Prize in Physiology, and when we said we didn't think any such thing he constructed a verbal helix in which scientific genius, physical beauty, spying, a Scottish accent, Ursula Andress's appearance Venus-like from the sea and Rosalind Franklin's descent into the murk of other men's careers, were made to spin bewilderingly before us. (I should say in passing here that this was by no means the last time he would ascribe skulduggery to the Nobel Prize which, incidentally, had so far passed him by.)

When, however, he was working, he would make his appearance late, dishevelled and preoccupied, and would actually put up his hand if anyone accidentally broke into a train of thought, no matter that it was a train no one knew he'd caught. Should one ask how it was going he would explain that even to refer to his novel's existence would compromise its mystery; but should no one refer to its progress at all he was quite capable of storming out of a room or making a scene in which he would accuse everyone present of denigrating his talent and belittling his achievement and refer with bitterness to other writers of whom it would appear we couldn't get enough. 'You are no better than the Nobel Prize committee' was a charge I had to suffer on many occasions — no matter that he was straddling me at the time — and it was all I could do not to remind him that he'd written three short and more or less identical novels about the sexual adventures of an unjustly neglected novelist working as a bus conductor in Bournemouth, and that if he thought he'd

95

ever be up for a fiction prize in Dorset, let alone Stockholm, he was living in cloud cuckoo land. As it was I had to step around his feelings as though they'd been mined. He'd show me a sentence he'd written and if I didn't like it he'd storm at me for supposing you can judge anything from a single phrase; if I asked to read more, in that case, he'd accuse me of a ghoulish desire to eat his work alive before he'd even given birth to it. 'I thought I was supposed to be the midwife,' I reminded him. His Maieutica, he'd called me when we got together. 'Medea, more like,' he said. I had no defence against this. Medea was my hero. But I'd never seen what she did as cannibalism. 'I'm not accusing you of eating babies,' he said. 'I'm accusing you of eating art.'

Well on that at least we could agree: eating art was worse.

When we spoke of art, of course, we were speaking primarily – no, let's be fair, we were speaking exclusively – of his. For all the grand statements he made in articles and public lectures about the ameliorative function of literature and the essential part the novel in particular played in fostering disinterestedness, he didn't have a good word to say for any living writer and wouldn't read a word they'd written. When he first cast eye upon my bookshelves he proposed a clean-up instigated by himself. 'What, like a book burning?' I asked with simulated naivety, and for a moment I believe he was prepared to consider doing precisely that.

Though he described irony as the first ingredient of any great novel, he was slow to detect it in human relations. Before he had time to reach for his cigarette lighter – he smoked, of course, out of the same writerly impulse that told him to wear a slouched felt hat – I came to his rescue. 'Maybe we should leave my books where they are,' I said, in return for which concession to my sensitivities I promised not to read any of his hated contemporaries in his presence. 'What about when I'm not there?' he asked. I was all sweetness. 'I hope there will not be a time when you're not there,' I said, taking my turn to straddle him. But I know for a fact that he would spy on my reading when he thought I wasn't aware of him; that he would enter the house silently in the expectation of finding me in bed, so to speak, with another writer; or would drop seemingly casual remarks such as 'Read any good books lately?' as though that would trick me into an inadvertent confession such as, 'A Clockwork Orange *and I'm relishing every word.'*

But it was laughter that infuriated him most. All laughter, as it happened, but above all my laughter when it was occasioned by words he hadn't written. I didn't ever say that it was highly unlikely to be occasioned by words he had *written* taking into account the absence in him of anything approaching a sense of humour. Why I didn't say that I am not sure. Not like me to spare a man pain when the instruments for causing it were so close to hand.

It could only have been that I felt pity for him. Which was also not like me. Did I suspect he might have had it in him to write a good novel one day? Did I want to be part of it if he did? Or did I simply want to see how long I could keep him before he'd be Houdini'ing it out of my life? Already, he told me, I had broken records. Normally he'd be gone within six weeks. From an affectionate or amatory point of view I wouldn't have bothered when he skedaddled. He didn't quicken my pulses. He was too short to be able to do that. You can't throb with desire for someone who comes up to your navel. And he certainly wasn't worth holding on to for the sex. Like many short men he thought it incumbent on him to start from my toes and work his way up tonguefully with agonising conscientiousness, as though we both had a year to kill. How he thought that would give him the illusion of height I never worked out. But at least, so long as I could blot out his questions – 'Is that good?' 'Have I missed anywhere?' 'Am I slow enough for you?'– I could think my own thoughts. Some days I was asleep before he'd reached my knees. So it's possible the whole thing held little for me other than lots of rest and free bus rides.

Then I arranged for him to give a talk to my sixth-form girls on the Novel and the Feelings (from Jane Austen to Him), the point of it being that readers had to come to fiction naked – emotionally naked, he meant, but he enjoyed the sight of the girls laughing behind their hands – and allow the writer to clothe them in hitherto unworn garments. What a charlatan he was, he who'd been going about in the same dreary emotional garb all his life. Knowing myself as I do, I suspect I arranged this talk as a trap, though even I didn't expect him to fall into it with such *promptitude. I'd arranged for tea and biscuits to be served after the talk, and as it was a warm evening the tea things were laid on a ladle table – no, a trestle table – under the laburnum trees. Half the girls needed to bend their heads to avoid the foliage, but Howie Houdini, I was pleased to notice, didn't. How he thought he could slip away with Joyce, our lump of a head prefect, without anyone seeing I can't imagine. But slip away he did, and see him I did, on his knees in the orchard with his head up her navy skirt. Knowing he didn't have much time he must have started higher up than was his wont, demonstrating, I didn't doubt, the difference between a writer's feelings and a reader's. He looked up, when he saw me, much as he would do mid-pleasuring me on my bed when enquiring if he was taking long enough. Few sights are more risible than a man pausing with his tongue hanging out to ascertain how he's doing, but if there is one it's a man pausing, with his tongue buried in another woman, to explain that things aren't what at first sight they may seem. I drove him home in silence – I haven't thought it necessary to mention that he didn't drive – and when he proposed making a cup of tea preparatory to our sitting down and talking over what had happened like adults, I dismissed him, as I thought for ever, with the words 'Hop it, Houdini.'*

It was at that moment that he looked at me with eyes of love and allowed a single tear to trickle down his cheek. What followed was an object lesson in the sexual management of men. He left the house but broke back in the day after. Would I forgive him? Would I give him another chance? In return for this solitary lapse – naturally, it meant nothing to him – he offered me a free pass: any novel by one of his contemporaries I cared to read and even laugh while reading and not a word from him. I said I thought his face up a prefect's skirt merited three novels. He cavilled but capitulated. Thereafter he knew he didn't dare object to whatever he caught me reading. I read and read and roared with laughter. This, I knew, began to interfere with his productivity. He began to complain about me to his friends. He pinned a print by Goya above his desk of Saturn devouring his son. But I hadn't finished with him yet. Once I'd read all the novels by those contemporaries he most envied, I began to sleep with them. Not every one of them, but as many as I could persuade to address our sixth-form girls and take tea and biscuits with me under the laburnum trees. He didn't last the pace. He was gone before I'd got through number four. And that should have been the end of him. But every six months or so I received a variation of a letter saying he'd found me impossible to live with, a vile and destructive woman, to whom he was grateful in one regard and one regard only, and that was that she'd forced him into writing darker novels and — for it seemed he was actually grateful to me in two regards — he had now found happiness in the arms of a woman he adored.

PS — for he hadn't finished with me yet — HOW WOULD I VIEW THE PROSPECT OF HAVING AN EXTRAMARITAL AFFAIR WITH HIM?

It is not uncommon for men who drag their wives' names through the mud and submit them to humiliating and financially crippling divorce proceedings to want an affair with them the minute either remarries. But Howie Houdini was exceptional in that he kept proposing adultery to me until we were both in our late seventies and only desisted on his decease, an event I read about in a small obituary in the Bournemouth Post *— a friend sent it to me — in which he was described as a familiar figure on the buses and a minor local writer who never quite found his talent.*

Though it would be tempting to look back on his louche proposals as a testimony to my allure, it is more likely that he'd been tormented all those years by the thought of who I might be reading and was desperate to know the worst, either by seeing with his own eyes their volumes on my shelves, or by having me shout down their names while he was lapping my feet.

18

The Widow Wolfsheim, who, at eighty-something, could pass for her own daughter, is alarmed to hear Shimi conversing loudly in her bathroom. She puts an ear to the door.

'Come on,' she hears him saying. 'You must be able to do better than that. Just a little bit more. For me . . .'

Who's he wheedling, the Widow Wolfsheim wonders. Can he have a woman in there? She knows that isn't possible. She had invited Shimi round for afternoon tea with ten of her widowed friends, each one of whom, extraordinarily, had cried off at the last minute. And she had dismissed her housekeeper for the afternoon. So there are only the two of them in the house. Who then is Shimi talking to in that enticing tone of voice?

Not a real woman, of course, but it's no less an insult to her if he's brought a fantasy woman to her bathroom.

She waits to be sure she isn't hallucinating, then she hears him say, 'Jesus God, is that really all you've got?'

Which is as far as she is prepared to allow this to go. She raps on the door. 'Shimi, are you ill?' she calls.

She has the voice of a woman who goes regularly to the National Theatre, the Royal Opera and Tate Modern. You can hear the raising of heavy curtains and the exchange of measured judgement in it – a confident, want-for-nothing voice, attractively hoarse on account of the chemotherapy. It would seem that everything works in the Widow Wolfsheim's favour. Even the cancer has added to her value. She has always been in demand for her voice and now more than ever she is called upon to act as a compère or auctioneer, as well, of course, as hostess, for the numerous charities – providing care for the aged, support for battered wives, housing for the homeless, and most recently advice to people undergoing chemotherapy – she tirelessly supports.

It wasn't for herself but for these greater causes that she originally reached out and drew Shimi Carmelli in.

But she was curious too – person-to-person curious, woman-to-man curious – about Shimi Carmelli's circumstances. She had rung him a couple of times and even got him to accompany her to one of her quieter charitable events where she was able to position him by her side and have a long talk. Where had he been all her life, she wondered. How was it that they had not encountered each other in North London before? And by what extraordinary circumstance did a man of his bearing, with those turbulent eyes and pleated cheeks, not only acquire his skills of divination but decide to employ them in a Chinese Restaurant on the Finchley Road, which wasn't . . . well, he knew for himself what it wasn't. She narrowed her fascinated eyes at him.

'It's a long story,' Shimi lied.

'Tell, tell!'

'I like Chinese food.'

'I cook a mean chow mein,' Wanda Wolfsheim said, before getting up to make the appeal.

And now here he is in her bathroom, if not talking to another woman then behaving very strangely.

'Shimi?' she calls again. 'Do you want me to ring for a doctor?'

'I will be out presently,' he says. 'I can't hold a conversation while I'm in a bathroom.'

On his emergence Wanda Wolfsheim crosses her legs. Over the years, men have gone blind watching her perform this manoeuvre. But Shimi is too flustered to notice. He is embarrassed by the fact of having had to talk to her in the course of his emergency ablutions. It is as though she has heard him in dishabille.

She taps the chair beside her as a sign for him to join her. She has laid the table for twelve so that Shimi shouldn't think she has inveigled him here on his own.

'I fear I'm going to have to leave,' he says. 'I'm not feeling myself. I'm sorry.'

She finds her deepest disappointment register. 'But you have only just got here.'

He apologises again.

She supposes it is because of the empty places at the tea table. 'I assure you,' she tells him, 'that it was never my intention for us to be alone. There has been no subterfuge, I promise you that. I am as abashed as you are.'

Shimi bows. He is indifferent to her intentions. It's himself he's worrying about. 'You cannot be expected to know,' he says gallantly, 'the things that embarrass me.'

She supposes he means a deserted tea table.

'We could go out,' she says, 'if you would be more comfortable. We can be at the Dorchester in twenty-five minutes. They'll clear a table for me in The Promenade.'

Shimi assumes they have good urinals in the Dorchester and that they'll be far enough, while not being too far, from The Promenade. 'All right,' he agrees. 'That might be better.'

That's if they get there in time.

He is in a better mood in neutral territory. The waiter pours them tea and the Widow asks to have her cards read. He can't go on doing this. He is running out of futures he can foretell for her and is frightened he might hit on one that has him in it. She pleads. She loves the way he handles a deck of cards. So – though it is strictly against the cartomancer's code to bastardise the cards this way – he agrees to show her a trick instead. What's one more defilement in a life of them?

He reaches for the miniature deck he keeps in the top pocket of his jacket, concealed by his scarlet handkerchief. She becomes a little girl watching him. There is something fatherly about doing card tricks. There is no reason in biology why a mother shouldn't do them just as well. But she rarely does. The mother whispers weasel words of truth to her children. The father enraptures them with deceit. Shimi is aware that his chest expands and his voice deepens, though not quite to Bernie Dauber levels, when he asks a woman to pick a card.

The Widow Wolfsheim, who knows what men want, leans into the deck, wiggles her fingers as though to select an expensive chocolate, and picks. Now memorise it. The Widow Wolfsheim memorises it. Now return it to the deck. The Widow Wolfsheim returns it to the deck. Men like a little flutter so she flutters.

Shimi shuffles the cards and raps the top one. Marvellously, the Widow's card slowly inches, face upwards, as though on a spring, from out of the pack. She puts her fingers to her lips. 'Oh!' she cries. 'How did you do that?'

'The quickness of the hand deceives the eye,' he says, his voice like gravel. If only all deception were so easy.

Wanda Wolfsheim has travelled the world and seen the majority of its wonders. In her time she was considered one of those wonders herself. But you would never guess from her amazement that she has ever seen anything to excel the prodigiousness of Shimi's dexterity with a pack of playing cards.

The fact that Shimi Carmelli's hands don't shake is a matter of remark among the Widows of North London. What other man his age is tremor-free in the company of exquisite women?

She asks to see another trick. Were he to propose sawing her in half she would trust him. She tugs her skirts down, imagining it.

I'm going to quit while I'm ahead,' he tells her, rising.

'I won't let you go,' she says with exaggerated playfulness. She makes a grab for his sleeve but Shimi is too quick for her.

'Conjuring is not exactly my thing,' he reminds her. 'If I'm to do another I must rearrange the cards.'

'I don't mind if the trick doesn't work,' the Widow says. 'It's the expectation that matters, not the consummation.'

Her eyes are pools of liquid fire.

'I am bound to be a disappointment on all counts,' Shimi says. 'But at least let me retire briefly to prepare the cards.'

On the bus home – he can't chance a walk after all that tea – he wonders if he did the right thing, refusing surgery. And only later remembers he has forgotten to rejoin the Widow at her table.

In her bath, lying up to her nose in bubbles, Wanda Wolfsheim thinks of Shimi. The rude man! But she cannot help herself – 'Come on,' she imagines him saying to her. 'Just one more time. For *me*.'

She steps out onto the marble floor, enfolds herself in Egyptian cotton and looks at her reflection. She dims the hundred little round film-star bulbs that light her. In the mirror it is harder to pass for her own daughter. Turning her back on herself, she takes three paces round her room. 'I am half-sick of illumination,' she says.

19

Speaking of pile-driving — I'm not certain anyone has been speaking of pile-driving but the phrase has just entered my head and that's narrative logic enough when you're my age — Piston Pete.

My pet name for a chunky Tory called Rory with a cylindrical chest which he would puff up like a pigeon's when following me into the trees. We did parks or cars — on the grounds that he could only take a woman on his own property. He was someone else's husband. 'I have enough to go round,' he told me, in case I was thinking about wanting him for myself.

'How far exactly do you extend?' I asked him.

He thought I was being ribald and didn't like it. When the piston was working he lost all instinct for play. Everything was deadly serious and incapable of being interpreted anything but literally.

'You mustn't worry about Flora,' he said.

'Who's Flora?'

'The night wife.'

This was in case I had night designs on him of my own.

I didn't.

When I say that eros deprived him of any instinct for fun or ambiguity I don't mean to imply he was a solemn bore. Out of hold, so to speak, he liked to joke, smiled for no reason much of the time, and generally took life genially. Hardly surprising, given how bounteous life had been to him, but I've met socialists who've been blessed with advantages as great as his and they have not succeeded in finding a genial way of giving thanks. Self-importance wipes the smiles off their faces before they've even formed. Sense of humour for sense of humour, you're always better off with a Tory. Somewhere in their booming cylindrical chests lurks a little germ of that amused self-indulgence without which a man will grow abstemious and turn every principle into a tyranny. Perhaps I've been unlucky in the socialists I've suckled – fathers and sons – but I've yet to stumble on one – and I'm not likely to stumble on one now – who's capable of admitting he's a fool without his trousers.

As a matter of interest, Tories understand more about personal loyalty too. They forgive quicker. Whereas socialists junk friends the way they throw out mouldy fruit. I see it in my sons. Sandy will drink with anyone. Pen is forever diving across the street to avoid a traitor. And so it was with their fathers. Perhaps because he betrayed effortlessly, Piston Pete factored betrayal into all his dealings. He certainly expected me to betray him. And maybe wanted me to, so he could start on the next betrayal himself.

I liked him anyway. He made me laugh.

But back to Flora . . .

'Flora, I imagine,' I said, 'will thank me.'

He paused as though to weigh the likelihood of that. 'I don't think she would,' he said.

No sense of the ridiculous, you see, when it came to wives and mistresses. But at least he respected the idea of a wife.

Where did I meet him? I think I must have taught one of his daughters. Maybe all of them. He had several. Good girls, he called them. I imagine he thought of me that way. Until his pigeon feathers began to fluff and he thought of me as very bad.

He owned farmland. Lots of farmland. Which he felt gave him rights over any woman who walked on it. Walk on his land and you became his by some ancient entitlement. There was affection in it. He was a man who loved what belonged to him. He once told me there wasn't a woman he saw he didn't desire. That's flattering to me, I said. He flushed the colour of the British Empire. He didn't mean it like that. 'There isn't a woman I see I can't have,' he corrected himself.

'Ah, that's all right then,' I told him.

'You're laughing at me,' he said.

'Yes, but mirthlessly. You aren't funny.'

He was hurt by that.

'I've always thought of myself as very funny.'

'Not when it comes to what you keep in your pants . . . or don't keep in your pants.'

That seemed to reassure him. Reassured meant ready to mount.

He liked the idea of himself as the paterfamilias of the nation. If he could have passed a law forbidding any other man fathering a child he would have. And it wasn't as though he especially liked the children he fathered. He'd do the rounds like a country doctor, check up on his latest issue, enquire as to its gender, ask its name, toss it into the air a couple of times, leave a cheque big enough to buy up a small village, and never be seen again. Rory the Tory. Lord Piston Pete. Duke of Smegma Magna was my name for him. Don't try that piston stuff on me, I'd warned him. I'm not an oilfield. He told me he couldn't do it any other way. He pegged a woman out and then drilled into her. He couldn't imagine how else to do it. You don't have to finish just because you've started, I told him. You can take a break. Smoke a cigarette. Even read the papers. I won't mind. We aren't up against the clock. (We were, of course. Flora's clock.) And I don't have to be subdued. I'm a willing participant. You might let me chase you through the trees some days.

'You chase me!' It was as though I'd asked him to dress up in women's clothing.

I was wasting my breath. He had only one object and only one speed, like a fast car with no gears. He pegged me out, then went into a spasm of ownership. 'I'm throwing precaution to the wind,' he shouted one afternoon in a lay-by on an approach road to Tonbridge. I was out of love with my diaphragm, and Piston Pete, by way of boasting, had declared himself out of love with it as well. 'Don't you dare throw anything anywhere,' I shouted back. But it was too late, he was in the grip of acute proprietorial ecstasy, and by the time he'd convulsed three or four times in the back of his Roller I was as good as big with child.

'Poor Flora,' he said, climbing off me.

'Poor Flora!' I repeated. 'Get out of the fucking car!'

'It's my car.'

'Not any more it isn't. It's our baby's.'

I made him walk home.

Nowadays he'd have kept a folded bicycle in the boot for just such emergencies. Like his son Sandy.

Not that he had far to walk. He had a house in every village in the county, and a woman with his baby in every one of those.

That, anyway, was how Sandy came to be born with a silver Roller in his mouth.

So why did I keep it? That's a good question. I was growing older – how old must I have been? Thirty-something . . . five, six, seven? Who knows? I could do the calculation but don't feel inclined. It's unhealthy working out how old you were when you made your mistakes. That way you never stop doing sums. Let's just say I was easier in myself, however old, about the untidy miracle of birth. There was always a way of handling it. And this one – timing's everything – I actually thought I wanted. A royal baby. Or at least a baby whose father was penetrating royals at the same time he was penetrating me. Let's not be indelicate, but these things rub off. When I say 'wanted' it I don't mean in the biologically needy sense. I mean 'wanted' as in let's for the fun of it see how it turns out. Too much is made of the maternal reverie. Curiosity can do just as well. You hold the baby up to the light, tickle it to see what it does, try it on the breast, and if you're not repelled you might even keep it.

Daddy would be paying after all. Unless Flora the night wife wanted to chip in.

The sperm chucker even put Sandy's name down for his old school in Smegma Magna. The one that taught him that it was sylish to wear unmatching socks and people the nation in his likeness.

Unnecessary as it turned out. Sandy was born the finished article. Didn't own an acre but acted as though he farmed thousands. Piston Pete Junior. People think Tory is an after-effect of education. None of it. Tory comes with the bone structure. It's in the rib cage. In the diaphragm – the thoracic diaphragm, not the silicone cap I'd omitted to insert. A Tory baby breathes with the intention of sucking in all the air that's going. This one pushed other babies out of their prams, chewed up their rattles, chased little girls through parks and expected to be loved for it.

And he was. Just not by me.

20

Funny thing. At a birthday party thrown for a fellow carer at the Fing Ho Chinese Banquet Restaurant just up the road from where she attends the Princess on the Finchley Road – carers on the Finchley Road now outnumber the cared-for by the ratio of two-and-a-half to one – Euphoria, laughing all the while, has her fortune read.

She excitedly tells Nastya about it afterwards but Nastya isn't impressed to learn that the method of divination was an ordinary pack of playing cards.

'I only trust tea,' she says. 'But not from bag. Only leaf.'

'What's so good about tea leaves?' Euphoria wants to know.

'I had mine read and they said I would come here.'

'To England?'

'To England. To London. To Mrs Dusinbery's. You name it.'

'Anything else?'

'A lot else. They said I meet titled man.'

'So they're not very reliable after all.'

'They also said I meet stupid African woman.'

Euphoria hopes for a kinder hearing from the Princess, who at least doesn't dismiss what Euphoria's been told because it didn't come from a tea leaf. 'So what's the damage?' she asks.

'I'm expecting—' Euphoria begins.

But the Princess interrupts her. 'Better not be a baby. I can't have any babies here.'

Euphoria covers her face. 'No, no, not a baby. A visit from my sister. I'm so excited, Mrs Beryl . . .'

'You shouldn't listen to what some fortune teller promises.'

'But it's coming true, Mrs Beryl. I ring her and she will be here. I haven't seen her since she was this high . . .' Euphoria puts the flat of her hand to where her breasts begin.

'And how high is she now? I can't have anyone here shorter than here . . .' The Princess put the flat of her hand to the top of Euphoria's head.

'I don't know, Mrs Beryl, but I won't be bringing her to your home.'

'Why not? She could help you with me if she's tall enough. Then I could get rid of the Moldovan.'

'She is not a carer, Mrs Beryl. She is training to be a linguist.'

The Princess is put out by the idea that Euphoria has a sister who's too grand to work for her. 'How old is she, this important sister of yours?'

'Nineteen.'

'Then she's too young. I can't have nineteen-year-olds here. She'll be fornicating day and night.'

'She's staying with me, Mrs Beryl.'

'Then she'll be fornicating day and night with your husband.'

'Oh, no . . .'

'Oh, yes. Haven't you been reading my diaries? You dare not leave a sister home alone with your husband.'

'I haven't come to the part about your sister yet, Mrs Beryl. I'm sorry to hear she fornicated your husband.'

'With. Fornicate *with*.'

'I'm sorry to hear that as well.'

'I'm not saying she did. As a matter of fact I never had a sister. What I'm trying to tell you is that it's unwise to give your husband the opportunity.'

'I am not worried that my husband would do that. He is too tired every night.'

'What about in the day?'

'He is working in the day, Mrs Beryl.'

'He won't be when your sister's there, swinging her legs.'

'He wouldn't break his vows. He's a good Christian.'

'That was what I used to think about mine, when he wasn't a good Jew or a good atheist. But a husband will do anything he is given the opportunity to do. It's in the nature of a husband. It's what the word means. *Hus*: fornicate; *band*: at every opportunity. He fornicates and then he cries.'

'Which husband was that, Mrs Beryl?'

The Princess wonders if she's being impertinent. 'All of them. Read my diaries.'

Euphoria looks downcast.

'So is that it?' the Princess asks, feeling she should cheer her up again. 'Didn't the fortune teller promise you anything nicer to look forward to other than a visit from a sister who'll steal your husband?'

Euphoria would like to say a long and happy life working here, but that wasn't quite what the cards said. They said she would meet the Queen a second time but she doesn't want to relay that information to her employer in case she tells her again that such a thing can never happen in this country. Best, she now decides, to keep the future to herself.

'No, Mrs Beryl,' she says, returning to her duties in the kitchen.

Mrs Beryl, meanwhile, wonders whether she is correct in saying she never had a sister.

Shimi's part-time employment at the Fing Ho Chinese Banquet Restaurant came about as a consequence of a falling out with Raymond Ho the restaurant's proprietor. No sooner did Shimi move out of Stanmore into a flat above the Fing Ho than he began to complain about the smells. Of course you must expect smells if you live above a restaurant but there had to be something seriously wrong with the Fing Ho's extractor fans because Shimi could not only smell the familiar plume of garlic, sweet chilli and ginger, he could smell the bean paste, he could smell the pak choi, Mr Ho I can smell the individual bamboo shoots. Raymond Ho responded with a complaint that dirty water from Shimi's sink or shower or washing machine or perhaps all three was leaking onto his customers. Shimi invited Raymond Ho upstairs to smell for himself and inspect Shimi's appliances. A polite and curious man, Raymond Ho looked at Shimi's bookshelves and saw several volumes on cartomancy. He wondered if Shimi was interested in maps. That's cartography, Shimi explained, cartomancy is fortune telling using playing cards. When he was a boy working in his father's restaurant, Raymond Ho told him, it was common for a magician or fortune teller to entertain the guests, a table at a time. For one reason or another this custom had fallen into disuse. Shimi remembered the table magicians from the Chinese restaurants of his youth in Stanmore. They embarrassed his mother, he recalled, but delighted his father and Ephraim. Magicians are like clowns, they fill some people with delight and others with terror. Shimi was of his mother's persuasion. Table magicians came too close for both of them. After an hour of these and similar reminiscences it was somehow agreed that Shimi would come into the restaurant three or four nights a week and read the fortunes of Raymond Ho's customers. Initially there would be no fee, but they would see how it went. In return Shimi could join the staff at the end of the evening and eat as much as he liked. Since Chinese was his favourite cuisine, and Chinese people with little English his favourite company, Shimi gave this extraordinary offer more consideration than perhaps it merited, and finally, precisely because it was the wrong thing for a person as morose as he was to do, he agreed to do it.

It turned out better than he could ever have imagined. Very quickly he learned the lesson known to people in the entertainment business that the best way to hide yourself is to put yourself on show. Certainly he was more of an enigma here, an aged but erect gentleman, possessed of arcane gifts, unfathomably from somewhere else, moving soundlessly and mysteriously between tables, with a silk handkerchief flowing from his jacket pocket and the knowledge of everybody's future in his hands, than he'd ever been while solving Uncle Raffi's sliding puzzles. Had the sphinx turned up at the Fing Ho Chinese Banquet with a pack of playing cards it would have excited less surprise than Shimi Carmelli did. Even the Chinese found him inscrutable. And then, when everybody but the waiters had gone home, he would settle down at a big round table with them, enjoying their badinage of which he understood not one word and helping them to polish off the leftovers. They laughed and laughed and it mattered not a jot that he didn't join in the laughter with them. He found a benign expression he didn't know he had and that was enough. The women touched him to make him feel loved. Li Ling, the prettiest waitress, even flirted with him a little – he thought. 'You smart,' she told him, fingering his jacket. And the men laughed riotously when he said something they didn't understand. This was life stripped of its superfluities, its comprehension and its verbs.

Shimi had thought he could only be happy in a cellar; this wasn't a cellar but I'm happy enough here, Shimi decided.

21

The Princess is lucky to be the age she is. Gadget free, she accepts boredom as a boon. Boredom becomes her.

But she has never liked the five o'clock part of the evening. It is too neither here nor there for her. It presses down on her with its indeterminacy, like an unwelcome guest.

It's the nothing hour when people pour themselves a drink to get them through to the something hour. She was a five o'clock drinker once herself, but she gets too drunk too quickly now and knows what getting drunk too quickly can do to a person. She has unhappy memories of drink, and of course those are the very memories that hang around longest.

Memory is a sadist.

You can shuffle memory like a pack of cards and the things you don't want to remember always come out on top. Shuffling is itself an admission that you can't pick and choose. You have to take the bad with the good.

She would love a drink. She's heard that said before. 'I would love a drink, Beryl.'

The things you don't want to remember always come out on top and the only son you would like to call you mother doesn't. That's the law of the shuffle.

It's no picnic trying to keep your life in order. But then it's no picnic not knowing where anything in your mind is. The sliding slabs of memory are up to their tricks again. They make themselves evident visually at first – spinning plates, like discuses imprinted with half-familiar faces and events, whizzing past her, stealing what's hers; and then, from the other direction, shapes she can't describe, rotating more slowly, as though inviting her to hop aboard, returning something to her, not the faces and events she'd lost, but the act of recollection itself, the recollection of recollecting. It is as though she is at the centre of a silent War of the Worlds, where what is being fought over is not territory but dimension, the very meaning of where and when.

She knows what has to happen, the space must clear, the rotating discs must slow and meet and become as one, like a total eclipse. Then she will be back in the present, knowing where things are, confident she can navigate herself again not only through her memory but her apartment, knowing which room is which and which direction she must go in to find it.

She lays down her stitching. Her eyes are tired. She unscrolls one of her school photographs but sees no one she recognises. It's because my eyes are tired, she reassures herself. Tomorrow. Tomorrow will be different.

She calls Euphoria to bring her tea. To her sense, Euphoria has never looked more beautiful, voluptuous and shining. It might be the dress she is wearing. An African print.

'Are you in love, Euphoria?' she asks.

'No more than usual, Mrs Beryl,' she answers.

'Do you know what Winnie Mandela said when she first met her husband?'

It occurs to her that Euphoria might not know who Winnie Mandela is or was. No doubt it's racist of me to think she should.

'No, ma'am.'

'She said *Yes*.'

Euphoria doesn't know how to reply. 'That's nice,' she says, after a moment.

In the silence that follows she plumps up the cushions on the bedroom chair. They are gold and show a sylvan hunting scene.

'They met at a bus stop,' the Princess pursues.

Euphoria goes in search of another cushion to plump.

'It's great love story. Let me correct that – it *was* a great love story.'

'Did something bad happen, Mrs Beryl?'

'Of course. Something bad always happens. But for a while, a long time ago, they were the future, they carried all our hopes, even mine and I had no hopes.' Unusually for her, the Princess smiles, remembering the hopes she was too grand to entertain. 'Do you know,' she continues, though she isn't really talking to Euphoria now, 'we all went through a phase of standing at bus stops where another Nelson Mandela might find us. That was where I met Pen's father. At a bus stop in Trafalgar Square. I had come up for a CND demo. I wasn't especially against nuclear weapons – I could imagine them coming in handy – but I wanted Sandy to see what a demo was like. He was about six and turning into his father. Already he believed in abolishing inheritance tax. It was time, I thought – in so far as I thought about it all – to broaden his education. This is a demo, that's Bertrand Russell, the philosopher and pacifist, those are people, this is a bus. Pen's father had been addressing the demo earlier in the day and came across to the bus stop. I can't say what brought him over. Maybe the slutty way I was standing, like a tart looking for business, regardless of the little boy whose hand I was holding. He seemed shy without a loudhailer and spoke to Sandy rather than me. "So, young man, have I persuaded you to join the campaign?" he asked him. "No," Sandy answered. His father would have been proud of him.'

'Where was Mr Pen?' Euphoria wondered.

'He was a concept as yet to be commodified in his father's consciousness.'

Euphoria didn't understand.

'Not born yet,' the Princess explained.

Euphoria looked embarrassed. The Princess imagined that she was picturing the conception of Pen there and then at the Mandela bus stop, with little Sandy looking on.

'Don't look so worried,' the Princess said. 'I've had a messy life but it's all worked out well in the end. Did I mention they made me Mother of the Year? You can go now. I just wanted to tell you that you look very fine today and remind me of a beautiful African woman. Winnie Mandela, if you've heard of her.'

'I heard of her from you, Mrs Beryl,' Euphoria says.

'When?'

'Two minutes ago.'

The Princess falls vacant.

Two minutes, two years, two hundred years . . . Why has she been talking about Winnie Mandela?

In fact, Euphoria wasn't far off the mark in imagining a hasty coupling at the bus stop. It wasn't love at first sight, but things were meant to happen after demos. It was how you knew you were having some effect. Pen's father accompanied the mother and son onto the bus, went home with them to their hotel, and went to bed with her . . .

Two minutes, two years, two hundred years . . .

The Princess gets out her diary.

It began, as it was to continue, as slumming. Was this my first bus ride since the war? Couldn't have been. But it was certainly my first bus ride since Piston Pete put his hand in his pocket to cover Sandy's travel expenses through life and, by maternal extension, mine too. A settlement, it was called. It gave him visiting rights, he thought. Visiting rights to me too. Droit de seigneur. *Fair enough so long as I was in the mood. I didn't stand haughty on my modesty. Though I did think that once in a while he might have done more than bring boxing gloves for Sandy and go a round with him. Once he even knocked him out. 'And now for you,' he said, turning to me and fluffing up his chest feathers. 'What, with the boy lying there?' 'He'll be all right,' he assured me. He believed that coming round from unconsciousness was a rite of passage in a boy's life. 'And finding his father pistoning his mistress?' 'Why not?' 'He's five,' I reminded him. 'The sooner the better,' was his answer.*

Where was I? Buses, that's right. Funny, the role they've played in my erotic life.

Cyril – I must give Pen's father his real name finally, and since I can't better ridicule it than it ridicules itself, Cyril it will remain – Cyril was perfectly happy to queue at the bus stop with me. He caught buses as religious men light candles. Buses legitimised him. Crowded buses in particular. He loved giving up his seat. If he had to stand for an hour he was in heaven. He coincided with my Shoreham-on-Sea period which made it difficult for him, as a principled non-driver, to get to me. I'd have bought him a bus with the Duke of Smegma Magma's money if he'd allowed it. But owning a bus was not the same as catching one and he averted his face whenever I mentioned it, as though to spare his nose affront, like a vegetarian sniffing a barbecue.

It amazes me to think now that I ever gave him the time of day. But these were the sixties. We all put up with nonsense from one another then. And he had looks of a sort. It was a dirty age for men, but he was like a green shoot. In retrospect I think of him – and for cheap political effect I speak of him – as smelly. He was no such thing. His views were but he wasn't. He told me once that he never perspired and I believed him. That in itself was no reason to fall in love with him, and I didn't, not exactly. You can't love a man who is niggardly with his sweat. But he didn't revolt me either. I can best describe what I felt for him as provisional attraction, as though I didn't at the time, but might one day, get the point of him as a man. It was neither admiration nor pity, neither warmth nor indifference, but a sort of considerate condescension. Which it turned out was exactly what he thought he was showing me. And the rest of humanity, come to that.

I came clean that first evening and told him there were two reasons I'd been standing at a bus stop: the first, to give Sandy the experience of riding in something other than a Roller; the second – because even I wasn't proof against popular romantic myths – in the hope of encountering another Nelson Mandela. 'Which you have done,' Cyril said, showing his little teeth. Joking? Yes. But then again not.

I had no choice but to ask, 'And how do I measure up to the Winnie you had come to the bus stop to find?'

It was a risk. But we were in bed by that time and I am a rival for any woman when my hair is down and my shoulders are bare.

'I find it helps,' he said, 'not to bring too many expectations to a relationship. It is unfair to the woman.'

I'd have vomited had there been a bucket handy. The way these men of the left pronounce the word 'woman'! As though, in the magic moment of their pronouncing it, all risibility flees the universe.

Abracadabra, bim salabim – WOMAN – now mirth be gone!

I could have called him a pious prig then and there and saved me a pregnancy, him expense and us both unnecessary grief, but I chose to give him the benefit of the doubt. Maybe he'd improve on further acquaintance. 'It is unfair to you, too,' I said.

He did something oddly self-effacing with his face, wrinkling his nose and pulling back his upper lip like a horse. I couldn't tell if it was a simper of apology or a suppressed bark of triumph. Later I came to understand that it was a simper of triumph.

I'd invoked the Mandelas for a bit of fun. Cyril didn't do fun. I've never met a man with so little flamboyance who valued himself more highly. His was the supreme arrogance of the introvert. In his view it wasn't colour of skin or quality of courage that separated him from Mandela; it was merely the intensity of the struggle. Mandela had had all the luck. He'd been dropped into a grander cause, that was all. True, he'd survived tough times on Robben Island, but making one's way up through the ranks of the Croydon Labour Party hadn't been a cakewalk either.

He'd bring his vests for me to launder. Not me, personally. Piston Pete had provided me with a person to do the washing. When Cyril discovered who was paying for his vests to be laundered he went into a blue fit. Well it's that or you'll go back home with them less odoriferous than you like them, I told him. This was a major test of his principles. Not my still letting an old lover keep me, and love me, come to that. If Cyril had felt any jealousy he would not have dared admit it. What he couldn't accept was benefiting in any way from money that was 'unearned'. 'What exactly does this ex-lover of yours own?' he wanted *to know. 'The country,' I told him. 'And how much does he pay the woman who does your laundry?' 'Not just my laundry, yours as well.' 'Yes, but how much?' I had to make it worse than it was. 'A pittance,' I said. 'And for that he expects sexual favours as well?' 'Aha.' 'From her or you?' 'From both of us.'*

Had I not been big with his child he'd have bussed out on me.

On a whim of mine – I had to dirty him up somehow – we made Pen on a pile of vests.

He was a considerate lover. Not passionate, but watchful and polite. It was as though he'd read how to go about it from a textbook. 'Don't impose yourself. Respect the other person. Sexual intercourse is the bedrock of a healthy society, and as such must be understood as an act of mutuality and cooperation.' Whatever you signalled you wanted, he endeavoured to give you, which was all very well if you knew. Call me an ingrate but in the end such deference makes you not want anything.

Cyril was as wrong about women as he was about everything else. You can over-principle sexual relations. Men who've systemised sex wear you out with their attentiveness when all along it's something else you crave. What is that something else? Ponderosity, I call it. The pleasure of unthinking weight, the bodily evidence that something grave is happening.

Just by the by, my preference for ponderosity over ecstasy has bemused most of the men I've ever slept with. They took it for docility, then quickly discovered their mistake. It isn't passivity that's driving this predilection, I had to tell them in case they thought they had to start slapping me. The weight of a man upon me was a purely animal necessity, a sort of challenge to me to reciprocate pressure, such as I imagine a horse must feel when ridden confidently. And whatever the rider thinks, the horse knows she can throw him at will.

My only regret is how infrequently this shared experience of power was achieved. Even as I flung myself down and burned up at them, clasping their flanks with my strong hands, I could sense their confidence ebbing. And decade by decade I sensed it ebbing further until it vanished altogether. I no longer speak from experience but I imagine the modern man to be all but weightless.

Cyril, anyway, to get back to him, was no horse rider. He disapproved of all cruel sports.

He left me, as he had to — and the irony was not lost on me — for Winnie Mandela. Not her exactly but in the ball park.

'I won't forget little Pen,' he told me.

'You're dead right you won't,' I said. 'And rest assured I won't let little Pen forget you.'

I was as good as my word. 'That's Daddy,' I'd tell the boy when he showed up on television. And when Daddy became a junior minister in the first Wilson Government I got Pen to write him a letter. 'Well done, Daddy,' he wrote. 'I'm very proud to be your son. I will be coming to stay with you this school holiday and look forward to doing stuff with you.' I didn't suffer him to wait for a reply. A week later Cyril found his son on his doorstep carrying a suitcase.

I'd dropped him off round the corner in the Roller.

When Pen was fourteen I made him a present of one of Cyril's vests.

'Have you been keeping this?' he wanted to know.

'Well how else would I come to have it?'

'I mean have you been keeping it sentimentally?'

'In a heart-shaped box, do you mean? No. I am not sentimental about your father's vests.'

'So why are you giving it to me?'

'He's becoming an important man. I thought you should understand the fundamentals of his ideology.'

'You don't like him much, do you?'

'Not much.'

'Did you love him once?'

'No.'

'Did he love you?'

'He's a socialist. Socialists love only one another. And then not for long.'

'So he doesn't love me?'

'You ask him.'

Whether Pen did ask him I don't know. Perhaps he told me and I forgot. I made a virtue of losing my memory when it wasn't in short supply. And relations between my sons and their fathers wasn't the kind of thing I made space in the lumber room of my mind to remember. It was enough, I thought, all things considered, that I remembered I had sons. But one way or another Pen worked out a method for winning his father's love. He became a socialist himself.

22

Euphoria, reading things she'd rather not, is mystified by the missing son. Mr Sandy she knows, Mr Pen she knows, and Mr Tahan she has heard mention of. But of Mr Neville, the poor little boy whose daddy was killed in the war, not a word is ever spoken. Did the war tragically kill baby Neville, too?

She has begun to hover, the Princess notices. Finding jobs for herself in the Princess's bedroom or in the living room when the Princess is in her armchair – plumping the cushions she's already plumped, straightening rugs, dusting photograph frames, all the while stealing glances at her employer as though expecting a request or gathering the courage to make one. The Princess wonders if it's all her fault for complimenting Euphoria on her beauty. Is she waiting be complimented again?

'You're not a housekeeper,' the Princess tells her. 'You're here to care for me, not the furnishings.'

'That's what Nastya says, Mrs Beryl.'

The Princess raises an eyebrow. Telling tales at school, are we? But she is more annoyed with Nastya than Euphoria. 'You shouldn't listen to that girl,' she says.

'I don't, ma'am.'

'She might want to marry a count but she comes from a Communist country.'

Euphoria nodded. 'I know, Mrs Beryl.'

'But she's right about some things. I'm a bit of a Communist myself. I too don't want you to be doing the housekeeping. I have a Spaniard or a Mexican for that.'

'She's from the Philippines, Mrs Beryl.'

'Wherever. So what's the problem? Aren't I enough to keep you busy? Don't you have enough to read?'

Well that's the point, Euphoria's expression seems to say. You keep me very busy, what with having to go through your diaries and filing cards and remembering who's who . . .

'Are you telling me my diaries are a chore for you?'

In shaking her head, Euphoria shakes tears out of her eyes. They fall like confetti.

'What is it, for heaven's sake?' the Princess asks.

Euphoria breathes in deeply. 'You remember saying I could talk to you about your diaries, Mrs Beryl . . .'

'I can't say I do remember that, no. I recommended that you make yourself acquainted with them, yes. Do you good. Your own culture is an oral one, I believe. Most admirable, but we like to write things down in this country. It's important that you get to grips with the way we do things. But I have no recollection of soliciting your opinion either on the contents or my prose style.'

'I'm sorry, Mrs Beryl.'

'Stop being sorry. Tell me what you were going to say. Is the story of my life disgusting you? I'm not surprised. It's disgusting me. You can stop if you want to. I'll give them to the tart. Nothing will disgust her.'

'It's Mr Neville, Mrs Beryl . . .'

'Is that a poem?'

'No, Mrs Beryl.'

'Is it a riddle then?'

Euphoria puts the duster to her face and makes to return to the kitchen but in doing so walks into the tea trolley she had earlier wheeled in.

'Are you hurt?' the old lady asks.

Euphoria shakes her head. 'I think you're right. I think it's better I don't read your diaries any more. They upset me.'

Whereupon, as though she too has been involved in a collision, Mrs Beryl recalls who Mr Neville was.

Left alone with her little boy after Harris died fighting the Italians, Beryl Dusinbery did as many others had to do in those years and moved out of the city to a safer place. She was fortunate in having her father's sister living alone in Ribblesdale, equidistant from Haworth and Kendal, the Brontës and Wordsworth, the mad and the sane. Enid was a village schoolmistress. Every member of Beryl's family educated somebody in something: pedagogy was in their blood. Without the Dusinberys the nation would have gone untaught. Enid wore her hair like Charlotte Brontë's in the famous engraving, severe but with the promise of steely abandon; though whether that meant she'd moved to the moors around Haworth to be close to someone she already revered, or had adopted the style upon arrival, Beryl didn't think it was polite to ask, and what Enid had looked like before moving up there she couldn't remember. Her own hair, in those days, fell down her back like a Rhinemaiden's as painted by Arthur Rackham. She was a strange vision in this quiet place, a spillage from an unimaginable world. Men lost their heads over her, neglected their farms and businesses, left their wives, took to drink, but she lost her head over no one. Any man worth knowing was in another country, killing or being killed. Only the elderly, the infirm and the pusillanimous were left. They had a nerve supposing she would unloose her hair to attract the likes of them.

The stone cottage was dark at all hours of the day and so silent, but for the jingling of a bell round the throat of a neighbour's goat, that she fancied she could hear the guns going off in Normandy. Enid was able to get her some part-time work at the little school and that was enough, since she didn't have to pay for her board, to keep Neville well fed and cheerful. She wheeled him to school and parked him in a corner of the classroom. Whenever he cried there was a five-year-old on hand to play with him. And back in the cottage in the evening there was Enid. It was good for him, growing up in this place, Beryl Dusinbery thought. She had that English belief in the moral and physical beneficence of running brooks and drystone walls, no matter that there was barely a healthy person in the country. But Enid noticed that she was never quite at ease with Neville, and caught her staring at him sometimes as though he were a disappointment to her. She wondered if Beryl would have preferred a daughter. No, Beryl told her, that was not it.

It. So there was something. Yes, Beryl conceded, there was something, but it's in me, not the child.

It was as though there were an anterior sadness in her that the boy corresponded to, a preparation for desolation that he confirmed. Had there been some catastrophic loss in the past that foreshadowed some catastrophic loss to come? She didn't mean when she was a little girl; she meant earlier than that. In the dawn of time, when the patterns for parenthood and happiness were being laid down. Before nations, before cities, before language. Nothing else could explain the piercing grief she felt on some mornings, waking up to realisation of herself and then the boy, sleeping by her in a wooden cot. Who was the grief for? Harris? Neville? The men over there being killed in their hundreds of thousands? There was a wrongness in it all, an ancient discordancy. And no, it would not end when the war ended.

Then the war did end and she was proved right. Still the waking to grief. By that time Neville had a bed not a cot. He was a boy, not a baby. He kicked balls and threw stones. And when she looked at him asleep she was not touched as of old. Grief? Was grief even the word for it any more? Imperceptibly, the sadness had turned into something more like distaste – not for him personally, no not for him, but for their relationship, their motherandsonness, the whole business of blood and connection, birth and nurturing, love. The horror, she told Enid, who was horrified to hear such words, of being human.

She had never, to tell the truth, much liked the physical side of being a mother. Did she have to? Unnatural not to love the maternal trance, the breastfeeding, the changing, the bathing, the mopping up of everything that came out of Neville's little orifices, but what kind of a concept was 'the natural'? If we were biological accidents then nature was an accident too. It meant no more than going along with the way things had happened to fall out. Only if there were a God with a purpose could 'natural' be accounted a virtue. And what God with a purpose would ever have allowed the dying that was going on only a few hundred miles away?

When Neville suddenly turned from a blooming if quiet child to a querulous and sick one she wondered if she were to blame. Had he sensed his mother's distaste? Could her reluctance to give him the love he had a right to expect have slowed his development, as though he meant to show he was as unwilling to go on with this charade as she was?

He began to look confused when anyone talked to him. He cried, he vomited, he held his head, he looked at her with unseeing eyes. There was brain impairment of some sort. She couldn't even bring herself to listen to what the doctor told her. The brain was the only organ she valued. The horror she had felt previously for the ordinary functioning of life was nothing to the horror she felt confronted with its dysfunctioning. That catastrophic loss she'd dreaded – here was the reason for it, here was the presentiment made actual, here was not just an apprehension of abhorrence but the monstrous thing itself.

It wasn't that pity for Neville eluded her. She pitied him to the centre of her soul. But didn't pity rot the soul? He had been delivered to her incomplete, impaired, and that impairment impaired and shamed her. She tore her hair. She thought she should pluck out her eyes.

'You are not a fit mother,' Enid told her.

The girl rounded on her aunt. 'I? Not a fit mother? How dare you!'

In the silence that followed Beryl could hear Harris saying, 'If it's a boy we'll call it Neville.'

23

He is on the Harley Street run, calling in to collect prescriptions, have his blood pressure read, his heart monitored, his cataracts checked, and the biannual service of his feet. He has his mother's feet. The moment the chiropodist gets to work on them he sees his mother's, folded under her on the sofa – frightened feet, he always thought, in hiding. His the same. Where has he allowed his feet to take him? Little Stanmore to Seven Sisters Road; the Finchley Road to Marylebone, North London park to North London park. You have surprisingly soft feet for a man your age, the chiropodist tells him. But then she doesn't know how carefully he's tended them.

Every specialist he sees will tell him the same: he's in remarkably good shape for his age.

Harley Street is like a social club for the infirm at this time of the morning. It can be hard to decide whether this is the last goodbye or the first hello. Are they gathering at the River Styx, waiting for the ferryman, or have they crossed over already? Is this what being on the other side is like – never knowing if you've got there yet?

Shimi doesn't like looking well amid so much affliction. Looking well is to invite retribution. Look well and you have to face the horrible drop in spirits that comes with realising you have so little time left to look well in.

He fills his lungs with air. He should be proud of his strong untried heart and dainty coward's feet. He should be dancing in the ballroom of the lonely with the Widows who are waiting at every corner of Harley Street for an invitation to take to the floor. Dance, Shimi, for Christ's sake. Dance with the Widow Wolfsheim whose legs are legendary and who has a ballroom of her own.

He can't picture himself dancing but he does suddenly remember he is meant to meet her for coffee. He looks at his watch. He is an hour late and when he gets to the venue she is gone. He knows what she'll be thinking. 'Once, Mr Carmelli, I can excuse, but twice . . .'

What's he got against the Widow Wolfsheim that she alone triggers forgetfulness in him?

She isn't looking for the earth from him. Yes, she'd like to show him off – the only unmarried man in North London who can zip up his own fly. (A hundred times a day, as it happens, but that's another matter.) But it's unlikely she wants it to go any further than that. Conversation and cartomancy will do her. So? What in God's name is so wrong with her?

He doesn't know. Yes, he does. She's too familiar. Not too familiar *with* him, too familiar *to* him. He has never, in some part of himself, not known Wanda Wolfsheim.

So it's himself he's bored with. He isn't Br'er Rabbit kicking in vain against the Tar Baby. He *is* the Tar Baby.

He finds a bench in St Marylebone Gardens and closes his eyes. It's early to be nodding off but that must be what he's done. A voice comes to him as in a dream. 'Would you help me, please?' But when he opens his eyes he hears it again . . .

This isn't happening now, it is happening when he is a younger, stronger man, but it might as well be happening this very minute. A hyperthymesic doesn't bother too much dividing yesterday and today. Shimi lives in a continuous present of dishonour . . .

He can't see anyone. He rises and walks, as though to his doom, in the direction of the lavatory – there's always a lavatory in Shimi's tapestries of woe, even if it's a lavatory he can't get to in time – then sees whatever it is, barely a person, a human wreckage, of no discernible age or gender, in a shabby wheelchair. An old blanket covers the place where the legs might just be, but it wouldn't surprise Shimi if the legs have gone along with just about everything else. Shimi cannot bring himself to look too closely. To tell the truth he is terrified of what he will see. Or, worse, of what he won't. Just the idea of injury is hard for Shimi to entertain, but the sight of missing parts disturbs him beyond all reason. For weeks after being approached in Oxford Street by a limbless beggar on a skateboard – a mere stub of humanity – he was unable to sleep. It is as though the more that's lopped off a person the more menacing to Shimi he becomes. He reasons that the problem is metaphysical: a limbless man gives the lie to the idea of an ordered universe. But it's more visceral than that. Shimi is only just held together himself. The horror of life is kept at bay only by the illusion of wholeness.

How extreme a case of insalubrity is now being presented to him Shimi doesn't want to know. There is a bad smell, though whether of a rotting body or unwashed blankets he cannot say. The voice, too, when it repeats its plea – 'I'm desperate, please help me' – is a history of ruination. A sunken chest cavity, torn vocal cords, a mouth clotted and malodorous.

Shimi instinctively puts his hands in his pockets to see if he has spare change, then realises in time that this is not the assistance he is being asked to provide.

'What do you want me to do?' he enquires, still not knowing if he's addressing a man or a woman.

'Help me with the toilet.'

Shimi goes cold. 'I think it's free,' he says.

Yes, he knows how that sounds.

'It's when I get inside that I can't manage,' the person says.

Manage!

What would be worse, Shimi wonders, helping a man, or helping a woman. He wants not to put a picture to the words, but a picture forms. Helping a man, he decides, pushing the pictorial details from him, helping a man would be far worse.

I am not capable of this, he acknowledges to himself.

Who doesn't wonder how he will be in the final extremity, when called upon to show extraordinary courage, or just extraordinary forbearance? Shimi has often wondered and never doubted he will fall short. And this isn't the final extremity.

He looks around to see if there are others better equipped to meet this trial, but there is only him, the chair, and the wreckage in it.

He makes as though to take the handles of the chair, but even that is a connection too far. An apology, he decides, will only make matters worse. An explanation, even supposing he can find the words for one, will make them worse still.

There being nothing else for it . . .

When he gets home he finds the message light winking on his answerphone.

No one ever leaves him a message.

Ephraim, he thinks.

A thought he hasn't had in over half a century.

When you fear the worst it will be the worst.

Shimi's mother used to tell him that. It was a piece of wisdom she'd brought all the way over from the Carpathians. As a little boy Shimi imagined the Carpathian Mountains as a place where everyone lived in dread of calamity, day and night.

Shimi's mother had prepared him well.

Ephraim is dead.

'Passed away' is the expression the slightly tetchy voice on the machine says.

'If that is Mr Shimi Carmelli's phone it is my sad duty to inform you that your brother passed away peacefully in his sleep two nights ago. I'd be grateful if you'd return my call so I'll know whether or not I've reached the person I need to reach.'

Shimi rings back and gets an answerphone in return. 'Yes,' he says, after the beep, 'you have reached the right person. But I don't know who you are or where you're ringing from. Can you tell me more about what happened? What did my brother die of? Do you have information about the funeral? I'd be grateful . . .'

He too is tetchy.

Two nights ago. Time enough for the cold to have reached Ephraim's extremities. The answer machines exchange warring messages.

Also waiting for Shimi on his old computer is an email offering him cheap bulk viagra.

It isn't viagra he needs. It's mandragora.

24

Is it my legs, the Widow Wolfsheim asks herself.

She examines them in front of a full-length mirror. The ankles are still elegantly engineered, the heel discreet, the ascent to the tibia gradual, the talus bone unobtrusive. A famous jeweller had once encircled the Widow Wolfsheim's ankle with his thumb and forefinger and vowed to make a charm bracelet in its honour. Her calves, too, are nicely rounded, strong without being muscular. Higher up there are the usual problems but she has had a lifetime's experience promising higher up without actually delivering it. No woman in London knows better how to get in and out of a car than she does. She has even made a video demonstrating the art for Age Concern though she isn't sure whether it has ever been screened.

Could be too much for the old men.

No, there is nothing wrong with her legs that she can see, but some of her mystique is gone. Never before has she been left at the Dorchester with the bill to pay.

She has overcome many personal losses and battled illnesses with courage, but suddenly she wonders if she has the strength to carry on. Honestly and truly, what is it all for?

It's only a momentary waver. She will find the strength. She is of that class of person deserving to be heroised by the age that demands so much of it – the elderly glamorous. Old women who try to hold on to their beauty have always been the object of satire, as though giving in to decrepitude and senescence is a virtue. But it isn't only vanity that will drive a woman in her eighties to preserve her looks; it can be a sort of ethical seriousness, an expression of gratitude to the gods for having once received the gift of youthful loveliness, a desire to contribute to the aesthetic good of humanity, an act of respect to those who care about the appearance of things, an expression of reverence for life itself. It is no coincidence that women who answer to this description are almost invariably as conscientious in the matter of charitable giving as they are in the matter of themselves. For duty is at the heart of how they live.

So she will carry on to the end – buying new clothes, visiting her hairdresser once a week, paying a personal trainer to keep her pliable and toned, having the odd sign of tiredness on her face ironed out and presiding over charitable events, though she sometimes no longer recalls what the initials of these events stand for.

There is another reason why she cannot afford her faint-heartedness to be anything but temporary. She doesn't just have grandchildren to think about; she has a parent. The Widow Wolfsheim is not the only Widow Wolfsheim. For her part, the older Widow Wolfsheim has long forgotten there is a younger. Her self-engrossment is of another order to her daughter's. She is not preserving herself to make the world a better place; she preserves herself because some inner demon of the sort that drives an infant makes her do so, regardless of any pleasure she gives to others or any inconvenience she causes them. Nothing in mind or body breaks the circle of her egoism. A hoop of indomitable will, weighing less than a one-year-old child, the older Widow Wolfsheim lies leaking in her own bed in her own house with lipstick smeared roughly in the area of her mouth, with the sole intention of outliving everyone she has ever known, though she cannot of course remember anyone she has ever known. She no longer recognises her daughter but her umbilicus is connected to her day and night by the latest 4G technology which she accesses on a giant telephone pad by jabbing at the letter E for Emergency. For the older Wolfsheim every hour is an emergency. Knowledge of who it is she is telling she is hungry, thirsty, lonely, needs moving, needs bathing, has long faded. A team of people attends to her wants but only the daughter she no longer recognises can satisfy the most important of them, which is to torment the daughter she can no longer recognise.

The younger Widow Wolfsheim accepts that this is nature's law. She hopes she won't torment her children when her turn comes but suspects she probably will. Just occasionally she turns off her phone, as she did the afternoon she had Shimi Carmelli round for tea. She is filled with guilt when she does this and always fears it will be the time the mother who is dead in every other way dies in actuality. But she must have some life to herself. That also is nature's law. Which is why she grows depressed when that life fails to materialise.

Though there are overwhelmingly good reasons why the younger Widow Wolfsheim should ignore nature, rip open the pillow and stuff the feathers one by one into the older Widow Wolfsheim's unquiet mouth, she doesn't do it. 'She will outlive me,' Wanda Wolfsheim often thinks. 'She will probably outlive my granddaughters, it is not impossible she will outlive the human race.' But she continues to answer her mother's calls, and when she cannot still the abuse she receives on the telephone she goes around to have more of it spat, as though from a babbling corpse, into her face.

She is not the only Widow in North London for whom this is the underside of life. Most of her friends are wired up to mothers born before the outbreak of the Great War. Though it is dressed in the language of motherly frailty and daughterly obligation, it might as well be the Great War refought: a battle between the dying and the as-good-as-dead for the last remnant of attention, the last gasp of air, the final word.

No relation is as pitiless as that between a mother and a daughter. But knowing that doesn't help. 'Bring forth men children only' was good advice.

For the Widow Wolfsheim and her widowed women friends these should have been the good years, the long-earned, long-awaited remuneration for tedious marriages to unfaithful men and the thankless chores of parenthood. The children are fled for good or ill and the husbands lie where the mosquito bite of illicit desire can no more be scratched. All that's owing to the Widows should now be theirs – forget honour, love, obedience, troops of friends: just quiet and the occasional gentle perturbation of the heart. But it would appear that humankind is forever to be denied happiness. The Widows are liberated from one enslavement only to be sold into another. Thanks to science and technology, those great impartial prolongers of what has no reason to be prolonged other than that it can be, they live longer only to suffer longer.

Somewhere not far away Beryl Dusinbery is working the words I know when one is dead and when one lives - She's dead as earth in fine black thread upon a black background. It is a shame that she and Wanda Wolfsheim can't get together to discuss this. They would probably have a lively time of it.

Wanda Wolfsheim puts on a pair of trousers and goes to Harrods.

25

Shimi pictures Ephraim passed away, getting colder by the second. Is there a limit to cold?

He puts his shaking hand to his throat where it's warm.

There's no recovering from the loss of a younger brother. Shimi might not have seen Ephraim for half a lifetime but his brother has always been a fixture of the heart. You don't see your heart either. But there it is, and there Ephraim was. To remain alive – that was the unspoken contract – the younger brother must not die before the older.

Those Carpathian superstitions. When you fear something is wrong, something will be wrong. And when one of you is ill, the other will know of it, no matter how great the distance between you.

Shimi blames himself for not sensing Ephraim's death, as a marked change in the universe, the minute it occurred. The sky should have darkened, volcanoes should have spat fire, his own heart should have burst when Ephraim's did.

So how long is it since the brothers met? Would they have known each other had they passed in the street yesterday?

What did Ephraim look like? Not at the moment of his death, but essentially, for all time. Given how much Shimi remembers, how can he not see his brother's face? There must be a reason he can't reassemble it from the fragments of the past. He mustn't want to.

He has no family photographs on his mantelpiece to help him, just postcards of far-away places, a collection of dusty phrenology busts – some antique, some of his own making – and a certificate of membership from the Society of Cartomancers. He stares at the mantelpiece, at the image that isn't there, at the space where Ephraim should have been. The atmosphere of Ephraim fills the space. That's sufficient, Shimi has always believed. The atmosphere of a person is all that matters. Who cares about the eyes and mouth? But he still wishes he could call back the face. Can he mourn him without the face? Can he even miss him? Then he remembers: buried at the bottom of his wardrobe is that commonplace biscuit tin of memorabilia everyone keeps for just such a day as this. Nearly thrown out, but not.

Once you've got rid of the biscuit tin the only thing left to get rid of is yourself.

He drags it out and there – miracle of miracles, absurdity of absurdity, at the very top of an unordered pile of frilly-edged black-and-white photographs and letters, they are – Ephraim and Shimi, unless it's Shimi and Ephraim, impossible to tell apart under the cowboy hats they're wearing, no matter that in life they bore not the slightest resemblance to each other, Ephraim and Shimi, Shimi and Ephraim, two apparently carefree pre-war boys of roughly the same age, fooling about in their garden in Stanmore, one in a wheelbarrow grinning, one pushing the wheelbarrow, grinning likewise.

Shimi, whichever one he is, grinning!

How old are they? Eight or nine, he estimates. So the garden is still paradisal. Shimi and his brother before the fall. Not the war, the fall. Shimi's Fall.

Was life nothing but grinning then?

He approaches the mantelpiece and moves aside a sepia postcard of New York, sent to him by Uncle Raffi centuries ago. This he replaces with the photograph of two brothers who are a mystery to him, having a good time. He wonders who took it, his mother or his father, and then remembers – his mother, of course it was his mother, chasing them with a box camera – Shimi's Kodak, it must have been – at her chest. Was that what they were grinning at – their mother running after them round and round the garden while one pushed the other in a wheelbarrow? Where had that memory gone? Too happy for him, was it? Too energetic for his memory of her? Has he invalided her over the years – invalidated her – to satisfy some invalid necessity of his own?

He falls into a chair with the tin on his knee. Normally it's only the past he cannot contemplate. Today it is the present. Other than his bathroom, there is little in his surroundings to give him comfort. Of no discernible period or style, his flat could be a show home for ex-spies or terrorists-in-waiting. There are no papers lying about, and no surfaces where papers could be laid. There are indistinguishable Mittel-European landscapes on the walls, a half a dozen Venetian water glasses on a papier mâché tray inlaid with shells, an old-fashioned stereo housed in a fifties sideboard with spindle legs. He sits in what at one time was called a cocktail chair, upholstered in turquoise felt. He seldom invites anyone back, though he has nothing to fear. There is nothing here to incriminate him. Unless that's what would incriminate him. Who, without something to hide or punish himself for, would choose to live like this?

Having put the photograph on the mantelpiece, Shimi gets up, takes it down and scrutinises it more closely.

Does Ephraim have this photograph too, he wonders?

Does? The word is *did*.

Did, *did* Ephraim have this photograph? Did he look at it ever? Could he tell which of them was which?

Where had he been? What had he been doing since Shimi had seen him last in Blackpool? Shimi hasn't thought about him often, but did Ephraim *ever* think of him? Did he wonder how the stock controlling and the phrenology busts were going? Did he remember anything about Shimi at all? And what did he, Shimi the memory man, truly remember about Ephraim? Could you be a good brother in retrospect to someone you'd made so little effort to think about?

He would like to say he doesn't know why or how they drifted apart. He has constructed an elegant edifice of mystification and sadness around their estrangement. It goes like this: *it's in the nature of separation without fracture that its history cannot be traced; because there's no event that marks it, there's nothing to remember; better to have had a fight; better to be left cursing or vowing revenge; this way is too upsetting; what you don't commemorate in love or rage might as well never have been.*

False, every word of it. However bloodless their separation, it could be traced to a distinct event. It was their mother's dying that did for them.

Aside from a pervasive absence of robustness – though in that case explain the newly excavated memory of her chasing them with her box camera – there'd been nothing wrong with their mother's health and suddenly there was. Disease went through her at the first mention of its presence. It just said its name – *breast cancer* – and, as though the verbalisation was fatal in itself, she capitulated to it at once. Emotionally, it felled her husband and her sons with the same immediacy. It was as though the timber of her family could not survive so much as a mention of her illness and split asunder, at the first breath of it, like a brittle log beneath an axe. Was that all it took? Had it been waiting to come apart ever since Shimi mortally betrayed it? Was the axe that cleft it, him?

She spent her final days in hospital. Shimi sat uselessly by her, holding back his tears. She had gone blind and would put out her hand to find his. 'Is that you, Shimi?' He couldn't trust himself to answer.

For the comfort he brought her, for the love he showed her, he might as well not have been there. Ephraim, though younger, did a far better job. Ephraim lifted her in bed, adjusted her night clothes, mopped her brow, made her comfortable, kissed her brow. Yes, it's me, Ephraim. I'm here, Mam.

Shimi uselesss by her bedside. Fastidious and ashamed.

It was worse than that. The invariable law of Shimi's memory – dig deeper and it's worse. At the end he wouldn't even admit to her that he *was* there. 'Shimi?' she would implore out of her darkness. And he would say nothing. He didn't dare risk answering, 'Yes, Mam, I am here beside you,' for fear she would ask something of him that he couldn't give.

There was so little of her left he dreaded touching her. What if she broke into a thousand pieces in his hands?

Was that why he and Ephraim went their separate ways? Because Ephraim had seen what an unnatural wretch he was? Or was it because Shimi couldn't forgive Ephraim his assumption of authority?

You could have helped me, Ephraim, Shimi thought. I was your brother. You didn't have to triumph morally and psychologically over me. Caring for a dying mother is not a competition. You could have said we'll do this together. But no, you had to be all man and all woman to her. And you wouldn't leave any room for me.

They didn't see each other much after their father decamped, and then they didn't see each other at all. Except once. And that was Ephraim's doing. 'Guess where I am,' he wrote on the back of a postcard showing donkeys on a vast expanse of empty beach with Blackpool Tower in the background. 'Why don't you visit me? Take yourself out of that rat hole for a weekend.' He left no address. Which could only have meant that he didn't really want Shimi to visit him. But then why send the card?

Shimi packed a bag and caught the train.

It was 1959. The year of the Mental Health Act, which he read about in *The Times* on the train north, and which interested him for no other reason than that it abolished the category of 'moral imbecile', a term he had come across in the *Encyclopaedia Britannica* in the Hendon public library when trawling through mental disorders of the sort that might just cover his infamous aberration. Moral imbecility stuck him as preferable to all other explanations. He'd even identified a moral imbecility nodule on his phrenology bust, just behind the left ear. Against any thought of gender uncertainty he had resolutely turned his back. It hadn't been uncertainty that had got him into his mother's bloomers, it had been curiosity. Idle, indecent, imbecile curiosity. Sex made everybody mad and it made adolescents even madder. And a boy could be a moral imbecile and still remain definitively a boy. Now, twenty years on, he was on a train to Blackpool reading in *The Times* that they'd abolished the category. No more moral imbecility. Did that mean they'd abolished the episode? Was he wiped clean of his mother's bloomers?

And where did that leave the nodule he'd identified?

He took the train without any idea where Ephraim was living. He had never been to Blackpool but from Ephraim's off-season postcard showing trams on an empty promenade – had his invitation been ironic: did he never really intend that Shimi should visit him? – he envisaged an abandoned, old-fashioned resort with an inhospitable wind blowing in from the Irish Sea. He didn't imagine it would be hard to find his brother if he asked around. Who in Blackpool would look the way Ephraim looked? The whole town must have known him.

He was right about the wind. But had no luck finding his brother. When he made enquiries, people just shook their heads at him. Ephraim Carmelli? Sounded like a clown. Had he tried the Tower Circus?

He found a boarding house that had time restrictions pinned to the bedroom door. Out by ten, back by eleven, no visitors. So this was what people meant by holidays. Shimi was surprised to find himself missing Little Stanmore.

Two girls in floral dresses picked him up on the promenade. He didn't understand their accents so he might have been wrong about their intentions. But they linked arms with him in the most companionable manner – they could have been his sisters – one on either side, and proposed he take them back to his hotel. It occurred to him they just wanted to get out of the cold. He told them he wasn't staying at what could be called a hotel exactly; it was more a reformatory. They were staying somewhere similar. So they led him to the dunes. He lay between them on the damp sand, shivering in their arms, and thanked them both when it was over. They laughed, not unkindly, as they repaired their lipstick, at his courteous manner. They seemed so taken aback by it that he could only assume people didn't say thank you where they came from. They didn't return the compliment. Which was fair enough. They didn't have much to thank him for.

He had liked the idea of being shared. It removed many of his compunctions. The extra diligence required took him out of his head briefly and freed him from the fear of giving a wrong impression. He had no responsibility to two. He didn't have to pretend to be someone he wasn't. But he accepted that there wasn't really enough of him to go round.

He bought them chips afterwards and when they parted they kissed him chastely on each cheek. It's possible that one of them said, 'No hard feelings.'

It hadn't been an ugly experience. He hoped it hadn't been unpleasant for them either. It left him feeling mournful, that was all. Disconsolate, as though the wind that had chilled his bones had chilled something inside him as well. Not his heart. Not his soul. It hadn't been as bad as that. Some other part. Something that had no name. Here where I should be able to have a good time, he thought, I can't.

Unless that *was* his good time.

The next day he saw them on the promenade linked to another man. They waved at him in the friendliest manner.

He waved back, hoping they'd found someone who was staying in a hotel this time.

Having nothing else to do, and the rain holding off, he wandered onto the South Pier where, not looking at anything in particular, he suddenly saw painted on a mocked-up gypsy caravan the words

SHIMI THE GREAT: CARTOMANCER
FORTUNES TOLD

26

This is what he can remember of the day:
    The nautical clinking of the boards on the pier.
    The spaces between them through which he could see the grey sea.
    A child blubbering over an ice cream it had dropped.
    Pellets hitting their target in a shooting gallery.
    The sound of pennies tumbling out of a slot machine.
    The laughter of a mechanical clown.
    A person shouting the price of donkey rides on the beach below.
    Gulls swooping.
    A logjam of angry charcoal clouds, threatening to burst.
    Women in headscarves.
    A merry-go-round with painted horses rising and falling.
    A row of empty deckchairs, their canvas seats flapping.
    A poster advertising the Rainbow Pierrots.
    A stall selling rock.
    A man complaining he could see nothing through a telescope.
    A woman saying you're hopeless, let me try.
    The smell of stewed tea and spilt ale.
    The girls waving to him.
    The question: had they waved to him today or the day before.
    His mournfulness.
    Two loose nails in the boards beneath his feet.
    The question: what were the boards nailed to?
    His balance going.

His wanting to apologise to someone.

His wanting not to be here.

The caravan.

The words.

His laughability.

The sensation, familiar to him when he stayed in the shower too long, scrubbing, of time falling from him, of not being the same person when he came out as he had been when he went in.

A deep sense of disappointment in himself for not being above absurd contingency. He had always unwrapped every new day as though it might go off in his face, or worse as though it would contain some material — a hateful letter, a soiled garment, dog shit, his own shit — that would reduce him to retching without end. And now here, in some unknown and yet utterly familiar dimension, whatever it was, was. And what, after all that waiting, was it? Nothing more interesting than blundering into his own future.

The smell of toffee apple.

The first spurt of rain.

Two seagulls fighting over a crumb of bread.

The sight of Ephraim with a rag tied round his head . . .

And after that, he wishes he remembered nothing.

The meeting went badly.

Ephraim told him he'd bought the caravan from a gypsy woman.

Looking at the upturned fish bowl on the table, Shimi snorted. What told him she was a gypsy? Did she give him a sprig of lucky heather?

I met her at Alcoholics Anonymous.

You're an alcoholic?

Why shouldn't I be?

Is that what you brought me here to tell me?

I didn't bring you here.

You sent a postcard.

I didn't think you'd come. But now you are here — you might as well know I'm a homosexual as well.

Shimi snorted again.

You find that funny?

I find it ironic.

Why? Because the homosexual should have been you? You don't have to be a mother's boy to be queer, Shim.

The sea gulping.

The rocking of the pier.

The wind flapping the sides of the gypsy caravan.

I don't care what you are, Eph. Just give me back my name.

To do what with? Where's the harm? I've put your name up in lights. Take it as a compliment.

So that's why you sent for me – to show me the latest thing of mine you've taken. Haven't you stolen enough from me already?

Like what?

You know like what. Like magic tricks. Like my sense of fun.

Sense of fun! You!

Like the war. Like our father. Like our mother. Like the air I breathe. Like God knows what else.

Ephraim shakes his head. What else do you have, Shim?

Shimi lets that echo. *What else do you have, Shim?*

The smell of sea spray.

The smell of cat's piss.

The smell of a mother decaying.

The answering machine has no answers for him but one: the date, the place, the time of the burial. Wherever Ephraim has been all these years, he is to be cremated in North London. Shimi hasn't attended to this. Shimi is unable to attend to any of the ceremonials of death. He will do his own dying when the time comes and that will be that. He knows the crematorium – what cemetery or crematorium in London doesn't he know? – and believes it to be non-denominational. He is relieved about that. Their mother had a religious funeral and the obsequies were too bleak and sonorous to bear. Die Jewish and you're dead longer even than for ever. Better a frolic with Jesus, expecting to meet your loved ones in a flowery garden soon, he thought – not that he would have wanted that for Ephraim either.

'My people!' his father had once heard Shimi say, after two of his mother's gloomy sisters had been to stay.

'They aren't your people,' his father told him.

'So who are my people?'

'You have no people. You have your mother and me. If you want to belong to someone else, take the trouble to find out about them.'

Good advice but Shimi never took it.

He catches a bus north but gets off sooner than he has to. He wants to walk to the crematorium. Sorrow a little in privacy, and walking's good for that. He is wearing his heaviest black coat and his best Nikita Khrushchev homburg – soft and low brimmed, a menacingly ironic hat, though he wouldn't own to such a mood. Whom does he want to menace? What is there to be ironical about? He is relieved that it's Blackpool weather, cold and overcast. Glad for Ephraim's sake. Funerals are never sadder than when the sun's shining. And he doesn't want to dishonour Ephraim by feeling falsely sad for him. After two sleepless nights, he is allowing Ephraim to drift back into his past again.

That's what Shimi does about anyone not himself. He howls for them, then puts them away.

But he knows he will lose control when he sees the coffin. And is stiffening himself against that. He hopes he will be dignified.

He also hopes there will be a urinal close by. After a long life of loss he is familiar with all north London's burial and burning sites but never before has he had to take conveniences into account. He cannot go under a bush. He cannot relieve himself in the presence of the dead.

There are more mourners gathered outside the chapel than he expected. He has been dreading finding no one there – poor bereft Ephraim leaving the world unlamented. But unless he has come at the wrong time to the wrong funeral it would seem that Ephraim is very much lamented. He only wishes the lamenters were dressed more respectfully. The modern way is not to overdo the formalities. We celebrate the ordinariness of life now, barely before it's over. Every occasion like every other. No black suits. No ties. Death too is an occasion to wear your trainers.

The gathering swells by the minute. Seeing no one he recognises, Shimi disappears further into himself. Who would he like to see here? In a moment of crazed dislocation he imagines his father turning up, hoping for a final reconciliation with his sons. He can't remember what he called him. Dad, papa, father, pop? But he soon comes to his senses. It doesn't matter what he called him. He won't be coming. Only imagine how old he'd be now. Shimi's own age comes as a shock to him every day he doesn't have a nurse or a chiropodist telling him how well he looks. Can he really be that old? He stands as though in a landslide of years.

Poor Ephraim – had he been feeling that too?

But poor Ephraim seems to have had a lot of friends. They are mixed crowd, of all ages, all classes, all colours, and, Shimi guesses sniffily, all orientations. Still there is no one here he recognises. When you're ninety, funerals are no longer opportunities for renewing friendships. The advantage of this funeral is that there will be no one here who recognises him.

The hearse is not here yet, so it is permissible to chatter idly. Knots of people who know one another shake hands and embrace. There is a lot of hugging of the modern sort, perfunctory hugging where once you would have settled for saying 'how do you do'. Two couples embrace more feelingly than that in a hugger-mugger of fondness and tears. A woman looks up at the sky and sucks on an electronic cigarette. Shimi realises he was wrong to think no one would recognise him. People are discreetly pointing him out. *There, Ephraim's brother Shimi* – unless they are people who have known Ephraim as Shimi and so think he must be Ephraim. But the brother, yes. Maybe at the end they came to look even more alike.

Shimi realises he has been dragging a foot nervously there and back in the gravel. Like a horse before a race. He wants the ceremony to start and then be over. Maybe he should have brought the Widow Wolfsheim along for company and support. At least she would have known how to dress for it.

A man of middle age, who Shimi has watched rubbing his hand over his mouth, as though trying to keep it steady, suddenly returns Shimi's curious stare. Shimi inclines his head. Does he want the man to come over? Yes, he thinks he does. He has a round sympathetic face – weather-beaten like a gardener's, Shimi thinks, with broken veins in his cheeks and rheumy eyes – and might be able to tell him how Ephraim had been and what he died of. Everyone here must know more than he does.

The man comes over and extends a strong hand. He appears reluctant to speak, as though words might turn too easily to tears. But he does manage to say, 'A good turnout.'

'Yes. I'm pleased for Ephraim,' Shimi says. 'I'm his brother, Shimi.'

'Yes. I thought you must be. I'm Mark.'

Shimi tries to estimate the man's age. Fifty? What could he have been to Ephraim? His carer? His gardener? His lover?

'Who are you, Mark?' he decides to ask. There's no point now sidestepping everything. 'Forgive me but I lost touch with Ephraim. I haven't seen him for more years than I can count. I don't where he's been. I don't know if he has a family. I didn't even know he was alive.'

'He isn't.'

Shimi steps back as though from a blow.

Very well then, now it's clear. He had wondered if people knew Ephraim even had a brother. Evidently they do. And just as evidently they don't think all that highly of the sort of brother Shimi has been. Could that be — well it had to be, didn't it? — because Ephraim hadn't thought highly of Shimi as a brother himself. Shimi stares around to see how others are regarding him. Is he the villain here? Shimi the Unforgiven. Does he deserve that?

He means to hold himself together. He is innocent. They walked away from each other. If there's blame, they must share it. Except that Ephraim isn't here to share anything. The living have to bear responsibility.

He prepares himself for more. 'Are you a friend of Ephraim's, Mark?' he asks. And then, a question difficult to frame. 'Or are you family?'

'In a manner of speaking I am both. He and my father were very close. Ephraim treated me like his own son.'

Very close. Shimi processes that. Is he envying his dead brother a friendship, whatever manner of friendship it was? What Mark equivalent will turn up at Shimi's funeral and say my father and he were very close. He will be lucky if the chiropodist shows.

But what does *very close* mean?

'And your father . . . ?'

'He died some years ago.'

'I'm sorry.'

'Thank you. But these questions . . . Do you really know nothing at all about Ephraim's life?'

The imputation is fair. Shimi's ignorance is shameful.

'Nothing. Apart from Blackpool.'

'Ah, that long ago!' Mark shakes his head. 'Well you should know my father and your brother met in prison.'

There is a stir among the mourners. The hearse has arrived. Shimi turns away. He cannot look at coffins. He never looked at his mother's. He doesn't want to look at Mark, either. He doesn't want to see Mark's grief. And just this moment he doesn't want more shocking information.

He stares at the ground and kicks more gravel. 'Can we speak afterwards?' he says as they mount the steps to the chapel.

'I would like that,' Mark says.

Why? So that he can impute more crimes of the heart to his father's friend's brother?

The chapel is already full to overflowing. As a rule the family of the deceased — the chief mourners — sit in the front rows. But no one has invited Shimi to be a chief mourner and he is not going to insist himself among those who are, whatever their relations to his brother. If Ephraim had family they would surely have sought him out. So if there is family here he must assume they don't want him to join them. Should he be upset by the insult to him in this? Yes, but he accepts he doesn't have the right. Not after so many years of silence. He was the older. He should have gone to find Ephraim. He shouldn't have left him out there on his own. Prison, for Christ's sake. He could have stopped that. Or he could, at the very least, have visited him there.

By the time he has finished looking around there are no more seats. A couple of people offer the old man theirs. But he would rather stand at the back.

Prison.

Among all the other things he feels this terrible afternoon must he feel shame as well? Shame is his element, but prison-shame is new to him. He knows no one who has been in prison. Has never talked to anyone who has been in prison. He might have the appearance of a wild Russian reprobate but to Shimi prison equals disgrace. His poor parents. What would they have thought? Long dead but that's not the point. Shame can haunt the dead. So will it be haunting Ephraim? He had laughed dismissively when Shimi had warned him that to put himself about as a homosexual was to risk arrest. That was just tight-arsed Shimi being tight-arsed Shimi. Ephraim had always been the high-wire artist.

It wasn't out of the question that he saw a sort of louche glamour in being behind bars. Shimi could see him standing outside Wormwood Scrubs reciting *The Ballad of Reading Gaol* and kissing Bosie.

What if, it occurs to tight-arsed Shimi to wonder, what if the mourners are all people he knew in prison? Old lags. Warders. Ephraim was a popular guy. You met Ephraim and you fell in love with his incorrigible grin. Shimi pictures him in his cell, dealing out cards, telling fellow inmates their fortunes and making them laugh. 'When will I be getting out, Ephraim?' 'You? For your crimes, never.' 'It says that in the cards?' 'What it says in the cards is that you ought to try keeping it in your pants, you old queen.'

Oh, Shimi!

But look again and none of that, not even the non-pantomime version, is possible. Few here are anything like old enough for a start. Shimi tries to imagine Ephraim as he was at the end. An old man like him. And where, apart from Shimi, are the men old enough to have gone through Ephraim's life with him? They could, though, couldn't they, be the offspring of people Ephraim loved. Like Mark, a sweet enough man who wants to make a connection with Shimi but can't conceal his contempt for him.

The service passes Shimi by. It is like being at school again. He cannot concentrate on what is being said. He had a wandering mind, his teachers said. They threw chalk and chalk dusters at him and still he looked out of the window, unaware. They called it daydreaming; Shimi called it thinking at his own speed. He remembers the A. E. Housman poem he'd read in class then couldn't get out of his head. Everyone else was onto the next poem. Why did Shimi have to keep pace with them?

'When the bells justle in the tower, / The hollow night amid, / Then on my tongue the taste is sour / Of all I ever did.' You couldn't read that and then move on seamlessly to Browning. He tries to remember if he ever talked to Ephraim about Housman's poem. Housman was a homosexual. Yes, he knows it's ridiculous to suppose that Ephraim was bound to like his poetry on that account. Shimi Carmelli is an old man from another age, but even he grasps that not every homosexual is interested in every other.

So don't 'Oh, Shimi!' him.

But on that question, how many of the mourners – how many of them *are*? Shimi wonders, not daring to look around.

Back at school again, Shimi barely hears what's being said, though every word should be precious to him. He's back in the tower being justled by the bells, tasting the sourness on his tongue. It's bad luck for him that he has recalled the Housman; the poet's sourness sets off Shimi's own. It is wrong he wasn't called on to help arrange this funeral. Wrong he wasn't given a seat at the front. Wrong he hasn't been asked to deliver a eulogy. What would he have said? He rehearses a speech. *Ephraim and I were very close when we were young. He had a great spirit of adventure. You should have seen him shoot down any German plane that strayed into Little Stanmore airspace. But he was possessed of great tenderness too. You should have seen him with our mother when she was dying . . .*

Meanwhile the coffin sits unlooked at on the belt that will convey it through the flames. And the reminiscences have begun. What good company. How he filled any room with his laughter. The lives he touched. The lives he saved. Shimi, standing smouldering at the back of the chapel, picks that up too late. *The lives he rescued?* Was that the word he heard? Rescued! A woman is unable to finish a story about her father and all Ephraim did for him. From the mourners' assent this story and others like it are well known. Agreement unites the mourners. In another place there would be applause. Shimi hears the words 'I was an alcoholic for forty years,' and this too can be vouched for by everybody here. 'I was given up for lost until Ephraim . . .' People turn to one another and nod. That was Ephraim.

Did he rescue them all, Shimi wonders.

A celebrant offers consolation for the non-religious. Shimi knows what he thinks of that. There is no consolation for the non-religious.

And now one of Ephraim's favourite songs. In the spirit of the event Shimi thinks it's going to be Leonard Cohen's 'Hallelujah', but it's Marvin Gaye. 'I Heard It Through the Grapevine'. Who *was* his brother?

Then comes the reading. From a South American novelist, though it could have come from the back of a greetings card. Have the honesty to do the thing you want to do and have the courage to be yourself. The end. I know what I would say were I speaking, Shimi thinks. I would say have the courage to be someone else. As Ephraim did? Yes, as Ephraim did. Because the stories about him describe another Ephraim to the one Shimi knew.

Then the hammer blow of horror when the belt bearing the coffin begins to move. There is more music. A heavy, jeering, mirthful beat. An assault on tears. The music of indomitability. 'Another One Bites the Dust'.

So is it all a joke?

'Eph's sense of humour exactly,' he hears someone say. And needs to get outside.

Back out on the gravel no one is in any hurry to leave. If anything, there are more people here now than before. There is universal agreement. A lovely, fitting service. Ephraim would have enjoyed it. Shimi looks for Mark. While he's searching, a somewhat lewd-looking man in his sixties with bad skin comes over to introduce himself.

'You used to know my father,' he says.

This isn't another joke is it? This isn't Ephraim's son? But no, no one could be so malicious, not even Ephraim's son, supposing him to have one.

'Remind me,' Shimi says.

'Perkin Padgett.'

Shimi slaps his head. ' "Peanut" Padgett!'

'I never heard him called that.'

Shimi apologises. 'Peanut' just popped into his head. It could have been worse. 'Penis' Padgett could have popped into his head.

'And how is your father?' Shimi wants to ask, but he can guess the answer. Instead he says, 'Your father and I were good friends. I don't remember him being a chum of Ephraim's, though.'

'They met in rehab.'

Shimi is relieved. Rehab is one up from prison. But for what offence did 'Peanut' Padgett need rehabilitating, apart from all round disgustingness of person? In a rush, he remembers the day 'Peanut' loosened his belt. Was 'Peanut', too, put away for consorting with another man?

'So did my brother help your father the way he seems to have helped everybody else?'

'He did, actually, yes. They weren't exaggerating in there. He was one in a million, your brother. You lost contact with each other, I gather.'

Gather!

'Yes.'

'Was there a falling out?'

'Not really. We just drifted apart. We were living in different parts of the country and had different interests. I don't know how Ephraim described it.'

'Pretty much the same way, I think. I didn't know him as well as Dad did, but I did hear him talk about you occasionally. I think he believed you disapproved of him.'

'For what?'

'He had some wild friends. Maybe he thought you disapproved of them.'

'Was your father one?'

'Dad? Wild? God, no. All he wanted after a hard day in his bookshop was to come home, watch television and open a bottle of sherry.'

'He had a bookshop?'

'Yes. The Book Worm in Borehamwood. You never went there?'

'Never. But I remember he was interested in books.' Obscurely, Shimi was pleased for him. An ambition realised lit up everyone associated with it.

But he was also envious. What ambition had he realised?

'His precious books, yes, though he neglected those when the drinking devil was in him. Enter Ephraim. He understood.'

'One of the last things Ephraim told me was that he'd started drinking. I didn't really believe him.'

'Oh, he drank all right. But he put it to good use. Same with his time in prison. Alcoholics Anonymous employed him as a Prison Liaison Officer I think it was. He was good with people who'd fallen a long way down the ladder.'

'Was Perkin in prison with him too?'

'Nah. Dad never had the balls to do anything bent.'

Then he must have changed drastically, Shimi thinks.

Mark comes over to join them and the two men shake hands warmly. Shimi suffers a second pang of envy. Ephraim died in a circle of friends. How will he die?

He succeeds in walking Mark aside. 'This prison thing . . . ?'

'You want to know what was he in for?'

'I can guess. But was he in there long?'

'Less than a year. But what do *you* think he was in for?'

Shimi straightens his backs and makes himself taller. I am Ivan the Terrible. I am Rasputin. He makes an easy come, easy go motion with his hands. What his brother was, he accepted. There's no shocking someone who's been where Shimi's been.

But Ephraim's friend is not deceived. 'Your brother loved you, you know,' he announces with odd formality, 'but he said you had a Little Stanmore mentality.'

Shimi reels as from a blow. 'If it's your intention to wound me,' he says, 'you have succeeded. Though that wouldn't be hard to do today. But yes, undoubtedly Ephraim was the bolder of the two of us.'

'I don't mean to wound you. I don't believe Ephraim would have wanted to wound you either. He wasn't that impressed with the way his own life had worked out. He worried for you, that was all. He thought you never properly got away from where life began for you both, and that as a consequence you took things hard.'

'He was probably right.'

'He said he wished you could have punished yourself less.'

'And *his* punishment? What was that? What was his crime?'

'Not what I think you think. Theft.'

'Theft! What the hell did he thieve?'

'A gypsy caravan.'

Shimi catches his breath. He has to stop himself laughing. 'He told me he'd bought it off a gypsy he'd met at Alcoholics Anonymous.'

'I'm sure he meant to. But the paperwork proved too much for him.'

'Let me get this straight in my mind. Do you mean he stole the business or the caravan?'

'Well the business would not have been much without the caravan. What he got done for was sneaking the caravan off the South Pier at Blackpool and towing it to Brighton.'

'You can't *sneak* a caravan off a pier.'

'As he found out.'

'And he went to prison for trying?'

'It was still the fifties, remember. I know that because 1959 was the year my dad went down. They took theft a little more seriously then. And the gypsy proved vindictive.'

Shimi does the calculations. 1959 was the last year he saw Ephraim. Had his visit in some way precipitated Ephraim's felony?

'And your father, if you don't mind me asking,' he asks. 'What did he get done for?'

Mark laughs. 'An act of gross indecency. 1959 for you. If you think things are bad today . . .'

Shimi rubs his eyes. 'Things are always bad.'

'I agree. Which is why we need men like your brother.'

Rather than men like you . . .

Shimi's done. Ah yes, my brother. Who was or wasn't a thief, who was or wasn't a homosexual, who was or wasn't an alcoholic, who was – well, there are no two views about this at least – a saint.

He puts out his hand. 'A pleasure,' he says. Which it hasn't been.

Enough's enough. Ephraim will be burnt to ash by now. There's nothing more to hang around for.

28

Some aspects of ageing are voluntary. Shimi decides to walk like an old man.

He makes his way heavily along the memorial avenue of shrubs and trees towards the gate, burdened by years if not by grief – he knows he has no right to grief. Plaques mark the places where the ashes of somebody's mother or father, sister or brother have been scattered. To the left of him is a separate, sadder ground for sons and daughters. And a smaller, sadder one still for babies. It's like an abandoned nursery. Dolls, teddy bears, greeting cards, propped against urns or just lying on the ground. For all the order, it is as though a hurricane has been through. Or Jesus, marauding for sunbeams.

Shimi keeps to the main path and breathes in the foliage. Briefly, the idea of being returned to nature consoles him. But what if you didn't come from nature in the first place?

On his way out, by the arched Gothic gate to the main road, he sees an old woman sitting on a mossy bench. Sometimes, talking of nature, the old on mossy benches can look as though they have grown there. This old woman doesn't. She is too alert, in her own way as much an enemy of growth and greenery as Shimi. Is she here for Ephraim or the next deceased? He didn't see her in the chapel. That, though, tells him nothing; there was much he didn't see and didn't want to see in the chapel. She doesn't look infirm, but there is a wheelchair parked beside her. She beckons Shimi who instinctively backs away. His record with people in wheelchairs isn't good.

Can she possibly know this about him? She rises, anyway, and waves her stick at him. She looks perfectly steady on her feet. 'Mr Carmelli!' she calls. 'Do me the goodness of at least acknowledging me. I am right, aren't I? You are the brother.'

The haughtiness of her manner, the authority in her voice, and the straightness of her posture, all things considered, reassure him. This is no human wreckage looking for assistance he can't give. Quite the opposite. Sinew for sinew, bone for bone, the human wreckage, this time, is him. There is something of the sibyl about the old woman, as though she is there, at the gate to her cave, to ward off the living and protect the dead. How many secrets is she privy to? How can she be so confident he is Ephraim's brother?

The moment he approaches she resumes her seat. He is not to consider himself an equal. As though obedient to her movements, a rook settles on the back of the bench. A leaf falls onto her lap. The woman looks up as though to castigate the tree from which the leaf has fallen and at that moment the sun which had put in a brief appearance is eclipsed by clouds. From the direction of the car park an African woman appears, leading a tiger. No, not leading a tiger, though Shimi doesn't see why not. In her tight, tribal-print dress she splashes the bleached-out cemetery with colour.

Shimi is easily cowed by authority, even when it isn't supported by the supernatural. 'I am Ephraim Carmelli's brother, yes,' he says, in the manner of one making a formal confession.

'You couldn't be anyone else. You bear the mark.'

'What mark?'

'The Carmelli mark. Ephraim spoke of it.'

Shimi is nonplussed.

'I am making light with you,' the old woman says. 'I suspect someone has to. You resemble him, is what I mean.'

'You knew him?'

'Of course I knew him. Why else would I be here? How else could I remark on the resemblance?'

'Well, if you mean to be original you have succeeded. I never thought we were alike.'

'That would have been because you weren't able to look into your own eyes. Come closer to me. Closer still. Yes, I look into yours and I see what I saw in his.'

What happens next, Shimi wonders. Does the rook peck the sockets of his eyes clean? Does the African woman disfigure him with her nails? Is this the moment when the ground splits at last, throwing up its accumulation of ashes?

He steadies himself by steadying his voice. 'I am touched that you see something of my poor brother in me. A part of him remains alive, in that case. But I am surprised by it. What of Ephraim is it that you see in my eyes?'

'You will have to give me a moment to find the words. Euphoria, my thesaurus.'

'Yes, Mrs Beryl,' the African woman says. But no book passes between them. Does this too pertain to the paranormal?

To describe what she sees in Shimi's eyes the old woman closes her own. 'Bravado masking affliction,' she says at last with satisfaction. It is as though she has passed a test she has set herself.

Shimi, too, takes his time.

'Well?' she asks. 'Do you intend to honour my description with a comment?'

Shimi sighs. He could do with a thesaurus himself. 'I cannot speak for his affliction but I can for my bravado. I have none. As you see, I quake before you. And your retinue.'

'Retinue? Retinue is good. That's you he's referring to, Euphoria. So straighten up. And stop holding on to that damned wheelchair, girl. Let it career away if it wants to. I warned you not to bring it. As for your bravado, Mr Carmelli, I'm in no position to argue with you about that. You must, at your age, know yourself. Ephraim had enough for both of you. He could stare down any misfortune. I have known many men but few of his character.'

'Thank you.'

'Why are you thanking me? It is no compliment to you that I praise him.'

The sternness of her manner dislodges the familiar rook.

'I thank you on his behalf,' Shimi says.

'You can no more thank on another's behalf than you can apologise.'

Shimi smothers a sigh. It's beginning to feel a long day. 'I am pleased he was admired, that's all.'

'Why, didn't you admire him?'

'Not enough.'

'Were you close? Let me rephrase: did you think of yourself as close to him?'

Shimi hears what she's not saying. That Ephraim didn't think of himself as close to Shimi.

'Not as close as we should have been.'

'And whose fault was that?'

Is he obliged to answer? 'Mine,' he says, obliged or not. 'Mine entirely.'

'You say that too quickly.'

'It's what I believe to be true.'

'It wasn't what he believed to be true. He said he ought never to have abandoned you.'

'He didn't.'

'Sit down,' she orders.

He sits. But not too close.

She regards him strangely, as though he might have dropped from the trees. 'Remind me what you were saying.'

'That Ephraim didn't abandon me. He did other things but not that.'

'Perhaps you misremember.'

'I'm not so fortunate.'

'Wait till you misremember everything.' But as he makes no reply to this, she goes on to ask 'Do you feel he has abandoned you now?'

'How could I not? A younger brother has no business dying before an older. But that's just fancy.'

She has a long face, almost as long as his. She uses the full length of it to show sorrow of which he would not have thought it capable. Could those storm-grey eyes shed tears?

'I understand you,' she says. 'It can be terrible when they leave. At least when some of them do. Others you can't wait to see the back of.'

'I hope you have not had cause to feel that too many times.'

'Do you intend to be impertinent?'

'I do not. Any more, I must assume, than you do.'

He feels it's courageous of him, standing up to an old person, no matter that he's an old person himself.

'You are ruder,' she says, 'than he was.'

'I'm affecting an effrontery I don't have. By nature I'm over-respectful.'

'Your mother got to you too, then? Certainly she had her way with Ephraim. She made a pleaser of him. He was a man who tried too hard to creep inside a woman's skin. You?'

'The same, only more so. She got a better deal with him. He didn't want to be her. He wanted only to protect her.'

'Did she need protecting?'

'All the time.'

'From?'

'Everything.'

She pauses as though she knows what that must have been like. Surely she is not in need of protection from *anything* . . .

He would like to be gone from here. But wanting always to be gone is what's made him the man he wishes he were not. He could run from this old woman and be spared her knowing condescension, but spared for what? To go home on his own and sob his heart out falsely for Ephraim? What would that serve? Why this always choosing ignorance over knowledge?

'May I enquire,' he says, determined to make himself stay a little longer, 'as to the context of your friendship?'

'*The context of our friendship!*' She puts her hands under her hair to spread it wide and laughs the laughter of a grand duchess. 'And my sons accuse *me* of being formal! Relax, young man. How intimate were we, are you asking?'

'I wouldn't dream of asking that.'

'Ask away. I have put coyness behind me. You must do the same –
for I have things I want to know from you. Don't look so alarmed.
The easiest way to answer you, for now at least, is to say I am the
mother of Neville Dusinbery, if that means anything to you.'

'I'm afraid it doesn't.'

'Well why should it? I'm not sure any longer what it means to me.
But it meant something to your brother.'

'He was friends with your son?'

'He was friends with me. He was the saviour of my son.'

BOOK TWO

I

They are at an octagonal table in Regent's Park, drinking tea from paper mugs. She has a blanket over her knees. She is struck by the brilliant blue of the sky, sharp daggers of dark cloud progressing with a sort of prearranged menace towards the sun, but then choosing to go by it. The sun survives another day. He, she notices, looks neither up nor around him. The world could be square to him, its edges finishing where he does.

But he has remarkably still hands for a man his age. She spills a little of her tea. He does not.

'You have forgiven me then for waylaying you,' she says. 'It crossed what's left of my mind that you might not agree to come.'

'It never crossed what's left of mine that I had a choice. You don't defy the Angel guarding the Golden Gates.'

'That's an elegant compliment. I'm surprised by it. Ephraim said he was the more poetic of the two of you.'

'Ephraim would.'

'So what did you see in me that you didn't dare oppose? Was I barring you from leaving the cemetery of death or welcoming you into the garden of life?'

'That's what I have braved my fears to find out.'

'I fear you overestimate me either way. I cannot keep you in or set you free. As for Paradise, I cannot even promise you a rose garden.'

'Oh well,' Shimi says.

As well as the blanket on her knees she has a large cashmere scarf about her shoulders. This she releases herself from in order to wind it around her more tightly. She has long arms, Shimi notices, and a determined grip, but whether the loosening motion denotes reserves of strength or frustration he cannot tell.

'At least you don't look as pained as you did when we spoke two days ago.'

It was a week but he doesn't want to embarrass her.

'I'm not going to make a stranger of the pain Ephraim's death caused me,' he says. 'It was enough I made a stranger of him. It isn't every day you lose a brother.'

'Nor every day you lose your friend. But this isn't a competition, is it?'

'Isn't there always competition around a death? Let's not go through the forms. From what you told me he was more a friend to you than he was, in any active way, a brother to me. Or I to him. So let's just agree you've won.'

'How thin-skinned you are. I am not laying claim to Ephraim's memory.'

'Well, I don't know how much you saw of him but it was more than I did. Strictly speaking I only ever really knew the boy, and I'm not sure how well I knew *him*.'

'So I'm to tell you what he was like? I was hoping you'd tell me.'

'What can I tell you you don't know? I last saw him in 1959.'

'He was already a formed man then. You're the one who knows what formed him.'

'I'm not sure I do. And why do you want to know that anyway?'

'For the same reason you want to know what he became. We both want the man entire.'

Shimi falls still. Some would say – the Widow Wolfsheim, for example – that at times he appears to fall out of the living world altogether. Beryl Dusinbery doesn't mind. She is a sometime absentee herself. But she does wonder where he goes. He would not have been able to tell her. On those occasions he is hurt, he goes nowhere. Just away. As for what's hurting him he has a lot to choose from. But right this vacant, suggestive minute it is probably the idea of there being such a thing as a man entire. Or rather the thought that it is not a phrase that has ever been, or could ever be, applied to him.

'I'd settle for less than that,' he says at last. 'I'd just like to know how he was. Was he happy. Did he feel he'd made a success of his life.'

'You call that less? How would you answer those questions of yourself?'

'I wouldn't ask them.'

Beryl Dusinbery leans forward and rests her chin on her hand. She could, at that moment, be seventeen. 'What if I were to ask them?'

'I'd tell you to wait till we knew each other better.'

'You think there's enough time left for that?'

'No. And probably not enough curiosity left either. Which is why I'd like us to concentrate on Ephraim, who interested us both. How was he when you last saw him?'

'Last? Oh – he'd been bedridden for several years. I never found out what was wrong with him. I have no curiosity when it comes to physical ailments. Mental derangements are another thing. But he seemed sane enough for a man. So there was nothing to help me overcome my aversion to the sick room. And he wasn't able to come to me. Don't ask me how long ago it is since we talked. Could have been a year. Could have been twenty. But that I didn't visit him in his sickness, whenever that was, must strike you as callous.'

'I've no right to any such judgement. Sickness appals me as well.'

'Good,' she says. 'So you wouldn't have visited him had you known he was ill?'

'Would he have wanted me to?'

'I can't answer that. He wasn't calling for you, if that's what you're hoping to hear.'

Shimi does something exceptional. He looks at her. 'If I shrink from your unfeelingness you will call me thin-skinned again.'

She takes his stare and returns it. 'What unfeelingness? Ephraim would have laughed at what I said.'

'The more tough Ephraim.'

'He was. Very.'

'Then there we have the man entire. I remember a tough young man and you remember a tough old one. During the war he went out armed with a wooden rifle and took on the might of the German air force. He didn't scare.'

'I'm talking about emotional toughness. He risked his heart.'

'By falling in love?'

'Don't be banal. He made friendships where others wouldn't have dared, he put his faith in people others wouldn't go near, he risked betrayal.'

'Already you are revealing to me a person I didn't know. We spent time together only when we were boys. We didn't have hearts yet.'

'Did you love him?'

'Boys in 1940 didn't love one another.'

'Boys have always loved one another.'

Shimi laughs a dry laugh. 'Is there any subject,' he enquires, 'on which you are not willing to pronounce with authority?'

'You find me rude?'

'I find myself wondering how Ephraim found you.'

'I am an authority on boys because I've given birth to many.'

'How many's many?'

'There you have me.'

'Well, I claim the advantage over you, when it comes to boys – however many you had – in that I *was* one.'

'But you will have forgotten what it was like.'

'I will never forget what it was like.'

'You are melodramatic about yourself.'

'I don't mean to be. I don't think I was unusual in being an unhappy child. It takes some of us longer than it takes others to recover from the psychic shock of birth.'

'So is that what you chiefly remember – being in shock?'

'No, being sad. Which I think is one of the after-effects of shock. I was sad all the time. I woke sad and I went to sleep sad. Vapid might be a better word.'

'I'll stay with sad. How did your parents respond to your sadness?'

'My father was away a lot, helping the war effort, but he hit me once.'

'For being sad?'

'For being odd.'

'And your mother?'

'Did my mother hit me? God, no. My mother was like me. Vapid.'

'You mean you were like her.'

'If you're saying I learnt my sadness from her you might be right. But it seemed to come from inside me. Ephraim had the same mother and he wasn't sad. He seemed to be lit from within. I was dark inside.'

'So that's why you say you didn't love him. You were envious of his light?'

'I didn't say I didn't love him. That makes me sound deficient. I said the concept of love didn't apply – to either of us. As I've told you, we were at a pre-love stage.'

'You've dodged my question about envy.'

A gust of wind causes Shimi to hold on to his hat and Beryl Dusinbery to wrap her cashmere angel wings even more tightly about her.

'This conversation,' Shimi says, 'is becoming too much about me. Isn't Ephraim the person we've met to discuss?'

'I am questioning the witness.'

'Which makes this not a conversation.'

'I won't mind you questioning me when it's your turn. I will tell you everything you want to hear and most likely more, but first you'll have to help me recover what I've lost. Don't look so alarmed. You won't be having to get down on your hands and knees. One word begets another. All you have to do is keep talking.'

'What makes you think I have the words?'

'Your brother did. Why not you? Jew-boys are made of words.'

'I'm only half a Jew-boy.'

'Half a Jew-boy is better than none.'

He blows air.

'I'm counting on you not to bother taking offence. Ephraim, rather wonderfully, was unoffendable. You could say anything to him. I'm hoping you are the same. I'd hate it if you turned out to be one of those men who isn't there in the morning.'

Shimi remembers the human wreckage in a wheelchair, that barely person rotting under unwashed blankets, who once solicited his assistance outside the urinal in the park. Then he remembers much else besides, of which the Widow Wolfsheim is a mere contemporary detail. 'I am more a man who isn't there the night before,' he says.

The Princess plays the coquette. 'Not a type I am personally acquainted with,' she says, tossing her hair and showing Shimi her throat. Once no doubt magnificent, it is furrowed now like a squeeze box. If I were a different man, Shimi thinks, I would find magnificence in it still. But he is who he is and does what he always does and looks away. Manners, he calls this. But it might be madness.

'It's getting cold,' he says.

'I'll order us more tea. Euphoria can get it. We were discussing envy.'

'We weren't discussing, you were telling. But yes, I envied Ephraim. What does that say about either of us? I envied lots of boys. Isn't envy like learning to walk? You want capacities others have. You watch and learn.'

'And ache . . .'

'Yes, yes, and that too. But to ache to be someone other than yourself is also part of growing up.'

'What if it doesn't stop?'

'You're in trouble.'

She thinks about asking if he is in that sort of trouble now. But holds back.

He thinks about saying that Ephraim must, in his way, have envied him. He actually stole my name, for Christ's sake. But he too decides it's a bit soon for that. You don't open the whole can of worms in the first hour.

'I am not running away, but I am growing tired,' he says instead.

She turns her face away like one rebuffed.

And she calls me thin-skinned.

2

'There are going to have to be ground rules,' the Princess says.

Euphoria, who is driving her employer around the parts of North London that have changed most rapidly in the last ten years, thinks she is referring to her motoring skills.

'I can't do anything about the bumps, Mrs Beryl.'

'Of course you can't, child.'

'Do you want me to drive more slowly?'

'You couldn't drive more slowly without stalling the car altogether. What's that there?'

'An office block, Mrs Beryl.'

'Why is it shaped like a coffee jug? Don't answer. You won't know. But what was there before? Don't answer that either. I have to do it for myself.'

The Princess is trying to put North London back to what it was, remember which shops and buildings used to be where, not only to recover the narrative of her life, but in the hope the exercise will be good for her brain.

The ground rules she is talking about – talking to herself about, because she isn't looking for help from Euphoria – relate to the exchange of opinions and recollections she's been enjoying – enjoying, is it? – with Ephraim's brother. They are rules as to style rather than content. How are these two ancient creatures to comport themselves in the inevitable event of misunderstanding, awkward-ness, discomfiture – Shimi Carmelli is a mine of the latter, in her view – to say nothing of those lapses and hiatuses when the discs of time spin before her eyes – she cannot speak for Shimi Carmelli's attention – and she doesn't know where or who she is.

Forgotten words from her childhood return to her. Why have they resurfaced suddenly? *And be ye kind one to another, tender-hearted, forgiving one another, even as God for Christ's sake hath forgiven you.* Cross-stitched, she sees them, in a churchy little wooden frame, though whether on the wall of the house she grew up in or her first school, she cannot say. Where have the words been all these years? Perhaps biding their time, like slow germinating seeds in the humid darkness of her soul. They've always been there, anyway. Their rhythm is like the rhythm of her pulse, no matter that she has never acted on them in her heart. 'As with Shakespeare, the King James Bible is written in our blood,' she'd tell the pampered girls she taught. Some confusion clearly as to which part of her the words claimed. They clattered about in her somewhere – that was enough. Did they similarly clatter about, she wondered, somewhere in Shimi Carmelli's person?

Be we kind one to another, she would like to urge him, but he might think she is lecturing him on usage or, worse, converting him to Pauline Christianity.

They came to an agreement, anyway, in the course of their third meeting in the park. They were both methodical by nature. She would leave life with everything labelled. Shimi would slide out of existence, probably screaming, but assuredly in the right clothes. Knowing this about himself he acceded to the old woman's rigours.

The ground rules agreed upon, then, were as follows.

1. In the matter of words, each will tacitly supply what the other fails to find.

The tacitness was important. She didn't want him shouting suggestions in her ear. As someone whose memory was not failing, Shimi would falter less often. But to be weighed against this was the smallness of his vocabulary relative to hers. There were deficiencies to be allowed for and forgiven on both sides. Be we kind one to another. She thought it worth adding that as a sub-rule.

1a. Be we kind one to another.

2. We are too elderly to stand on ceremony, whether in the matter of bodily dysfunction or attention deficit. One might spend an unconscionable time in the bathroom only to return to find the other asleep. Neither departure from conventional good manners is to be deemed a personal slight.

3. Forgetfulness or no forgetfulness, there is to be no tolerating repetition. Even a failing brain can be disciplined to recognise a sentence taking shape that it had only a moment before delivered in an identical manner. Tender-heartedness must prevail, but neither party is obliged to be bored by the other. The phrase 'It must be getting late' is to serve as a *terminus ad quem*. But mustn't be repeated.

4. Having no one to answer to or worry for as regards example, precept or embarrassment, our colloquies need admit no impediment to personal confession, whether that confession takes the form of looking back or looking forward, reminiscence or velleity. This is not meant as an encouragement to soppiness by either party.

5. Notwithstanding the latter, neither is, under any circumstance, to look for the renewal of sexual feelings.

6. Either of us might die at any time in the course of words exchanged or sought. This is not to be an occasion for guilt, remorse or even sadness on the part of the person left alive.

7. She will not go to his funeral. He will not go to hers.

3

In her heyday Beryl Dusinbery had been able to drive the thought of any other woman out of a man's mind. It wasn't infidelity she conjured, it was oblivion. The man who woke up in Beryl Dusinbery's arms hadn't betrayed his wife, he had forgotten he had a wife.

Shimi Carmelli is long past the age of any such abandon, as Beryl Dusinbery is long past the age of being its occasion. But she has occupied Shimi's thoughts to a degree that has surprised and bemused him. It is Ephraim, of course – how else to explain what's going on? – he's really been thinking about. Ephraim, in Beryl Dusinbery's own words, the saviour of her son. Saviour! What the hell did that mean? Beryl Dusinbery has no other allowable function in Shimi's life but to enable thoughts of Ephraim to resurface – if he was truly a saviour, to surface for the first time – and float. Away? No, just float. On her own account, though, there can be no pretending she hasn't made an impression. For three mornings running the first thing Shimi has seen when he rubs his eyes on waking is the old woman with the flowing white hair sitting on the bench in the crematorium gardens, peremptory and yet halting, flapping her cloak like an angel opening and closing its wings.

Barring his way or beckoning him in?

That he still cannot decide.

So a letter from the Widow Wolfsheim comes as an unruly surprise. Wanda Wolfsheim? Does he even know a person of that name?

Yes, yes, he thinks so – but in another life.

The letter contains a list of acceptances for the charity event which the Widow Wolfsheim had, in that other life, pencilled Shimi in for. He scans the list. The Widow Adler, the Widow Ansky, the Widow Atzman, the Widow Berenblum, the Widows Celia and Cynthia Bloch, the Widow Chomsky, the Widow Carlebach, the three Widows Cohen, the Widow Fackenheim, the Widow Foxler, the Widow Glassman, the Widow Glueck, the Widow Goeschel, the Widow Greenwald, the Widow Haffner, the Widow Hoffman, the Widow Hildesheimer, the Widow Leemis (married out), the Widow Ostropova, the Widow Lady Khan, the Widow Lerner, the Widow Lyons, the Widow Minsk, the Widow Molotov . . .

. . . and for the time being leaves it at that.

One name in particular has arrested his attention. Hilary Greenwald, née Shlosberg, to whom, before the advent of Harvey Greenwald, he was very nearly betrothed. Or rather, to whom he was very nearly betrothed at about the time that Harvey Greenwald was very nearly betrothed to her as well.

They had met when Hilary dropped into Shimi's of Stanmore. She didn't buy anything.

Something made him ask her out.

'If that's an invitation intended to lead eventually to marriage, you must give me time to choose wisely,' she told him. 'For starters I need to know what you can offer me.'

She must have said the same to Harvey Greenwald.

Hilary Shlosberg had briefly been a Tiller girl, which meant that she was tall. She had also worked as representative for a cosmetic company, giving away items in Selfridges, which meant that she was always well made-up. For some reason Shimi sees her in a bell-hop's costume topped with a cute hat. Why such a vivacious beauty wanted to be with Shimi Carmelli, who made and sold phrenology busts for a living, was anybody's guess. Shimi's own guess was that she had confused him with his brother.

Over the course of six or seven meetings Shimi had tried to explain he wasn't a rich man and couldn't give her any of the things she was entitled to expect, or indeed that Harvey Greenwald, by all accounts, was in a position to shower on her, but Hilary Shlosberg had stopped him each time, laying a finger on his lips. 'I want to know what you can offer me in the way of devotion,' she explained. 'I want to know how eagerly your heart beats for me.'

Shimi knew better than to say his heart didn't beat eagerly for her at all. But as it didn't, he was hard-pressed to say something that would help her to choose wisely, except in the sense of wisely not choosing him.

'This is not a decision I can make for you,' he said.

'Yes you can,' Hilary Shlosberg said. 'You can tell me you love me.'

'And that will do it, will it?'

'It will if you can convince me that you mean it.'

In the event, this was the worst thing she could have said. Shimi was unable to convince himself he meant anything.

Hilary Shlosberg waited. And waited. And waited.

'Well?' she came to his shop to know at last. Shimi busied himself under the counter, unable to look at her.

'I'll need a bit of time to work my position out on this,' Shimi said. He meant about the propriety of competing with another man for the hand of a woman he wasn't sure he wanted. But he would have felt the same even had he been sure he wanted her. The very idea of jockeying disgusted him. He had watched film footage on television of refugees fighting over a bowl of rice distributed from the back of a United Nations truck. I'd rather starve, he told himself. The Underground the same: travellers elbowing one another aside as though afraid of missing the last train out of hell. I'd rather stay on the platform and burn, he thought.

So Hilary Shlosberg married Harvey Greenwald and thereafter never knew a day's happiness in her life. Even the pleasure that might have attended the births of her sons was marred by the fear that they would turn out to be filthy lying scumbags like their father.

In the event, only two of them demonstrably did. The third, after a marriage almost as bad as his mother's, vanished into the world of Hare Krishna, reappearing occasionally in Oxford Street wrapped in one of his mother's sheets – which she wouldn't have appreciated his dyeing orange – wearing sandals and white socks, with his head shaved but for a single lock of hair, and banging a tambourine.

I'm only glad Harvey isn't alive to see it, Hilary told those 'friends' who reported the sighting. But they all knew she was glad Harvey wasn't alive to see anything.

Once in a blue moon, Shimi ran into her, in a park or a supermarket, where they nodded civilly to each other. Hilary noticed that Shimi was always alone. He suspected that she took his single state to denote an inability ever to find anyone he loved as much as her. Without doubt, she imagined him to have regretted his indecision every day for nearly fifty years. Though she would have been within her rights to jeer at his life of embittered loneliness as no more than he deserved, she found compassion for him. The poor man. And who was to say that hearts which had been broken couldn't be fixed? She was in good working order, and so, from the look of him, was he. As an ex-Tiller girl she had legs very nearly as elegant as Wanda Wolfsheim's and, by and large, her lips were her own. As for Shimi Carmelli – only look at the erectness of his bearing. By the most modest computation of probabilities there were still twenty, fifteen, ten years left to them, though he'd better get a move on if they were not to run out of years altogether.

The thought of meeting Hilary Greenwald's expectant expression at Wanda Wolfsheim's filled Shimi with apprehension. For how long can you go on letting someone down?

Thinking about her affects him strangely in relation to Beryl Dusinbery. Absurd as this appears to him, it is as though he has been asked to choose again, and once more fails to cast his vote for Hilary.

A butterfly doesn't beat its wings in China without Shimi feeling it is his fault or at least reflects badly on him. So having three women jostling for space in his head prompts the question: Which is the greater sin? Failing to love other people or failing to love oneself?

Everyone's a loser in my world, Shimi thinks.

★

Marking time – she couldn't say what she is expecting, but she is full of impatience – the Princess stitches Emily Brontë.

Cold in the earth
and the deep snow
piled above
thee

She knows Brontë Country, had walked it in her grief long ago, and for many years had only to put herself into daydream mode to see it all again. The parsonage with its square blank front and two Spartan chimneys standing up like ears. The sounds of madness issuing from Branwell Brontë's bedroom. The barking of dogs and screams of beaten cats. The snowy churchyard. And the moors around, beautiful when blanketed with purple heather, but dead as extinguished hope when the wind whistled through the ruins and the drystone walls. Dry stone – does she have silks chill enough to render those?

These days she can't bring the place back to mind without the help of illustrated books. And even those don't always work. In the end the deep-snow death poem does the trick better than any photograph or drawing. Brown hills, heath and fern leaves. Far, far removed, cold in the dreary grave.

She was nothing but a girl then and the grave elsewhere, in some corner of a foreign field . . .

She doesn't stitch the things there are to see. She stitches the thoughts that no longer hover, the forgetfulness, memory's rapturous pain, only she isn't sure she is up to the rapture. She stitches a path – not a real, pitted, potholed, frozen path following the soft contours of moorland, but the eternal path from bliss to desolation. She has always loved the idea of trodden, winding paths: the setting out, the expectation of arrival, the no less exhilarating expectation of getting lost.

It is killing her but she can't remember with whom she walked just such a path as she is embroidering. It needs to be more tangible, after all. Thread by thread she brings it back, renders its barren meander, the way it loses definition in mud and grass and then recovers itself, drops and rises, promises and disappoints, but still she cannot reanimate the person. Who was it? When was it? All her life ago.

This has been going on too long, she thinks, but doesn't mean it. The art of life is to make art of life, she believes, and art isn't only vivid recollection. Art is also a blank. The sin – against art and life – would be to make up what she no longer possesses. Stitch sunlight where there was none. Soften the stone. Prettify the path. No.

My life is three-fifths blank. Very well. That too is a story. You could say that is the only story.

Don't try to rescue. Leave the dead to bury the dead. And the misrememberers to misremember.

All else is a lie.

But making the best of loss is false as well. The unforgivable illusion is to believe that what is irretrievable is irretrievable for a purpose: all for the best in the best of all possible worlds, even the world that's fled your mind. Make art of that and you might as well be colouring in at an old people's home.

She stitches with the divine impatience of the artist, not to recover what's been before it's too late, but impetuously, not to lose the urgency of living in the present.

It isn't about her, it's about making.

Purple silk for the heather. Brown silk for the barer hills where heather has not flowered. What colour for the cold, cold headstone?

> All my life's bliss
> is in the grave with thee

No, it isn't about her, but it's hard to keep her out of it.

Or him.

Thee . . . thee – who was that, is that?

4

The same park at the same time of day. Not the same table, but similar. The Princess, like a winter bird, is plumed extravagantly against the cold. On her head a burgundy velour scarf tied into a turban in the style favoured by Edith Sitwell – she has a feeling the vatic poet gave it to her but she can't remember when or why – and on her shoulders a voluminous scarf embroidered with Egyptian hieroglyphics as worn by Cleopatra in Rome.

'So,' she says. 'You've seen my notes. I propose we clean the slate and start again.'

'We'd need to be meeting on a bench in a crematorium to do that. With ravens flying about your head and a native girl leading a tiger.'

She doesn't know what he is talking about.

'I'm being fanciful,' he says.

'Please don't be. We've a lot to get through.'

'Is this a chore for you?'

'It will be if you play the fool.'

Shimi feels passingly sorry for himself. She's right, he is playing the fool. He thought it would be fun to do so for a change. Clearly he has no gift for it. Clearly she has no gift for it, either. Just for the tiniest moment, like a squeeze of silvery light in a charcoal sky, he wonders if he'd be having a better time with Hilary Shlosberg. Which, if nothing else, proves he made the right decision not to marry her. He is not capable of constancy. He cannot be faithful to himself for five minutes at a time.

'Let's start again, then,' he says, remembering the ground rules. Be kind.

She rearranges her person. 'From the beginning,' she says. 'Your first memories . . .'

'Of anything or of Ephraim?'

'I suspect your first memories are of Ephraim – the rival child – but you'll tell me if I'm wrong.'

'What if the first memory I have of him is actually a memory of a photograph?'

'It won't be. You will be interpreting that photograph.'

'So how do you suggest I stop interpretation getting in the way?'

'Leave that to me. You just talk.'

'When I learned that he'd died I found a photograph of the two of us as children, running around the garden, being cowboys. We were indistinguishable.'

'And that surprised you?'

'Shocked me. Upset me.'

'Why?'

'We looked indistinguishably happy, which is not how I remember it. And in appearance he was not how I remembered him. Unless it was I who was not how I remembered me.'

'So in the photograph are you prettier than you remembered, or is he less?'

'Pretty isn't a word I'd use for either of us.'

'Why not? Are you word-squeamish?'

'We were being cowboys.'

'Ah, so you're gender-squeamish.'

'I am of the age I am. Girls are pretty, boys are handsome. He's a he, she's a she. It's sadism to expect me to change the way I use words now.'

'Did you think of him as more handsome than you? More of a boy?'

'Can I agree to that without you taking me to mean I felt *less* of a boy? I thought he was more mischievous than me. I'm talking about life principle – I grew up believing he had more of it.'

'At what age?'

'From the earliest age.'

'At the earliest age you wouldn't have been using phrases like *life principle*.'

'At the earliest age I wouldn't have been using any phrases. Why don't you let me finish answering the question you ask? I thought people found it easier to connect with him than me. He had a round, cheeky face. I had a long, miserable one, like a horse waiting to be shot. Ephraim was a live wire. I depressed people. He enthralled them. He enthralled me. I was struck by his energy and charm.'

'Struck? Struck down?'

'Now you are being my analyst. No, I wasn't struck down, or struck dumb.'

'But you must have hated him for his energy and charm if those were qualities you believed you didn't possess.'

'No,' Shimi says, shaking his head. 'Hated him, no. Admired him, more like.' But is he telling the truth? He cocks his ear to the past. Down the corridors of the years he hears a song. He is in the air-raid shelter, awkward and ashamed, hating the odour of humanity, feeling the nodules on his porcelain model of the human skull. People are laughing. Not at him. They are laughing and clapping because Ephraim is marching up and down, with his wooden rifle over his shoulder, singing. Can Shimi bring the song back? He strains his memory to bursting. If his brain had been made of porcelain it would have cracked by now. But he gets there in the end. If it's there to be remembered, and it's painful, Shimi will remember it. And what now echoes down that corridor of the years, down the hollowed corridor, down the cracked steps, down into the stifling air-raid shelter, are the words. 'This is the Army, Mr Jones.' A song they'd both sung, like little soldiers, to please their mother. A private, family song. But performed today, for the whole world, by that shameless attention seeker, that charming purloiner of what was not strictly his to perform alone – Ephraim the Indefatigably Lovable.

Very well, since the ground rules insist there must be no

impediment to personal confession, he confides to Beryl Dusinbery his jealous memories of Ephraim entertaining wartime Britain.

She closes her eyes while he talks to her. This gives him the opportunity to scrutinise her face more closely. He hadn't registered the depth of her brow before and imagines fingering it – impersonally, that is, in his guise as phrenologist. Nor had he noticed how the lines on her face are not the usual fine intersection of tracks etched on parchment by experience, happy or otherwise, but deeper, more vertical grooves like the dried-up beds of once free-flowing rivulets. Until now he hasn't imagined her capable of tears, but what else could have made these marks? Or is he being sentimental? Are these the grooves, in fact, made by an habituated scorn? Is hers, if anything, a too-unwatered face?

But she's listening to him, with her eyes closed, so intently, rocking slightly while he speaks, she could be down there in the shelter, not wanting the all-clear to sound because the little boy is such a joy to watch. Ephraim shoulders his wooden rifle, meets the expressions of mirth of which he is the cause with mirth of his own, grinning at his own effect, the rascal, the urchin, the wily schmoozer, but most of all shining with the reflection of pleasure in Beryl Dusinbery's face. That's when it occurs to Shimi that they'd been lovers, Ephraim and Beryl, long long ago.

He stops and waits for her to return to now, to him, Shimi, the lesser brother.

She opens her eyes, as though on command, to the very disappointment Shimi has been anticipating for her. He is not, he thinks, the person she wants to open her eyes and see.

'Such powers of recall you have,' she says.

'You are welcome to them.'

'That's a tactless thing to say to someone who can't plug the holes in her memory fast enough. Don't wish away the most precious thing you have.'

'What if it doesn't feel precious to me?'

'Then you're a fool.'

There is silence between them and then, as though to illustrate how hard she can find it to hold consecutive thoughts, she says, 'What did Ephraim think of the way you dress?'

It's as though she's only just noticed herself.

'That's an extraordinary question. There isn't *a way I dress*.'

'You're telling me you just fall out of bed that way, wearing your art critic's bow tie and looking like Raskolnikov in that silly hat. What happened to the one you were wearing when I last saw you? The René Magritte hat?'

'The weather's turned.'

'You have a hat for every season?'

'I have a hat for two.'

'You shouldn't be wearing either in my presence. Did no one teach you to take your hat off when you're in the company of a woman?'

'I wouldn't be wearing it if we were inside. I did tip it. I have tipped it every time I've met you. And then I tip it again when we part. But it's too cold to remove it out here.'

'I don't believe you. I think you just like being in fancy dress. I fancy you have a band leader's jacket at home.'

'Funnily enough I don't.'

'Does your bow tie swivel?'

'Not if I can stop it.'

'You're more of a dandy than Ephraim was. He was a dandy in his head; on the outside he was confident enough in himself not to dress like a band leader.'

'I'll have to trust you on that. I can't see him in clothes. I only see his face.'

'He had a lovely face. Like a fallen angel. But repentant. You are like him but then not. You aren't as attractive.'

'You don't have to tell me that. I know I'm not. I never was.'

'You could have been. You have the features. You should have got away.'

'Getting away would have fixed it, you think?'

'It would have made you less wary. You'd be handsome if you dared to relax your face.'

'It's a little too late for that.'

'It's never too late for anything. Let your face go. There's nothing wrong with your bone structure.'

She hasn't seen the nodules on his skull. She doesn't know what he knows. She doesn't know that bumps are fate.

'Well, you're right about getting away,' he says. 'I should have. The opportunity never presented itself.'

'You mean you never presented yourself to the opportunity. Ephraim said you were a frightened, burdened man.'

'And he of all people was in a position to know. I was burdened by him.'

'Because he was the person you couldn't be?'

'You seem to want that to be the case, so let it be the case. But I was the older and felt responsible for him. Not when we were boys, but later.'

'Yet you didn't see him for more than half a century. That was an odd way of showing responsibility.'

'You don't have to see a person,' Shimi says, tapping his chest, 'for him to be *here*.'

She leans forward, gripping the table. She seems to want to locate the part of Shimi's chest where Ephraim is lodged.

But she can't find him there.

'He'd defeated the Germans single-handedly,' she reminds him. 'What did he need you for?'

'Nothing. I needed him. I needed to feel concern.'

'About what, though?'

'He told me things about his lifestyle that troubled me . . .' He pauses, wondering if he's said enough, then remembers the ground rules. 'His drinking . . . His homosexuality . . .'

He sounds very old to himself.

'Has it ever occurred to you,' Beryl Dusinbery says, 'that he was having you on?'

'There's been time for everything to occur to me. Was he?'

The Princess draws herself up in her chair and regards him, in silence, inscrutably.

They pause for Nastya to fetch them more tea and ginger cake from the counter.

'Ignore the way she stares at you,' the Princess says when the girl withdraws. 'It's not an invitation. She looks at every man like that. I think she is smitten by your hat. It probably reminds her of her great-grandfather.'

'Unless I remind her of my brother.'

The Princess counts time on her fingers. 'She has not been with me long enough for that. But the other one tells me she has seen you before. At some Chinese Restaurant, doing conjuring tricks. Is she delusional?'

'About the conjuring tricks, yes, but she might well have seen me working there.'

'Well I'm amazed she even got that right. What were you actually doing – washing up?'

'In a strictly amateur way – except that they feed me – I go from table to table telling fortunes.'

'With a wicked pack of cards like Madame Sosostris?'

'Who is she?'

'She reads the Tarot in T. S. Eliot's *The Waste Land*.'

'I am, as you would expect, more prosaic. I use an ordinary deck of cards. I practise what's called cartomancy.'

'*What's called!* I know what cartomancy is. It's woman's work. All divination is woman's work. Didn't they teach you about the sibyls at school either?'

'What's the force of your "either"? If you mean Madame Sosostris, there you have me. But you can't get to my age without encountering a sibyl.' He thought of making a joke about a Widow he knew called Sibyl but thought better of it. Two, however, could play at impatience. 'I wonder,' he said, 'if another of our ground rules could be that you don't castigate me for my lack of education.'

'It's too late to add another ground rule. Be grateful I still have the patience to pass on to you what I know. Attend before it goes. The sibyls were priestesses. There were ten of them but the one that matters is the Cumaean sibyl who asked for eternal life but omitted to mention she also wanted eternal youth. You can see why she might interest me. She withered to next to nothing, and hung upside down in a bottle, pleading to die.'

'Why upside down?'

'What a curiously incurious question. Why don't you ask why no one broke the bottle? Ephraim would have.'

'Ephraim, Ephraim . . . Wasn't breaking people out of bottles his big thing?'

'So what's yours – watching while they struggle?'

'No – averting my gaze.'

'But leaving them there?'

He doesn't think he needs to answer that.

'Speaking of your brother,' the Princess says, after a pause, 'wasn't he something of a diviner in his time? Also cards, as I recall. Clearly it ran in the family. Was it from him you learnt it?'

Shimi reduces his slice of cake to a thousand crumbs. He is aware of the Princess watching him.

'It's getting late,' he says, rising.

5

Suddenly, Shimi feels he has too much to do.

Wanda Wolfsheim is ringing him at all hours. Is he still up for the event.

Why can't he say, 'No, Wanda, I am not'?

But no: he must leave her swinging in her glass bottle.

Why?

He's not sure he can explain it to himself but if he were to try, he has a feeling it would have something to do with Beryl Dusinbery. He has never been a decisive man. If he were to be decisive now, and deliver the Widow Wolfsheim an unequivocal 'no', could it not be interpreted, by himself, as an unequivocal 'yes' to Beryl Dusinbery? There is no reason on earth that it should be. The moral dichotomy exists in his own head only. He could even locate the nodule for it in on his cranium. A no to Wanda Wolfsheim equates to a yes to Beryl Dusinbery. As for what it would be a 'yes' to exactly, he has no idea. Beryl Dusinbery hasn't asked for anything other than his attention. What else could she ask for? What more could he give? But dismiss it as he might, he is in the grip of a crazy logic: by keeping the younger Widow guessing he continues to hold the older at arm's length.

'Do you know who else has just written to say she's coming?' the Widow Wolfsheim confides. Even over the telephone Shimi feels her breath hot in his ear. He could tell you the blend of coffee she's been drinking. Wanda Wolfsheim is renowned for her telephone manner. I like people to feel I'm in the room with them, she says. Shimi feels she's in the shower with him. But he accepts that without Wanda Wolfsheim's social skills the world would be a worse place than it is. Over the years her telephone manner has persuaded wealthy people to cough up millions for her charities.

'Who?' Shimi dares to ask.

'Shirley Zetlin.'

'Do I know her?'

'Well she says she knows you. She is so keen to come I am not sure I should allow her to.'

He is, of course, only pretending he can't remember Shirley Zetlin. He remembers everyone. But it's a prerogative of old age to pretend your memory's failing. Perhaps the only prerogative of old age.

Shirley Zetlin . . . Christ!

And then there was Bernie Dauber, who had decided some time ago to check out Shimi's prostate the old-fashioned way and, while he had Shimi at his mercy, seize the chance to discuss Dickens's characters with him. 'Why do you Brits, who can't make a decent cup of coffee either, find those names so amusing? Sweedlepipe, for crying out loud. Wackford Squeers! What kind of goddam name is Wackford Squeers?'

Shimi wasn't going to get into a critical discussion of Dickens's merits while lying on his side on an extra-large sheet of kitchen paper with Dauber's gloved hand up his anus. He tossed in a few of his own to speed things along – M'Choakumchild and Sergeant Buzfuz – and said it beat him why anyone found anything amusing.

But now Dauber feels he has to greet him with a Pumblechook or a Fezziwig every time they meet. And frankly Shimi has more important things to talk about. How is it that he is urinating less, or at least with less urgency? Can whatever it was that was wrong have reversed itself without medical intervention.

He drops in for a quick consultation. To hell with the money.

Dauber wants to know if Shimi's circumstances have changed significantly.

'My brother's died.'

'Were you close?'

How many times is he going to be asked that?

'Yes and no. But could closeness have a bearing on my bladder?'

Dauber scratches his head. 'If you were very close I'd expect you to be returning to the john more. Deep distress can do that. Not close should make no difference. I'd just be thankful if I were you.'

'I'm thankful, but there is one other thing. I have struck up an acquaintance – I don't know what else to call it – with a woman who appears to have known my brother well. She's older than me . . .'

Rather tactlessly, Dauber allows his jaw to drop. Older than Shimi Carmelli? Older than Shimi Carmelli and the object of romantic, even if not erectile, interest?

Shimi notes the doctor's surprise. 'To the old,' he says, 'the old do not look old.'

Dauber makes the face of a man innocent of offensive imputation. 'That's a grand thought,' he says. 'Do you mind if I write it down?'

'I am not saying I'm going anywhere with this. And I'd expect her to say the same. To be frank, I'm not even sure we like one another much. But it's a way for both of us to stay in touch with Ephraim.'

'Your brother?'

'Yes.'

'And to her he was what?'

'I've no idea. I'm trying to find out. But what I'm wondering – what I'm asking you – is if this could have anything to do with it.'

' "It" being going to the john a lot.'

' "It" being *not* going to the john a lot.'

'Well again I'd expect it to have been the other way round. Agitation and excitement would normally make you go more.'

'Then by your reasoning it must follow that I'm neither agitated nor excited.'

'Unless you're lying.'

'Why would I lie to you?'

'Not to me. To yourself.'

Shimi rolls his eyes.

Dauber looks at his watch. 'Don't be guided by me on this,' he says. 'I'm not a shrink. You must know what you feel.'

'I guess so,' Shimi says. But no, he doesn't know what he feels.

'Nathaniel Winkle,' Dauber adds as Shimi is on the way out.

The restaurant, too, is a problem waiting to be solved. Hasn't he now entered the twilight of his career as a cartomancer at the Fing Ho, no matter that it was in the twilight of his career that he began there? It's partly the Widow Wolfsheim's importuning that is the cause of this dissatisfaction. Life would be easier if he put his cards away altogether. 'I've retired,' he could tell her. But there's something else. Beryl Dusinbery. That's to say Beryl Dusinbery's carer. He isn't gratified that she's reported seeing him doing his stuff at the Fing Ho. What if she comes again? What if she persuades the old lady to accompany her? That the prospect of this should alarm him is something he can't adequately explain. Would he rather Beryl Dusinbery were uncontaminated by knowledge of what he does? If so, wherein lies the contamination? Does he see her as a higher being, too rarefied to know what he gets up to on the Finchley Road at a time civilised men his age are tucked up in bed reading *The Waste Land*? Does he fear her seeing him demeaned?

But then what about Ephraim who'd been to prison, taken to drink, and rolled in the gutter with God-knows-whom – how had she reconciled herself to that?

Glamour is the difference, he decides. Ephraim had been disreputable – Shimi is merely humdrum. And there is another consideration. The Fing Ho isn't what it was. The world isn't what it was. Though he continues to astonish the elderly and the widowed by what he seems to know just from looking at a deck of cards, he accepts that in the era of the spectacular media illusionist and soothsayer – traversing time and space through the miracle of video and television, deploying microchip technology to do in half a second what a hundred old-style performers like Shimi couldn't do in half a century – his brand of close-up prognostication is old hat. People can now look deeper into their futures on their mobile phones than he can with a thousand packs of playing cards. More and more, these days, diners at the Fing Ho Banquet Restaurant politely look away when he approaches their tables. Once upon a time high-flying banqueters waved twenty-pound notes in the air to get him to come to them and deal the cards or read their destiny among the contents of their duck pancakes; now, harder to impress and more concerned with hygiene, they will pay that much to get him to stay away.

The consequence of this is that he's standing around more, not knowing what to do with himself. Another of the cultural changes to which the Fing Ho has succumbed is the public commemoration of birthdays. For ten seconds at least five times a night the restaurant comes to a stop, the lights dim, a cake is brought out, and the waiting staff gather round the celebrant's table to sing 'Happy Birthday'. There is, Shimi believes, a silent pressure building on him to join in. Not least as he is the only one who knows the words. But for him, of course, joining in is quite impossible.

He is lucky that the proprietor of the Fing Ho has a soft spot for him and remembers to invite him to join the staff for a left-over dinner at the end of an evening, no matter how little satisfaction he has given or how many waitresses he has impeded. 'My father employed you, I employ you,' Raymond Ho tells him.

'I can't go on taking your charity, Ray,' Shimi says.

'It's not charity, it's tradition.'

Shimi knows what tradition means. It means he is the elder statesman of the establishment now that Raymond's father, who started the place and was also called Raymond, but later sat with his back to the kitchen, staring sightlessly out into the street, has departed it in body. Shimi is just as useless, revered only because he has stayed alive. The Chinese have a deep respect for old age. As well as for people who live above their restaurants and don't complain about the smells.

He should have stopped long ago but he hasn't. The staff whose laughter he still can't fathom and whose conversation he still doesn't understand have been like family to him. Li Ling, who used to finger his jacket and tell him he was smart, has long gone. But there's another Li Ling now, the original's daughter, who also finds him amusing and fingers his jackets in the same sisterly way.

So he is ashamed of himself for being ashamed of working there.

And now, as though that's not enough to keep him awake at night, the reappearance of Shirley Zetlin.

'Will you walk with me,' he recalls Si Zetlin saying to him in a gravelly whisper. Shimi can still smell the schnitzel on Si Zetlin's breath. They'd been eating lunch at adjoining tables in the Bukovel Cafe, just a short walk from Swiss Cottage Underground Station. Shimi loved it at the Bukovel, less for the food than for the languages that were spoken there. Not the language of psychiatry which so many of the Bukovel's regulars spoke with fluency – this was lost on Shimi, who didn't believe in psychological explanations of anything – but Russian, Hungarian, German with a Viennese accent, Czech and the despondent Carpathian crooning with which his mother had failed to soothe his anxieties. If the Bukovel was still the sanctuary for exiles it had been since first opening its doors in the 1930s, giving solace to the dispossessed of Europe, for Shimi – a man dispossessed in London – it worked the other way around, making him feel at home in the dark woods and barren mountains the speakers evoked. It didn't matter whether he talked to anybody. It was enough just to listen. In fact it was better. Talking to a person always led to misunderstanding.

Si Zetlin and Shimi were on nodding acquaintance, that was all. Other than the Bukovel's schnitzel, the two men had no common interests. Zetlin wore a football supporter's scarf, and flew to Las Vegas to see Barbra Streisand. He looked women up and down in the street. He asked favours of virtual strangers, such as Shimi Carmelli.

'Will you walk with me?' were four more words than either had ever spoken to the other.

Shimi would rather not have, but he'd been brought up to be polite. What Zetlin wanted could be summed up in a sentence. He wanted Shimi to disburden him of his wife. For one evening, initially, and then they'd see how things panned out. That wasn't, of course, how he put it. Slipping his arm into Shimi's in the old European way, he told of his wife's longing to be a card reader and her admiration, in particular, for Shimi's skills. He brought out a photograph of her from his wallet. This is her. Shirley. He couldn't believe Shimi hadn't noticed her at the Fing Ho and been aware of the intensity of her interest. Did he think she was going for the chow mein? No sir: she was going to see Shimi. So the favour was this: would Shimi give her lessons. Would he, at the very least, take her out to a dinner – Zetlin even had a time and place in mind – and talk to her about it. There would be a fee, naturally (though the niceties required Shimi should not discuss money with her).

Shimi didn't believe a word of this. He had certainly noticed, and heard, Shirley Zetlin. Overflowingly buxom like a Bavarian waitress, she wore low-cut Oktoberfest blouses and interrupted her own conversation with loud laughter, as though she couldn't wait for anyone to find her as entertaining as she found herself. If she had left her husband far behind in this race, she still had many friends and admirers. The question, therefore, had to be asked: what could cartomancy possibly add to her portfolio of charms?

But sometimes an instinctively suspicious man will choose – for no good reason other than boredom with himself – to act entirely out of character. Maybe he was more than usually lonely that week. Maybe he half-hoped that he was wrong and Shirley Zetlin really was an admirer of his. Maybe the Bukovel imposed a loyalty to Si. Maybe something in Shirley Zetlin's effervescence struck him as desperate.

They met, anyway, at an intimate Italian restaurant in Chelsea. She wore a blouse for bending forward in and Shimi began by explaining, in some detail and at some length, the history of the *ars cartomantica* – how, although it was Chinese in origin, the modern version was Southern European, especially popular in Italy where women wanted to learn who their future suitors would be and what their husbands were up to. That might not have been a good early note to strike. Shirley Zetlin withdrew her blouse from the table, sat as far back in her seat as she was able, and yawned.

'Is this your only subject of conversation?' she said.

Shimi reeled as from a blow.

'It is hard for me to avoid the conclusion,' he said after ten minutes of hostile silence in which she wouldn't look up from the wine list, 'that you are not, after all, interested in what I do. I must assume that you are here under an equally erroneous impression.'

'Si said you liked me.'

'Liked you?'

'And that you could get us tickets for Barbra Streisand.'

'And you would compromise your honour for that?'

'Don't get any ideas,' she said.

'Believe me,' Shimi said. 'I have none.'

Their expressions were those of natural predators eyeing each other in the jungle.

They waited to see who would strike first.

Shimi wondered if this was the longest Shirley Zetlin had ever gone in her adult life without laughing.

Eventually it was she who rose from the table in a flurry of frills. 'I will kill my husband,' she said.

'Kill him for me too. I presume the purpose of this ruse is to give him time away with his mistress.'

What happened next Shimi could never have expected. Shirley Zetlin fell back down into her seat, covered her face and began to sob into her hands.

A cold wind rattled the shutters of Shimi's soul. Afterwards he would wonder what other men would have done. Taken her in their arms? Apologised, though the first blow had been cruelly struck by her – bored out of her life, was she; how bored did she think he was? Patted her hand? Admired her blouse? Told her there were worse husbands in the world than Si? Told her that some men wore women's underwear?

But he did none of those things. It would seem that I am even more callous than I am inept, he thought.

He sat, immovable and unmoved, as the tears flowed, until at last the restaurant manager suggested he take the lady home.

'Call her a taxi,' Shimi said.

He could have been ordering the removal of a dead animal.

He put her into the taxi without a word. And then walked the several miles home.

Back in his bathroom he scrubbed away the night.

But he hasn't forgotten any of it.

And now she wants to come and see him do magic tricks in the Widow Wolfsheim's ballroom.

6

The Princess has a change of plan.

'I think you should come to me,' she tells him.

He isn't sure what that means. Sit next to her? Come into her arms? Move in with her? 'As in . . . ?'

'As in come to me. Why are you acting dumb?'

'Come to you how?'

'Come to my abode. Live a little.'

Shimi is still unsure what all this means.

Amused by his perplexity, she throws wide her arms, making a web of her embroidered shawl. 'I see what you are thinking . . . *How do I resist the lure of the spider woman?* Most men, I have to tell you, have never tried.'

Shimi is not going to say I am not most men. He inclines his head in tribute to her powers.

'Rest assured,' she goes on, 'you are safe from being eaten alive.'

'What aren't I safe from?'

'That's a big question. How do you feel about scrutiny?'

'Anxious, but I can take it.'

'Sarcasm?'

'I am glad to be the occasion of it.'

'Interrogation?'

'I am growing accustomed to it.'

'Then you have nothing to fear.'

'But no reason to change our base of operations either. Surely we can continue scrutiny and interrogation perfectly well here. And there's a nice enough room inside.'

Here is still Regent's Park. They are at the same cafe. They are becoming so familiar the staff know them. 'Have a lovely day,' an Italian waitress tells them when they leave. 'I hope you've had a beautiful weekend,' the same waitress says when they return.

'I cannot bear the stress of their expectation,' the Princess says. 'How lovely can a day be? Do I dare tell her that I didn't have a beautiful weekend? I'm nearly a hundred. It's a miracle I have a weekend at all.'

A Polish waitress overhears her. 'Ah!' she says.

'Ah what?'

'It's nice you had a beautiful weekend.'

'They fool me to the top of my bent,' the Princess says.

Shimi is growing accustomed to the way she puts things. 'They intend no harm,' he suggests.

The Princess recoils in surprise. 'Understanding doesn't become you,' she says.

'It's a good thing then that I have so little of it.'

Unlike Ephraim, he means, but she knows what he means.

'Between us,' she says, 'we can squeeze out about as much sympathy for our fellow beings as a mosquito carries in its heart.'

'And yet here we are.'

'What is that supposed to mean?'

'Here we are deep into ripe old age.'

'Did anyone ever say that showing compassion played a part in keeping people alive?'

'Yes. My doctor. The kind of heart live longer, he tells me. I have a friend' – he means the Widow Wolfsheim – 'who gives me fridge magnets reminding me that the person who puts others first is left standing last.'

'Do fridge magnets warm your fridge?'

He smiles at her. 'I have also read,' he goes on, 'that having a pet can add years to our life.'

'What about a pet grievance?'

He sighs. 'I think my friend would say that doesn't count.'

'I bet she would.'

'Who says it's a she?'

'No man ever gave another man a fridge magnet. Or cared how long he lived. So what's yours?'

'My what?'

'Pet grievance.'

'It will take too long to tell it. The moon will be out before I'm finished.'

'Then come back to my flat. It's warmer there.'

They take turns complaining of the cold, as though at any time they can only generate enough heat to warm one of them. Today it's her turn to freeze.

His ears prick to the word 'flat'. She hasn't used it before. He's been imagining her in a mansion.

'Do we need it to be warm? We could wear more clothes.'

'How could *you* wear more clothes. You already look like a bear.'

He smiles. The bird and the bear. This is not the first time he's smiled today.

'I like it out here,' he says.

'Describe it.'

'What do you mean describe it?'

'If you like it out here you ought to be able to say where here is. What's the tree we're under called? What kind of cloud is that? Do you ever see the sky? Do you even know there's a sky up there? Without looking down, tell me what surface we are on – grass, gravel, a Persian carpet? What's the table we're sitting at made of? What can you smell? What can you hear? What bird is that?'

'I like being *me* here – what's wrong with that? I'll bet that tree couldn't tell you where it is. Doesn't mean it's not enjoying being here. Not everything has to be put into words. Not everything has to be known to be felt.'

'Ephraim used to say that.'

'Well, we were brothers.'

'But so different. You with so much energy for yourself. Ephraim with so much energy for other people. He should have had a bit more of what you have.'

'But I don't have the saving grace.'

'What do you call the saving grace?'

'I call it what you call it. The grace to save another's life.'

Or at least the grace to try, he muses, back in Little Stanmore with his wasted mother trembling in their house of fear.

'You've grown grave,' the Princess says. 'Did he save you?'

'No. But he would have saved our mother if he could have.'

'Don't all boys want to save their mothers?'

'I will need another lifetime to think that one through. And then another lifetime to punish myself.'

'You are a glutton for it. Saving lives isn't everything. Saving one's own is just as important. Maybe more. That was at the heart of my argument with Ephraim. He wouldn't save himself.'

'From what?'

'His demons. Alcohol for one . . .'

'I thought he gave that up.'

'Yes, but he bore the mark of Cain. He helped others achieve what he'd achieved, but seeing yourself for ever as a man who has given up drinking isn't exactly a liberation from it. He never freed himself.'

'You sound embittered,' Shimi says. 'Was the other side of his being a saviour that he let you down?'

The Princess looks at him with hooded imperiousness. It is like meeting the stare of a hawk, Shimi thinks. But she is hearing something, far away.

Now, he decides, has to be the time to ask. 'Was he your lover?'

'What if I tell you I can't remember.'

'I won't believe you.'

'That's hardly gallant.'

'I put my brother's honour first. I don't want him to be forgotten as a lover.'

If it's bitter he's after, she does him a bitter laugh. 'I wouldn't concern yourself about that overmuch. There are many who won't have forgotten him. They crowded the chapel, you saw so yourself.'

'I take it you mean men and women?'

She shrugs. 'I don't care about any of that. It wasn't the indiscrimination I regretted, it was the profligacy. He kept nothing for himself. The profligacy tired him – morally. He didn't like how he lived. He didn't like himself.'

'Am I to take it that he didn't like himself after he became your lover?'

'You can take it any way you like. I repeat what I have said to you. I don't remember.'

'You have spoken to me of other lovers.'

'Only the ones I remember.'

'What determines, do you think, who you remember and who you don't?'

'Ah – if only I knew that.'

Something vaporous has fallen about her. Shimi decides he will take advantage of that. 'How did he save your son?'

She slowly cranes back her head and looks up to the sky. Dark, heavier-weight clouds are on the chase, chivvying whatever's softer than themselves out of the way. It is no sky for gentle dispositions. Shimi lowers his eyes and takes in the arch of the Princess's throat. She must have been a charmer, he thinks again. Lucky Ephraim. Or not.

She is a long time looking. 'What was it you asked me just now?' she enquires, coming back.

'How did he save your son?'

She seems to be on the point of disappearing into the sky again but thinks better of it and pushes her face close to Shimi's. It is a provocative action. She could be wanting Shimi to kiss her. Or she could be wanting him to slap her.

But she has a definitive answer to his question.

'He showed him love.'

7

They keep coming back to love. Could that be accidental?

Accidental or not, they are united in drawing back from the subject the moment it arises.

It takes a couple more conversations in the park, on which the sky is darkening earlier and earlier, for him to ask if the love Ephraim showed her son was the love she hadn't.

'Well it could never have been the same order of love, could it?'

That isn't what he means. She knows it isn't. 'I am not implying,' Shimi rushes to assure her, 'that your love was in any way deficient.'

'Yes you are and you are right to. My love was in every way deficient. Perhaps most of all by virtue of its being too great.'

Shimi blows air. 'That's not a paradox you'd permit me to utter,' he says.

The Princess, too, blows air. She shivers under her shawls. 'Very well,' she says, pointing a finger at him – this is something he must take note of: sit up at the back. 'I had my first child when I was a mere child myself. It was shortly after the war started. Women had children because they thought they'd never see their husbands again . . . In my case I was right.'

'I'm sorry.'

'You are always being sorry for things you didn't do. Which makes me wonder what on earth you *did* do. Assuming you were alive then, what was happening to you while I was labouring to bring forth Neville?'

He doesn't want her to stop the minute she has started. This is her story not his. He'll come to his love-deficiencies later. 'Go on with you,' he says.

'I can keep. And I don't want you to feel left out. I know how hard it is for a man to listen to a woman.'

'It is hard for a man to listen to anyone. I never heard a word that was said to me at school.'

'That's because I was never your teacher.'

He looks hard into those grey Atlantic eyes. She has warned him she has no sense of humour. He has warned her the same about him. But there is a sort of choking underwater mirth in her which, frankly, he prefers to humour. When none of it's a joke, then all of it is. The mistake is to go looking for laughter. Yes, he wishes she had been his teacher.

'Don't look at me like that,' she says.

'Why not?'

'It reminds me.'

'Then I'll look away.'

They fall silent, listening to Nastya, at the other end of the park, on the phone to the Eastern Bloc.

'Go on with what you were saying,' he says at last. 'You had your first child . . .'

'At seventeen. A son. Sons are what I have. This one . . . Remind me why I'm telling you this?'

'We agreed we couldn't talk about love—'

'Love!'

So she can do a passable expostulation after all.

He raises a placatory hand. He hasn't forgotten. Ground rule five. *Neither party is, under any circumstance, to look for the renewal of sexual feelings.*

'You told me,' he goes on, 'that Ephraim saved your son by showing him love. Whereupon conversation ceased. We agreed we couldn't talk about love until we'd cleared the obstacle to our talking about love.'

'And what was that?'

'Our unwillingness to talk about love.'

'And then what?'

'And then we agreed to turn unwillingness to our advantage and talk about it after all. Beginning with yours.'

'Are you dead sure of that?'

'No, but I think no harm could come of it.'

She thinks about it. She is more malleable than he has seen her before. 'So where were we?'

'In the first year of the war?'

'Ah yes, then. And what – just as a matter of interest – were you doing at the time? Go on. Spill.'

Shimi laughs. Wildly for him. *Spill!*

She wonders what has amused him.

'No,' he says. 'You have the floor.'

'I relinquish it. Go on. What's amused you?'

It astonishes him how easily, after eighty years of incarceration, the confession slips out of his mouth. 'You asked me where I was. In my mother's bloomers.'

She barely blinks.

The story of his mortification. Told again and again like an ancient saga. Homer reciting the *Iliad*, a little differently each time. Except that Shimi's script never varies.

'It is a long, long time ago,' he says.

'Everything is a long, long time ago.'

'And yet it could be yesterday.'

'Everything could be yesterday.'

She couldn't be more receptive.

The bloomer episode – though to call it 'episodic' was to minimize its significance – marked the death in him, he tells her, of three qualities commonly deemed essential to an emotionally successful life. A capacity for critical introspection: for he has not cared to discover what else his nature harboured. Sociability: for he has wanted no one to know what he had done, has never mentioned it to a

living soul until now, and is frankly bewildered that he is mention-
ing it to her. And anything remotely resembling a capacity for fun:
for while it is true that nothing could have been more ridiculous
than the sight of himself in his mother's bloomers, from that moment
on a sense of the ridiculous is not to be dissociated from
abhorrence.

She shakes her head impatiently at most of what he says. 'Why do
you find yourself so interesting?'

'I know,' he says, 'that what I've described isn't all that unusual . . .'

'If you are going to make a speech,' she says, 'in favour of gender
fluidity, I don't care to hear it. I am weary of men who tell me they
are getting in touch with their feminine side. I've yet to meet a man
who's in touch with anything else. And that includes the brutes, half
of whom are only brutes in order *not* to get in touch with their feminine side.'

He assures her he has no intention of making any such speech.
'I just mean that there are many lonely, unamused, self-disgusted
people in the world. They get by, rubbing along with one another,
at a distance, without ever discussing it. Some even marry and have
children—'

'Retching all the while in secret?'

'I wouldn't go so far as that.'

'So how far would you go? Not so far, I take it, as to do it
yourself?'

'Retch in secret?'

'Marry and have children.'

'You know perfectly well I haven't.'

She shrugs. 'It seems a good time to be certain,' she says. 'But
what makes your disgust of a different order? Don't you think you
might be somewhat vain of it?'

'If you mean vain about my relentless introspection, you might
be right. But I allowed what I did to engulf my feelings for my
mother and, believe me, there is no vanity attached to that.'

'What part did she play, other than by being your mother?'

'None. Absolutely none. That is precisely why I have stepped out of the charmed circle of the family. I am not fit. I didn't only desecrate her, I blamed her for what I did though she never asked me to be curious about her in that way. She didn't invite me to try on her bloomers or leave them out for me to find. She wasn't party to my grossness.'

'You never spoke to her about it?'

'And say what? Your bloomers depress me, Ma. I was hoping for a garment of surpassing preciousness, but I found a worthless, hide-ously ugly thing made of cheap, dispiriting fabric, the lace worn and discoloured—'

'*Dispiriting fabric*? What a refined sensibility you have! How have you managed to pass the blame from you to your mother's drawers? Your brother told me you were an artist.'

'Laugh at me all you like. But beauty wasn't the only issue. Self-regard was. I mean her self-regard. How could she put something so horrible on her body? Did she see herself as an old lady?'

'You think there is an ugliness incident to old age?'

'That isn't what I'm saying. I felt she'd given up on being an attractive woman.'

'And there you were, little man, wanting to turn yourself into an attractive woman in her likeness. How inconsiderate of her to have denied you the opportunity! Would you have felt different about what you'd done had she owned expensive silk lingerie?'

'Never mind me, didn't she owe herself, didn't she owe my father, more erotic respect?'

'I think it was your father's job to express that. It isn't a son's role to feel a father's disappointment for him.'

'I don't see why not.'

'No, of course you don't see why not if it's your ambition to grab all the revulsion going. And it does appear to me that the guilt you say you feel for being disgusted still plays second fiddle to the pride you take in that disgust.'

'If I take pride, then that's my sickness.'

'Tell me something else – why, if you found your mother's knick-ers so offensive, did you try them on?'

Shimi winces. It matters what words you use. 'I can't answer that. It's possible I needed to submit my sexual curiosity to abhorrence, to feel disgusted not just with myself but with her.'

'Yes, but why?'

'I can't answer that either. It could, for some people, be a psychological, even a biological necessity. Perhaps it does the job of a taboo. So close and no further.'

The Princess falls silent. 'I wonder,' she muses, looking up at the sky, 'whether it works the other way around.'

'How do you mean?'

'Whether a mother might feel disgust for her children for similar reasons.'

Never having had children, Shimi says he doesn't know.

But he isn't really thinking about that. He is thinking it is a pity he never had this conversation earlier, but for that to have happened he would need to have met Beryl Dusinbery earlier. So that's two pities.

It's never too late for anything, she said to him the other day. Is that true?

'Better late than never' has always struck him as such a tragic phrase. He smells the dry desert of wasted years in it. But it beats 'Better never than too late.' By a whisker.

It's her turn – it was her turn before he snatched it from her – but she is grown tired.

She has to go. Nastya will take her home. 'Let's meet tomorrow,' she says, 'but not here. I've had enough of here. Let's take a slow walk in the church grounds together – you know the church, opposite the cricket ground, where the graves are. I'll see you at eleven, by the play area.'

When they meet he apologises for the rudeness of his self-absorption the day before. He didn't mean to tire her out. He apologises too for touching a nerve – if he had.

'We meet to touch nerves,' she says. 'There is no other point to us.'

He can feel a 'but' comin . . .

'It is too public here,' she says. 'There are too many children.'

He is slightly miffed. 'You chose this place.'

'I know.'

'And you didn't stop *me* yesterday.'

'You are incapable of being public. You are too gnomic to be indiscreet. Or even understood. "Bloomers," for heaven's sake. No one in that park but me was old enough ever to have heard the word. You could shout your confession from the top of the Post Office Tower and you'd be giving nothing away.'

'Don't tell me you think your conversation is accessible to the multitude.'

'I don't know about the multitude. It's the children's ears I fear for. Come to mine. Allow an old woman the indulgence of recollecting in comfort with her aides-memoire around her. This is no place for us. There are graves everywhere.'

'You chose it,' he reminds her again.

'That's why. Now I unchoose it.'

She had listened patiently to him. He cannot, now she is possessed of the very quick of his shame, deny her anything.

He agrees to come next time.

She writes out her address. He admires her courage. After ninety you stop writing where others can see your hand shake. She is shakier than him, but then she hasn't been shuffling playing cards all her life. Not too bad, though. And the letters are upright.

The shock is that she lives almost directly opposite him. He thinks of her as living in Kensington or Chelsea. There is nothing of the Finchley Road about her. But as they're neighbours, how come they have never seen each other?

This innocuous question is followed by a disturbing one. Did Ephraim visit her there, or even live there. And did that mean that for a while — for God knows how long — the brothers had been neighbours?

Let one frightful question out of the cage and more come snarling after. Did Ephraim know his brother was living opposite? Was he indifferent to that fact?

The Princess is less amazed to discover what she grandly calls their propinquity. Amazement isn't her style. She lacks the punctuation. But it's possible that she isn't surprised because she knew, and she could only have known because Ephraim had told her.

He searches her expression, beseeching surprise out of her. 'Good God,' she says at last, 'you live on the other side of the road! Isn't that extraordinary.'

She's unconvincing.

8

'So here you are, then.'

'Here I am.'

The first thing he does is remove his hat.

Nastya glides in from the kitchen and takes it.

'No thieving,' the Princess says. And then to Shimi, loud enough for the girl to hear, 'In her country that would feed a family of ten.'

'In my country,' Nastya says from the hall, 'we wouldn't be seen dead in such hat.'

The Princess calls her back. 'That isn't how I've trained you to speak to guests. Apologise.'

'I saying it in nice way. Such hat is Russian. Soviet imperialist hat.'

'I understand,' Shimi says. 'I'm sorry if it revives unhappy memories.'

'But I like clothes,' Nastya says, looking him up and down. He is wearing a soft, double-breasted woollen suit under his coat. Brown. And a maroon bow tie. She wonders if he might have a title. 'You buy in Savile Row?'

'All right, that's enough conversation,' the Princess says, shooing the girl away. 'I'd have preferred the black one to be here,' she confides in a loud voice. 'An altogether better thing. But she's seeing the Queen.'

'Does she see her often?' Shimi wonders.

'Who's to say. It wouldn't surprise me to discover they take tea every other afternoon. We are living in a strange world. We used to invade them. Now we give them the run of our palaces. Won't you sit down?'

There are embroidered throws on ornate Italian chairs. Vintage palm tree lights of the sort he has seen at the Royal Pavilion in Brighton cruelly illuminate the room. One has a bare-breasted alabaster native woman reclined beneath, indifferent to a lizard making its way up her thigh. He tries to guess how Euphoria feels about her. The walls are filled with photographs of men, most in black and white. Shimi wonders if they could have been taken by the same photographer, so alike are the poses they strike, so many Second World War airmen, squinting in a melancholy manner into the heavens, but it's clear they span too great a period for one photographer, unless the one photographer is Beryl Dusinbery – lover, he assumes, to them all.

Are these their goodbye photographs? Is that what their valedictory expressions betoken? She snapped them one last time and kicked them out. One even has *Au revoir* written across the bottom. He rakes the wall. 'No,' she says, guessing who he's looking for, 'he isn't here.'

She is robed – the expression is not too grand – in a caftan a great queen might have given her. The words I am fire and air are embroidered at the hem.

'I had no idea,' Shimi says, 'that the Finchley Road hid such riches.'

'I trust you mean riches of the imagination.'

She knows what he means. He means her.

'Day three of this,' he says when they are both seated. 'You had your first child . . .'

'I had my first child when I was a mere child myself. It was shortly after the war started. Women had children then – interrupt me if I've already told you this – because they thought they'd never see their husbands again. I now know what you were doing at the time. I've been giving it my consideration. Perhaps the gathering atmosphere of uncertainty affected you as well. Perhaps it frightened you into fearing you might never see your mother again. Perhaps—'

'Nice try,' he says. 'But we've done me . . . You had your first child . . .'

She coughs and makes as though to take smelling salts from the back of her hand. 'I had my first child when I was no more than a child myself . . .'

And continues, without interruption from herself, until she is in Brontë Country with her father's sister Enid. A village schoolteacher. All her family were schoolteachers. Without the Dusinberys, she enjoys repeating, the nation would have gone untaught. You might wonder what had brought Enid to this wild place. The same, in her view, as brings so many teachers to remote places. The same as brought me. The deranged governess tradition. The longing to go a little mad while holding on to what keeps you sane. The advantage of going a little mad in the classroom being that the pupils don't pay particular attention, since in their eyes all teachers have a screw loose. With so many men away, fighting or dead, the moors wore an even more funereal aspect than usual, Enid told me. Picture me wheeling my pram over Penistone Hill. The sole living thing visible for miles around. Things, I should have said. But Neville was asleep and unnoticing and so might as well not have been there. I see what you are thinking. I was already disconnected from my child. I won't deny it. Was I more interested in my effect, how I looked in the landscape – as an artwork, never mind who saw me – than I was in Neville? Without a shadow of a doubt. What was there in Neville to be interested in? He ornamented my pram, that was all – the widow and her baby, specks on the lonely landscape, striving against the needling, horizontal rain. It was a kind of happiness, wheeling him with no destination in mind, knowing I contributed a little to the picturesque when everything else in the world was shapeless and without colour. Otherwise I grieved the days away, in a revulsion from this lifeless place, from the death everywhere, yes, from Neville, and from myself for feeling what I felt. I had always been a morning moping girl, alive at night when the light was artificial and the spirits false, but when I woke to face the whole cycle of natural recurrence again, the morning spilled like bile into my stomach. I'd have spewed myself out of my mouth had I known how. After Neville, this nauseous sensation of being at one with things I abhorred – as though I no more belonged to a bright world of choice than a garden worm rooting blindly among garbage – disabled me for the day. I'd had no morning sickness while I was carrying Neville, but I had it now. Milk burst from my breasts. Shit poured out of Neville. Only on the moors, wheeling the pram, discordant among the forms of nature, could I feel myself.

Men, of course – those with no appetite for war, those with no fight in them – would pursue me down the lanes but stopped short at following me onto the moors. Fearing finding themselves alone with me they went home to their wives.

In another age they would have burned me.

But wherein was I a witch?

I darted my gaze at no man.

I desecrated no host.

I blasphemed against no religion.

I wasn't a heartless mother.

I protected Neville against all harm except the harm of being with a mother who couldn't love him.

In fact, what she felt for the boy was more piercing than love. She couldn't get over what she couldn't feel. She couldn't have worried for him more, grieved for him more, felt a greater anguish at her heart, had she loved him to distraction. She watched him grow as though from a distance, waiting for something to change, and then something did.

There was an impairment – whether in the child, or in her, or in what functioned, or didn't function, between them, she couldn't have said. But suddenly he wasn't quite as other children. It didn't help that she thought of it, whatever it was, as her doing. A revulsion, whatever its roots and rationale, is still a revulsion. When I turn away from this child, I am turning away from myself, she said. That was no comfort to the boy.

'You are not a fit mother to this child,' Enid said.

Beryl Dusinbery felt she'd been waiting a hundred years to hear these words.

'Then you take him,' I replied.

Shimi waits. And waits . . .

'And?'

The Princess also waits, as if the story is as new to her as him. Something in her expression suggests she wouldn't mind if he told *her* what came next.

But a deal's a deal. He hadn't left her to wonder what happened after he went rooting through his mother's dirty laundry. *His life happened*, and he's told her that.

'If you're waiting for an end there is none,' the Princess says.

'But there is what happened next.'

'What happened next was that I said "In that case take him," and she did.'

'Which you didn't expect?'

'Which I hadn't dared hope.'

Shimi wonders if she is making herself out to be a worse mother than she was. He understands the impulse. Leave yourself with nothing and who knows – some unexpected scrap of mitigation might just turn up to show you in a new light to yourself. That it doesn't, doesn't prove it won't.

'And?'

'You haven't heard enough yet? You're as bad as your brother. He liked to squeeze the tears out of people. He thought we were all better for a little cry.'

'Then no, I'm not as bad as him.'

'I hope not. Because if you're waiting to see me shed a tear you'll be waiting a long time.'

'I know you better.'

'You don't know me at all.'

'I know our common nature.'

'There is nothing of nature in me.'

'Nor me. Which is why I know you.'

'Then have your "and". *And* I never saw him again.'

'Not ever?'

'Never, never, never, never, never.'

★

216

Shimi falls quiet. How long is never? And what's a decent interval of time to come back from it?

Finally, though even finally is too soon, he says, 'But didn't you say Ephraim saved him?'

'Yes, Ephraim did save him. But that was later.'

'Yet still you didn't see him?'

'Ephraim didn't think it would be a good idea.'

'Was that decision Ephraim's to make?'

'He was a high-handed character, your brother. But Neville must have gone along with it.'

'So Ephraim didn't meet Neville through you?'

'Through me? It's all *through* me.'

'I meant in the course of knowing you.'

'You're asking me to piece together what I never fully grasped because I never chose to grasp it. Forgetting isn't always involuntary. But it went something along these lines:

Ephraim met Neville before he met me. Found him is a better way of putting it. I picture them sleeping in a doorway together. But I have no evidence for that. I hadn't left the boy to rot up there exactly. I sent money to poor Enid but she couldn't cope. And when she died I found other ways of getting money to him. Wasted by all accounts, thrown away on the usual forms of stupefaction. I am tolerant of most delinquencies, but not that one. Before the image of the hypodermic needle my small supply of pity dries up altogether. Ephraim was different. Human ruination excited him. Perhaps because he'd tried it. Whether he was himself gasping for air in prison when he first met my son, or had become a paid fisher of men by then, I can't remember. I don't do dates. But he combed his hair, deloused him, set him up in a room of his own, found him a job, showed him affection, taught him we were all better for a little cry. He contacted me after.'

'After what?'

'Sequentially – after Neville attacked and robbed him.'

'Why did you have to know about that? What did Ephraim want you to do – reimburse him?'

'It's a little more complicated. After Neville battered Ephraim he was beaten to a pulp himself.'

'What goes around . . .'

'Don't be flippant. We're all bound upon a wheel of fire.'

'So you do feel pity?'

'I accept the terrible mechanism of retribution. That isn't pity.'

'And Ephraim, whom you still hadn't met, and who you say did show pity, was still conscientiously keeping you up to date?'

'You've misunderstood. There was one communication. He found my name in Neville's papers, such as they were, after.'

'Is this another *after*?'

'Must you be so literal minded. After is after. After Neville followed through the logic of his own life and took what was left of it. There! Now you know. And don't scrutinise me, please, for evidence of grief or guilt. What I have of both is my concern and I won't advertise it.'

Shimi is afraid to bow his head in case that shows as collusion in a contrition she is not going to let him see. Better to meet callousness with callousness. But that's not the word either. In time the heart hardens as the skin hardens. It has to. Or you end up like him. Shimi the Shamed. So who is he to judge?

'So Ephraim didn't entirely save him?' he says.

'That idea seems to please you. He saved him a bit. No, he saved him a lot. He saved him enough.'

'Enough! But not enough for you to see him again?'

She looks around her room as though taking in objects that are unfamiliar to her. 'These are old wounds. I try not to think too closely on them. I enjoyed hearing about him – enjoyed? no; appreciated – I *appreciated* hearing about him from Ephraim.'

'But that was only after he'd died?'

The Princess laughs. It is, Shimi thinks, one of the most horrible sounds he has ever heard, like something precious dying from the world, like the last cry of the last of a threatened species.

Nastya, already preparing tea, comes running in with a tray

spilling tea to see what's happened. 'Put it down there and get out,' the Princess says.

'You're thinking,' she goes on, 'that I was better able to cope with him dead than alive. You are right. But your brother had the gift of words. He made him *come* alive. I see what you are wanting to ask. Were *they* lovers? I don't know and you shouldn't want to. Love's love. And now you.'

'Now me what?'

'Now what terrible, unforgivable crime of the heart do you have to confess?'

'I already have.'

'Don't make me laugh. So you dressed up in your mother's knickers—'

'Bloomers.'

'Don't fight me. Knickers. I'm trying to make this as bad as possible for you. But it's still nothing. So you made yourself look ridiculous in your own eyes. I find it hard to credit that this is really all you have to offer me – that you don't like the feel of cheap underwear on your skin. To be candid with you, neither do I. Now tell me something truly bad. I've booked my passage to hell. What have you done to ensure you'll be joining me there? Who have you murdered?'

'So there you have it,' Shimi says, after painting the scene of him by his mother's bedside, unable to help her, unable to touch her, unable to answer her when she called for him. A thoroughly useless, sterile, nugatory boy.

The Princess laughs to herself. *Otiose*. There's always a reason why a word crops up.

'Still not contemptible enough for you?' he wonders, since she seems not to be attending.

'Not bad,' she says, returning to him, 'but not the worst story I've heard. Not everyone has the stomach to nurse. So no. I'm still waiting for you to confess to something truly hideous. So far it's just been knickers and nausea. As things stand I'm still going to hell alone.'

Shimi eyes her steadily. 'Shortly after she died, I masturbated.'

'While wearing her . . . ?'

'No. While wearing nothing.'

'Well that was progress at least. I hope you still succeeded in disgusting yourself.'

'Of course.'

'There you are then. Lesson Two: this whole shame thing was between you and your biology not between you and your mother.'

A silence long enough for a man to make his passage through life from birth to death and back again.

'It was the morning of her funeral.'

9

The sons are worried for their mother. They keep their ears to the ground, which is to say they sit in the kitchen and talk to Nastya when they visit, and they gather that their mother is talking of moving a man in.

'Talking of?'

'I hear serious discussion.'

'How serious?'

'In low voices.'

'But what are they discussing?'

'They speak too low for me to listen. But once I come in with tray and hear speaking about children.'

'Whose children?'

Nastya shrugs. 'Maybe they have children together . . .'

'Are you saying they are planning to have a family?'

Nastya laughs. 'I think Mrs Beryl is too old.'

The sons say they wouldn't put anything past her. But does Nastya mean they were talking about children they'd already had?

'This is what I think when I come in with tray.'

Pen and Sandy exchange glances. It is not news to them that their mother has lived a variegated life. The idea that they might have brothers and sisters out there in the constituencies has crossed their minds and they have discussed it from time to time. But they have counted on her hardness of heart to keep them out of their lives. She has forgotten her lovers, she will have forgotten her children. That she remembers them − Pen and Sandy − is remarkable; ascribable, they have assumed, to her feeling something more than the usual indifference for their fathers, or at least to one of those fathers having made unusual provision for her upkeep; but then it is true she doesn't always remember them either.

Pen takes Sandy aside. 'You don't suppose this could be Tahan's father suddenly turning up?'

Sandy shrugs. Anyone's guess.

Tahan is the mystery brother they do know about, though they were always half-inclined to think of him as a foundling, so late in the piece was it that their mother produced him as if from behind a curtain. They were both making their way through university at the snail's pace dictated by political ambition, one as President of the Oxford University Conservative Association, the other as President of Cambridge Universities Labour Club. Though the older could be said to have stolen a march on the younger, the younger was able to present himself as treading hungrily on the older's heels. Either way, they both stayed in student politics longer than was good for either of their careers. The cares of office kept them apart from their mother for long stretches, but when they were able to synchronise their diaries to squeeze in a visit home for an afternoon they found Tahan playing with their old toys in their old room. 'Don't ask,' the Princess warned them.

They felt they had the right to know if he was their brother.

'It would appear so,' the Princess said.

'So who's the father?'

'I've told you, don't ask.'

Tahan's presence made no appreciable difference to their relations with their mother. Sandy did say he hoped she would give him a happier childhood than she'd given them, and Pen hoped he'd be sent to a comprehensive school instead of somewhere with a house system, but neither was able to come up with much of an answer when she reminded them of the advantages they enjoyed − indeed were still enjoying − as a consequence of an unloving home life and an elitist education.

'How old is this man?' Sandy asks, turning again to Nastya.

'Old, old man.'

'What do you know about him?'

'Euphoria says he's card player. If you want truth from me, he's Russian agent. When they play chess he's winning.'

Russian agent they don't mind. Russian agent could be useful. But they think it unlikely. Card player is more worrying. Card players go through their own fortunes and then any other fortune they can lay hands on. If he were to tell their mother she once bore him a family, in affectionate remembrance of which could she lend him a couple of hundred thousand quid, who's to say she'd refuse him?

'How often is he here?' Pen asks.

'Irregular. Once in week.'

'And how long does he stay . . . on average?'

'Sometimes all day, coming at lunch.'

'But he goes home at night?'

Sandy shakes his head at his brother. Are they worrying about her honour now?

The conversation is interrupted by the appearance of their mother in a Japanese kimono which she wears as a day-time dressing gown. She has been napping and wants tea.

'What have you been plotting in here?' she asks.

'Is that your way of saying hello to us?'

'I'll say hello when you tell me what you've been up to.'

'We've been asking how you are.'

'You could have asked me.'

'You were asleep. And anyway, you make light of your troubles.'

'I don't have any troubles. Nastya, what have they been getting you to tell them?'

'About condition of workers in my country.'

'What workers in your country? I thought they were all over here getting free treatment on the NHS.'

Pen rolls his eyes. Sandy doesn't.

It occurs to them both, at about the same time, that they could always just ask her directly. Mother, are you, er . . .

So Sandy, as the older, takes a deep breath and plunges in.

'Mother, let's not beat about the bush. It has reached our ears—'

'Reached your ears!'

'It has come to our attention—'

'That's worse. Nothing comes to anyone's attention without them going looking for it first. What are you snooping around the ladies of my bedchamber to find out – who the new man in my life is? Don't ask this one – she wants him for herself.'

Nastya snorts.

'So there is someone?'

'Would you want there not to be? Must I pass my final days alone?'

Pen reminds her she has family. Her sons, their children, their children's children.

She tells him not to go all biblical on her. She's seen her children's children's children, remember. Not often – *aber macht nichts*, she sees them often enough. They have sticky fingers and greedy eyes. Or maybe the other way round. They are hardly the generations of Adam. And on the evidence so far they are not going to provide her with the verbal stimulus she needs if she is to remain among the living.

'We could provide you with a conversationalist,' Sandy says.

The Princess laughs her most hollow laugh. 'Would he be someone from your party?'

'If you like.'

'Or you could have someone from mine should you prefer,' Pen suggests.

'You don't do conversation in your party.'

'That wasn't what you said when you let Blair kiss you.'

'He had a silver tongue, so you got rid of him.'

'A silver tongue is not necessarily a truthful one.'

'That could be your father speaking. If that's an example of the conversation you're offering – no thank you. *Truth!* Where did you get the idea from that I'm looking for truth? I've done truth. I've thrown truth screaming out of my bed.'

'So what are you looking for, Mother?'

'That's not the question you mean to ask. What have I found is what you really want to know.'

'And?'

'All will be disclosed when I'm in the mood to disclose it. In the meantime why don't you go back to your seats and leave the management of my last days to me. If you are worrying about your inheritances – don't.'

With which she flaps her kimono, as though to clear the air of an unpleasant smell, wraps it around her, and strides back into her bedroom like an Amazon.

A moment later she returns to pop her head around the door. 'I forgot to say hello,' she says. 'Hello.'

Without any doubt she's getting stronger.

From her bedroom window she sees them leave the building and then look back up at it. They remind her of Laurel and Hardy – the fatter one bullying and exasperated, the thinner one wondering why it's always him that's being blamed. She wonders if it's ever occurred to them to see themselves this way. Of course it hasn't. They have political careers. Before they go into politics, she thinks, all prospective candidates should be interviewed in public by their mothers. Then none would be elected. She could watch these two for hours. It's like a silent movie. Looking down on people in the street is a bracing exercise. Human activity, viewed from above, must always look foolish and pathetic. As flies to wanton boys are they to the gods. She is sorry when they vanish from her sight. Not maternally sorry. Diabolically sorry.

The brothers find a place on the Finchley Road to have coffee. They don't get on well. But then they have never been shown an example of family love. Sandy makes as if to dust the chair with his handkerchief, then asks Pen if he'll volunteer a corner of his vest. Do they know they look like Laurel and Hardy after all? They could be circus clowns emptying slop buckets on each other.

'Very funny,' Pen says. 'I don't possess a vest.'

'But that's only because you don't believe in private ownership.'

'Whereas after seven years of Conservative austerity yours is the only class who can afford a vest.'

'Which is why we are distributing them to the poor through vest banks.'

Having got this coltish ritual out of their systems they can settle down to talk. Sandy loosens his tie. Pen turns off his mobile phone. They comment on how good it is to catch up. They meet in Westminster frequently, but that's different. Blood might not be thicker than water if your mother's Beryl Dusinbery, but at least here they can play at being brothers.

'She looks well enough,' Pen says.

'I agree. Marvellous. Are you attributing that to the card-playing Russian?'

'It's possible.'

'Then perhaps we should welcome him into the family.'

'Shouldn't we find out a little more about him first?'

'Are you afraid he will make off with the family silver?'

'I didn't know there was family silver.'

'I've been keeping the fact of it from you. I know how you feel about inherited wealth.'

'I have never said my children's children shouldn't be left a teapot to remind them of their great-grandmother.'

'What about you? Don't you want a little something to remember her by?'

'I have a little something to remember her by. I have my damaged psyche.'

'I won't tell anyone. But as regards the Russian, is there any reason to fear he has his eye on our teapot?'

'There is if he's a gambler.'

'But then if he's making her happy he's relieving us of a duty. I don't see you coming up here once a week to supply the harridan with verbal stimulus.'

Pen accepts that readily enough. You can't show more love than you were shown, whatever your politics. 'I still don't think it would do any harm to talk to him,' he says.

'Ask him if his intentions are honourable?'

If nothing else, the idea is worth a laugh.

Their anxieties are premature. Shimi has no intention of moving in with Beryl Dusinbery. Where would be the point when he lives across the road and can easily nip there and back whenever he is required, whatever it is he's required for? And for her part, the last thing Beryl Dusinbery wants is another live-in boyfriend. But then again . . .

She is surprised how much time she puts into weighing the pros and cons of it. No, she doesn't want another live-in boyfriend. The technicalities don't bear thinking about. But if she is to give it a final whirl she will never do better than a man for whom the intricacies of intimacy – the undressing, the watching, or the not undressing and watching, the tasteful concealments, the dimming of lights, the blind swishing of garments – have been so fatally compromised. Nothing like damage to make a man discreet.

She must have voiced her vacillations out loud.

'But then again what?' Shimi wondered.

She had thrown her head back, showing him her swan's neck of yesteryear, and laughing her rasping, blood-flecked laugh. 'But then again, neither of us is getting any younger . . .'

'Is it the idea of me nipping across the Finchley Road that amuses you?' Shimi asked.

She didn't tell him that it was the image of herself sliding seductively out of her slip at ninety-nine that had amused her.

'Were I given to merriment,' she said, 'it's possible I'd find the thought of you "nipping" anywhere diverting, but I won't capitulate to gaiety of that sort and neither should you. Age is not a comedy. Which is not to say it's a tragedy either. Let's agree to call it cataclysmic and have done. Be advised by me, Mr Carmelli – resist all attempts to render you heroic or picturesque.'

'I don't think I need to be reminded how unheroic and unpicturesque I am,' Shimi said.

'You're as picturesque as you need to be, though not, I grant you, in motion. In this you are unlike your brother, who moved well. But you're still here and he isn't. I don't congratulate you on that. Don't let others congratulate you on it either. I know your sex and how susceptible they are to flattery. Fight it. You are not amazing for your age – even I am not amazing for my age – and anyone who tells us we are is taking an unpardonable liberty. We must never lower our guard. We must never let them sweeten us. Once we're sweetened we're done for and they will have what they want.'

'Who's they?'

'Who do you think? Our enemies. The young.'

That hadn't been the only almost-moving-in conversation. But Shimi had quashed all the others, pleading the strange unsociability of his temperament. He was a man who suddenly just vanished from a room, he told her, in case she hadn't already noticed. And not only in mind. He didn't announce when he was taking off, where he was taking off to, or why. He simply slid away. He left questions unanswered, he broke up parties, he caused hosts to worry what they'd done wrong. Where was he going? He didn't know himself. To take the air. To catch his breath. To check his fly front. To keep an engagement he'd omitted to mention. Was everything all right, Shimi? Fine, fine. He'd be back in a moment. Or maybe he wouldn't.

As for actually *sharing a house* – that he had always found impossible, no matter how many rooms and floors the house had, no matter how short the period he'd have to share it. How did people do it – sleep on a couch, sleep on the floor, wake early in a house that slept late, or sleep late in a house that woke early, use someone else's bathroom, shower using someone else's soap, climb into someone else's bath, sit on someone else's lavatory, use paper not made from Canadian wood fibre pulp or washed in the clear waters of the Niyodo River? And all for what? To save a few pence on accommodation. If there were no hotel nearby, Shimi did not accept the invitation. Hospitality was knowing what not to ask of a guest. The word for pressing your amenities on others was not bountifulness, it was barbarism.

This partly explained why Shimi had not travelled much.

The Princess had listened to this with her head to one side, her eyes yellow like a parrot's. From time to time she bit her lip, as though to stop her mouth from opening and words escaping. Once she even covered her eyes as though to spare him her mocking parrot scrutiny. But when she did speak it was with a respect that seemed to take even her by surprise. 'This is a madness which in my experience is rare in men. The men I have known would lie down with a dog were there sexual or financial advantage in it. Had you not told me you were unusually close to your mother I would have guessed it. She made an unexpected man of you.'

'Made no man of me, is that what you're saying?'

'There's more than one way to be a man, even though I seem to have met only the one sort. You should be kind to the memory of your mother – something I have never told a man – and take pride in the exceptionalness she gifted you.'

'My hypersensitivity?'

'I wouldn't call it that. A more sensitive man would be less final about not moving in here. He might at least promise to think about it. But don't get me wrong – I'm not offering.'

This would invariably lead to his telling her about his bathroom and why he couldn't be parted from it. She had never met a man who could talk so long and so passionately about a bathroom. She hypothetically offered to have a bathroom built in her apartment that would be the mirror image of his own, but it could only be the mirror image of his own, he explained, if he could wander out of it confident he would not encounter – or be encountered or at any point heard by – another living soul. Still hypothetically, she offered him his own half-floor with its own landing, double doored against intrusion and insulated against all sound. 'You will be as a God in there. You will reign alone and supreme.'

'My bathroom in the sky?'

'Exactly.'

But she was unable to budge him.

And in the meantime, yes, the arrangement was ideal. She would send Euphoria across the road to ring his bell when she thought of something new to tell or ask him, or when she felt as to words what a wintry tree must have felt as to leaves – robbed, denuded and lonely – while he, between times, could lock himself in his bathroom and think his life through. He had, he realised, while waiting for Euphoria to ring, a genius for continuity. Closing in on his ninety-first year, he was who he'd always been.

IO

Preparations for the Widow Wolfsheim's charity gala — A NIGHT TO REMEMBER — starring North London's own Shimi the Great, were going according to plan. All that could go wrong now was London's own Shimi the Great.

He didn't like the billing. In what sense was he 'London's own'?

'Would you prefer it if we said "Little Stanmore's own"?'

'Why do I have to be anyone's own?'

'Just Shimi the Great then?'

'I haven't been called that since I was a child.' Not counting, he thinks, the time his brother Ephraim the Rapacious stole his identity.

'Anything else not to your liking?'

'Why is it called a Night to Remember?'

'It's a pun, Shimi.'

'But what are we remembering? I'm not a memory man.'

He was, of course, but not in the sense — in either of the senses — Wanda Wolfsheim meant.

'And you've insisted you're not a fortune teller . . .'

'So what in hell's name am I, you are asking?'

'Yes, what in hell's name are you?'

He showed — his old card-performer's gesture — the empty palms of his hands. Search me.

'It's a little late,' she said, 'for you to be doubting yourself.'

'Hardly late. I've been doubting myself since I was born. It's you who claims to know who I am.'

'Very well then – *this* is who you are.'

'Who?'

'Shimi the Great. But I'm not calling you a cartomancer and phrenologist. No one will come if I call you that.'

'You told me you've sold all the seats.'

'I have, but they'll send them back. Can't I call you a magician?'

'No.'

'A wizard?'

'No.'

'A card sharp?'

'Definitely no.'

They settled finally on Card Reader. Let Shimi Carmelli, Card Reader, Look Into Your Future.

'Snappy,' Wanda Wolfsheim said. Her patience was wearing thin.

She had also, Shimi couldn't fail to notice, taken to wearing jeans.

It was Nastya who saw the notice in a charity-shop window. 'Tell me that's not the Russian,' she said to Euphoria.

And it was Euphoria who passed the information on to Beryl Dusinbery. 'Will you be going, Mrs Beryl?' she asked in all innocence, and with that the cat was out of the bag.

'It wasn't your intention, then, to invite me to the Widows' Ball,' she challenged him at the first opportunity.

'It isn't a ball.'

'Did you suppose I couldn't afford a ticket?'

'I thought you wouldn't be interested.'

'Not interested? After all I've told you about the sibyls.'

'I am no sibyl.'

'No, but I am. You could at least have made an enquiry. *My dear, much-respected Mrs Dusinbery, I will be looking into people's futures Sunday evening next, I wonder if you are at all curious about how I do that and whether you might want your own future read.*'

'Your answer would have been no.'

'As to the second part, you are right. As to the first you are not. How could I not be curious? You are an old man on an old woman's errand. You have no observational skills whatsoever. You take no interest in anybody's life. You barely notice other people exist. And yet you say you have acquired the art of looking into their futures. You must see how fascinating I find that.'

'Their futures are abstract.'

'Not to them they're not.'

'Their futures are independent of who they are. They are no more responsible for the cards that fall than they are for the bumps on their heads. So it isn't my job to register their appearances or characters. They are irrelevant to their futures. What you, as sibyl, should know is that prophets aren't humanitarians. They are misanthropists who tell the future because they prefer it to the present.'

'All the more reason I'd have liked to see your misanthropy at close range.'

'You've seen my misanthropy at close range.'

'But not when its object is other people.'

'Does that mean you'd like me to get you a ticket?'

'The decision has to be yours. If you fear I'd put you off your stride . . .'

What he feared was that she'd put the Widow Wolfsheim off hers.

He accepts it might have been a bad idea to prepare her. 'A neighbour of mine has asked me to get her a ticket. She turns out to have been a good friend of my late brother's. She won't be any trouble.' Why was it necessary to tell her all that? *She won't be any trouble!* Why the reassurance? Why should she be any trouble? People introduced as not being of any trouble invariably turn out to be trouble.

And it isn't as though Wanda Wolfsheim isn't anticipating trouble enough with Hilary Greenwald and Shirley Zetlin coming. Here, she accepts, she has been her own worst enemy. Boasting of her intimacy with the only bachelor in London who can do up his trousers has been unwise. She fears she has stirred a nest of sleeping vipers.

Shimi Carmelli, for his part, has always kept himself to himself. Neither Hilary Greenwald nor Shirley Zetlin would have seen much of him in recent years. Shirley Zetlin, by all accounts, has purposely stayed away from the Fing Ho Chinese Banquet Restaurant and it would never have occurred to Hilary Greenwald, who is a fine diner, to go to such a place; so neither of them would have known, or much cared, whether Shimi Carmelli – out of sight, out of mind – was alive or dead. But Wanda Wolfsheim has resurrected him. Suddenly she is hearing rumours that although Shimi broke Hilary Greenwald's heart more than half a century ago, she has not entirely given up on the prospect of a reconciliation and remains, when allowances are made for all that she has been through, a fine figure of a woman with a scarcely diminished inner glow. As for Shirley Zetlin, it is true she has been nursing no such fantasies; not only has her heart never skipped a beat for Shimi Carmelli, she believes him to have been instrumental in some obscure way both to the break-up of her marriage and a loss of personal confidence from which she has not yet entirely recovered. She would very much welcome, she has made clear, the opportunity to spit in his face. But Wanda Wolfsheim has been alive too long not to know what a spit in the face can lead to. Her assuring both these women that Shimi is not the man they take him for, indeed not a man they should take for anything, since his attachment to her is well attested, can only be said to have made matters worse.

By way of precaution the Widow Wolfsheim has had a dress made for the occasion by Azagury.

And now Beryl Dusinbery.

Who is this woman?

She has heard talk of Shimi being seen in Regent's Park in more than usually animated conversation with an extravagantly demonstrative woman rather older than a man in his condition has any need to be so attentive to. No one in her circle has any inkling who this woman could possibly be. Her description rings no bells. Tall, aquiline, imperious, fine-boned, educated. Could be a stage actress of another era is one guess. A feminist poet. A mistress of Ernest Hemingway. A once-famous traveller in Arabia. An heiress to the Nivea fortune. The illegitimate daughter of Pablo Picasso. The 'tall' part intrigues and worries Wanda Wolfsheim. None of the North London Widows is tall. Is that what's intriguing Shimi Carmelli? She would like to know more about her legs but she is shawled from head to foot and the Widow Wolfsheim draws comfort from that. No woman shawls what she would like a man to see. As for directly confronting Shimi himself, that would be impossible. She is too proud to admit to curiosity. And Shimi, anyway, is not the most candid or observant of men.

It wouldn't signify, probably, had he not invited this woman to the Night of Memory. But that he has, signifies to Wanda Wolfsheim a great deal. She is beginning to wonder how good an idea hosting this event was. But the tickets are sold, the chairs are in place, and the caterers are booked. There are many trials in the Widow Wolfsheim's life and this is proving to be another of them.

★

Shimi Carmelli has been feeling pretty much the same about it. There will be people here he would rather not see. There is a person anxious to accompany him who he would rather have stayed at home. Why he wants to keep Beryl Dusinbery separate from his other North London life, or his other North London life separate from Beryl Dusinbery, he cannot explain. But people whose lives are governed by shame are often compartmentalisers; secrecy is their medium and secrets are easier to keep the more separate rooms they have to lock them away in. Shimi is prey to many dreads; the greatest of them is everyone he has ever known getting together to discuss him. This is a solipsist's fear. Flip it and Shimi's greatest dread is everyone he has ever known not having a word to say about him. Can this possibly mean that the shames Shimi has taken such pains to hide are shames he would like the world to know?

It shames him even to pose that question.

Over and above such considerations is concern about his inundatory bladder: a problem which, as he reported to Dr Dauber, went away in the first weeks of his absorption in Beryl Dusinbery's effusive conversation, but has since returned.

'Why now, when I am about to perform before my most discriminating audience?' he wants to know.

'The answer is in the question,' Dauber tells him. 'But I shouldn't worry. Nature – otherwise known to you and me as adrenaline – will come to your rescue. How often have you seen a speaker leave the stage or run out of a live television studio to take a leak? It just doesn't happen.'

'They're a self-selecting sample, Doctor. People in a really bad way know better than to subject themselves to the test. They stay off the stage and don't appear on television.'

'Would you describe yourself as being in a really bad way – this minute?'

'No, but I fear I will be.'

'That's the very fear that adrenaline cancels out. You'll be too high on the excitement of performance to notice it.'

'No performance of mine was ever exciting. It's lasting out that worries me. And then there are the social issues.'

'What social issues?'

'Meeting people.'

'Meeting people sends you to the john?'

'Meeting these people will.'

'Why? Who are they? Hollywood moguls? Talent scouts?'

'In a manner of speaking, doctor, talent scouts are exactly what they are. They're elderly widows.'

'Then they'll be rushing to the john too.'

'That won't help me. Please, can you just prescribe me something?'

'What's wrong with what I gave you last time?'

'I want to shock my body with something new.'

'And the widows won't do that?'

Shimi throws him the look of a thousand-year-old man.

Dauber writes him a prescription for oxybutynin chloride. 'Don't overdose on them,' he warns.

'Why? What will happen?'

'You'll get confused.'

Shimi adds another hundred years to his expression.

'All right – *more* confused.'

They don't go together to the Widows' Ball, as the Princess now insists on designating it. Shimi has to be there early for sound checks and the like. The Princess follows with Nastya providing an arm to lean on, should an arm to lean on be necessary, but she isn't planning to lean on anybody. She is once more the belle of the ball. She would have preferred the company of Euphoria but it's Nastya's turn to be on duty and the girl will not be denied the opportunity to dress up. 'Don't expect there to be any dukes there,' the Princess warns her. Nastya puts on her shortest dress just in case.

The Princess, too, has given thought to her wardrobe. It dismays her that she's losing memory of the clothes she owns. Every time she slides open a wardrobe door it is as though she is entering an enchanted place. What are these garments? Such occasions they must have graced! Slowly, as recognition dawns – more painfully when it doesn't – she is pulled back into sadness. So this was her, was it? Her past, when she doesn't have her diaries to consult, is like dancing with skeletons. To see again the dresses in which she did dance with them only adds to the ghoulishness. They hang, in her imagination, as though from wasted shoulders. But she is resolute. One by one she pulls them out, all the way back to engagement parties and weddings and May Balls. The more sardonic her recollections, the better able she is to see the figure she cut. In this one she refused a proposal of marriage. In that one she discovered the father of one of her children – maybe – pleasuring another woman in the bushes. Seeing him, again, bent as though over a wheelbarrow, with his trousers down round his ankles, brings back to her how fine she looked in plunging black velvet with a diamond choker round her throat.

Oh, the elegance and absurdity of the long life she's lived. Her sadness vanishes. Yes, she will find something that is dead right and she does — a ceremonial *furisode* kimono that is a replica of that worn by the soprano Birgit Nilsson when she sang *Turandot* at Covent Garden. For a chill Princess a still icier Princess's robe. The story of how she came by it has been amplified over time, but what she will tell the Widow Wolfsheim is that she admired the *furisode* at a post-gala performance dinner some time in the 1960s or maybe even the 1950s, whereupon the soprano, examining her from head to toe, declared she'd make a better Turandot than her. 'I cannot sing,' Beryl Dusinbery replied, but Nilsson swept that consideration aside. 'Your appearance alone would riddle a man to death,' she said. And Beryl Dusinbery returned the compliment. 'Were I the Prince of Persia I would have died at your hand rather than find my way out of the labyrinth of your desires,' she said. The women exchanged chaste kisses. They must have looked like snowy egrets embracing. A copy of the gown arrived in a chauffeur-driven Bentley a week later.

She is gratified by Nastya's appreciation of her when she's dressed.

'You look million dollars.'

'Then let's go before I depreciate.'

'I take chair?'

'Only if you intend to sit in it.'

The girl takes a photograph of the Princess with her mobile phone. And then a selfie of them together.

Shimi doesn't appear until everyone is seated. He has stipulated no stage. He will go from table to table and describe the cards he deals so that even those unable to see can participate in the drama. He says a few words about the ancient art of cartomancy — its origins in China, its passage through the Middle East to southern Europe, the significance of some the key cards — which to watch for, which to welcome, which not to — and why it's forbidden ever to defile the pack by performing conjuring tricks with it. Divination, he explains, is more august than magic.

Shirley Zetlin has heard all this before. The most boring and insulting night of her life. But if she'd been inclined to heckle she is constrained by the immediate proximity of Wanda Wolfsheim, who is not going to let anything untoward take place. To that end she has seated Hilary Greenwald on the same table. Next to Beryl Dusinbery, who has not found a headdress to complement her *furisode* but has put her hair up and slid a pencil through it. The Turandot reference is not lost on Wanda Wolfsheim. Without doubt it's overdone, but when did that ever bother a man?

Shimi is well-served by his abstractedness. He notices little of the room, the flower arrangements, the guests. The cards engross him, as does the matter about which he consulted Dr Dauber and for which he has swallowed more pills than is recommended on the box, but then the box doesn't know the stress he's under. So far so good, but the evening has just begun. He pushes back the sleeves of his jacket, as though to demonstrate he is concealing nothing, but it is a gesture designed more to show off his cuffs than prove his probity. His wrists are the part of him he likes best. They are manly he thinks, not scrawny but strong, and yet refined. He has countless pairs of cufflinks, many with his initials engraved on them. Tonight he is wearing a simple gold pair, oval with chain links. The Widow Wolfsheim has bought him cufflinks very similar, but these were a present from his mother.

At the Widow Chomsky's table the ace of clubs is the first card up. 'Ah!' Shimi exclaims as though the devil or the god of love has come among them. The Widows gasp in mock collusion. Shimi's explanation that the ace of clubs is the card of matrimony evokes great mirth. 'I think there's been enough of that at this table,' the Widow Chomsky mutters in a loud aside. It is all, he explains, about combinations. For example, the three of hearts, which he deals next, combines with the ace of clubs to denote a beauty parlour. The Widow Chomsky's friends laugh again. They all spend too much time in beauty parlours already. 'Perhaps you are about to inherit one,' he tells the Widow Chomsky. But when a six of spades appears, which either promises a new car or warns of problems with a mobile home, followed by a two of spades, the card that augurs employment difficulties, a little of the sparkle leaves the table. Has Shimi forgotten to bring his A-deck? There will be a raffle before the evening ends and Wanda Wolfsheim has asked him to ensure he leaves the guests in open-handed spirits. Shimi lowers his voice to a guttural Russian and finds cards that presage the fulfilment of secret wishes, faraway places, romantic journeys, good health, great-grandchildren. He is not a comedian or a flirt, but he feels confident with the cards in his hands and his wrists on show. He diffuses an old-fashioned courtliness, reminding the Widows of their fathers, so that when he conjures felicity or fortune from the cards, they see no reason not to believe him; but he is also Ivan the Terrible, so at the mention of a journey the Widows see themselves in a speeding troika, scarfed against the snow but exquisitely vulnerable to temptation.

He visits a couple more tables before he finds himself at Wanda Wolfsheim's. It takes him a moment or two to realise who else is sitting with her. And once he does, a wave breaks over him and he is flooded with a panic indistinguishable from sorrow. Why are there women here who, with good reason or not, think the worst of him? Why them, of all people? What is this trick Wanda Wolfsheim has played? What are these poisons that will never leave his body? It is as though the hour of judgement is at hand and he is being read to from the Book of Past Transgressions. It wants only his mother to be here and he would fall on his knees and beg forgiveness.

The wave tosses him to and fro. He can't, he realises, go on with the cards. He puts a hand on the table. Eyes are on him, but none he wants to look back into, except perhaps – there is always a perhaps – Beryl Dusinbery's, and she is too grandly attired to be a comfort to him. Yes, he thinks again, it only wants his mother to be here, and in his confusion – for things are losing their distinctness quickly – he sees her. His mother with a pencil in her hair . . .

He puts another hand out to keep himself upright, feels a surge of terror whose source he thinks is his bladder, notices his cuffs and is pleased at least that they have not disgraced him . . . perhaps if he can keep them above the rising tide . . . and then crashes to the floor.

It is the Princess who cries the loudest – like a scream from a Greek tragedy, the Widow Wolfsheim thinks disconsolately – the Princess who, indifferent to the rustiness of her joints and the cumbersomeness of her garment, is the first to leave her seat, the Princess who is the first to kneel by him, the Princess who cradles his head.

BOOK THREE

I

There was no need for hospitalisation. She took him back to her apartment and put him in the guest bedroom. He was confused still but not so confused that he didn't, at the threshold, pause to ask whether there was an en suite.

'Of course there's an en suite. What kind of place do you think you're coming to? You're on the right side of the Finchley Road now. In my apartment the en suites have en suites.'

'I won't stay here long,' he promised her.

She promised him he would.

'I'm as right as rain,' he told her when he next opened his eyes.

'How long do you think you've been here?' she asked him.

'Twenty-four hours.'

'Then you're not as right as rain. You've slept for forty-eight.'

It suited her that he didn't know what day it was. She'd found the sharpness of his faculties uncanny. It equalised things between them a little that he should be bewildered as to time. A man who remembers everything and a woman who remembers nothing – that wasn't quite the way it was: she recalled plenty when she chose to; but it was near enough to being true to worry her. She had put her trust in no man. The present she commanded – no one did the present quite as she did – but she couldn't with equanimity gift him everything before that. It left her back uncovered.

'It would suit me if you had a little fall more often,' she said.

A 'little fall' was how they described what had happened to him.

'Why is that? So you can go on looking after me?'

'Don't call it that. I am not a mother-hen.'

'What should I call it, then?'

'Extending our opportunity.'

'For?'

'It would be gross to name it.'

'And how would whatever it is be helped by my having a "little fall" more often?'

'It would mean we'd be hazy about the same things. You remember too well. You don't surprise yourself often enough.'

'Why should that be a problem between us?'

'Who said it was?'

'You implied it.'

'No, you inferred it.'

'You should try a little fall yourself, Mrs Dusinbery. It might render you less pedantic.'

She waved the criticism away as though it were a tiny flying insect. 'I don't need a fall. I'm hazy enough. But you – you could do with some blurring at the edges. A man who knows the course of his life so well that he is never a surprise to himself shuts down the future. You too often have the air of someone who knows how it will end.'

'Then I give a false impression. What you see is fear. I dread the candle going out without ceremony or fuss. Just pfft . . . I dread it ending in a little nothing.'

'Then we must make certain it's a big nothing. I haven't moved you in for something small.'

'So you admit you've moved me in?'

'For the time being.'

He looked at his watch. '*Time being!*'

'There's the faint-heartedness I'm talking about. You think you're coming to the end because you've told the same, unvarying story to yourself a thousand times. Risk another story. Risk another end. For me, if not for you. I refuse to allow you to know me as you know yourself.'

246

'Then I would be better living across the road.'

'That doesn't follow. Aren't we in this for the challenge? Anyone can spring a surprise when you see them only once a year. Real genius is taking someone's breath away when you're with them every hour.'

'You're asking a lot of yourself.'

'And of you.'

'I am more surprisable than you think. I might not strike you as sizzling with expectancy but I am not closed to the future. Right this minute I would call myself suspenseful.'

'This must be the consequence of your little fall.'

'Not so. I inherited it. My mother and her sisters were like musical instruments, a xylophone orchestra of women, each waiting for the hammer to hit the others. Dread was the only music they heard. Something going wrong for one of them meant something going wrong for them all. I'm past the age of waiting for something to go wrong. It already has. So now I'm on edge waiting for the opposite assurance – not that everything will suddenly turn out right – it was only a little fall – but that there's a shape to it all, like the end of a good mystery story, when you see why everything happened as it did.'

'Please don't tell me you're waiting for a blinding flash.'

'Blinding, no. A gleam, that's all. A glimmer.'

'Of truth?'

'I wouldn't go that far. Just some gentle reassurance.'

'What of?'

'I don't know. If I knew, maybe I wouldn't need it. I can only put it in opposites. The opposite of dying like that oyster in your embroidery, vanishing down an open throat. With no one listening.'

'I'll listen.'

'That's not enough. I want to be told something. I want to hear my name. I want an old-fashioned blessing.'

'Then I'll bless you.'

'And I will receive your blessing with the deepest gratitude. But you're an interested party. You can't speak for impersonal nature. And anyway you don't believe any of that.'

'You mustn't make assumptions about what I believe from my embroideries. They're fictions.'

'We're all fictions,' he said, without quite knowing what he meant. 'Maybe all I'm waiting for is someone to tell me that I'm not. A kindly acknowledgement of my reality. Noted in passing. My presence ticked, as in an attendance register. Shimi Carmelli? "Here, miss." Only of course I won't be here, I'll be gone. But at least, if I'm ticked . . .'

'What?'

'I'll be happy.'

'Personally happy?'

What was she asking him to say? That he was happy with her? That she *made* him happy? He could almost say it – almost, almost say it – but he couldn't quite.

What he did say was, 'Yes, that as well. But would you believe me if I said metaphysically happy. Accepted into the scheme of things. You're aren't an aberration, Shimi. What you did you did because that's what people do. Even what people are expected to do. With all your faults you are of humanity. You aren't here today and gone tomorrow—'

'Well you're certainly not that.'

'Laugh all you like, but you know what I mean. I'm looking for that great assurance – *You aren't that oyster, Shimi.*'

'You make me regret I embroidered it.'

'Don't say that. It doesn't become you to regret anything. If there are to be regrets they should come from the other side. God, nature – whatever you call it. Sorry for how we made you. That's what I'm hanging on for – a celestial apology. A gesture of understanding at least. A pair of hands coming down from out of the clouds to hold my head.'

'Your head? Don't you mean your hand?'

'No, my head.'

'Why your head?'

'I don't know. To stop stuff falling out. To make sure I go with everything still in there.'

'Hasn't keeping stuff in there been the cause of all your sorrows? I'd have thought you'd want to have it shaken out of you at the end.'

'No. I want to go whole, full of me, to nice music. Maybe Horowitz playing Schumann.'

'If your head is being held you won't be able to hear any nice music.'

'I'll hear it in my soul.'

She looked rather longingly at him. Sad for him. Sad for her. Did she want to hear him say it would be her he'd be listening to as he finally floated away? Not the Music of the Spheres, but the Music of Her?

He could *almost* say it.

'With the arm of the universe around you?'

He could *almost* say no, with the arm of you. But he repeated what he'd said already. 'With the hands of the universe holding my head.'

She knew her limits. She couldn't compete with the universe. But she took responsibility for him anyway. 'Then I have my work cut out,' she said.

He offered to move back across the road, but she assured him that would not be necessary. Here/there, life/death – same difference.

2

'They've been doing their homework on you,' she tells Shimi.

'Who?'

'Who do you think? MI5? My boys.'

'And what have they found out?'

'They've uncovered your Russian connection. They know about your spying.'

'Do they know I play the balalaika and married Solzhenitsyn's daughter?'

'I've told you, everything.'

'I bet they don't know I solved sliding tile puzzles in a cellar on the Seven Sisters Road for most of my life, close to the pub where Trotsky and Lenin drank warm beer, reading Charles Kingsley's *The Water Babies*?'

'Where Trotsky and Lenin read *The Water Babies*?'

'Where I did.'

'That's, if anything, even more bizarre. *The Water Babies*! You! You grow more interesting by the hour. Why have you not told me this before?'

'I want to eke out my secrets.'

'Well you've certainly eked out this one. I know where you were born and brought up, I know where you went to school, I know your mother's drawers, inside and out, I know the air-raid shelter where you learnt to resent your brother, I know your Chinese restaurant,

I know your bathroom, I know your Widow friends, but *The Water Babies*? Why? Did you have a water birth?'

'In a manner of speaking, I did. It had been a stinking hot summer. My mother was bathed in sweat when I was delivered. The tarantula, presumably, was looking for water.'

'Tarantula. What tarantula?'

'The one that ran over my baby feet. It's a story I tell.'

'So it's a lie.'

'Define a lie . . . If I remember a tarantula there was a tarantula.'

'You'll tell me next it ran off with the afterbirth.'

'It did actually.'

'And so you sat in your cellar solving sliding puzzles and reading *The Water Babies*? What a gift for pathos you have.'

'As did Charles Kingsley. I loved that book. It was an heirloom of the heart – my mother's very own copy. She used to read it aloud to me or we would look at the illustrations together. They showed a little Victorian chimney sweeper swimming with grown-up fairies. They took him in their arms and gently washed the filth of his occupation off him. Is that all a bit obvious?'

She says nothing.

But she has a thought. Is that the role she has been appointed to play in the tainted life of Shimi Carmelli? Is she one of the fairies armed with a bar of soap?

'I am very glad,' remarked Euphoria bringing in hot chocolate, 'to see that Mr Shimi is looking better.'

The Princess peered long and hard at Mr Shimi. 'I've told you about encouraging familiarities with the staff.'

Euphoria took two steps back.

'I want them to feel relaxed with me, that's all.'

'Why should they feel relaxed with you? They don't feel relaxed with me. You aren't, I hope, planning some Leninist shake-up of the domestic arrangements just because you were both admirers of *The Water Babies*.'

'I don't like "Mr Carmelli" – "Mr Carmelli" was my father.'

'It's not the mode of their address I object to. It's their assumption of intimacy.'

Euphoria feared it was all her fault. 'I'm sorry, Mrs Beryl,' she said.

'Just address your concerns about Mr Carmelli's health to me in future, and stop talking to my sons.'

'I'm not the one who talks to your sons, Mrs Beryl.'

'Then we know who that leaves.'

Euphoria hesitated.

The Princess subjected her to a searching look. 'I sense the enormity of some moral struggle in you,' she said. 'Are you thinking of betraying Her Majesty's secrets?'

'She isn't only talking to them in the kitchen, Mrs Beryl,' she said.

'Who isn't? The Queen?'

'Nastya, ma'am.'

'So where is she talking to them?'

Euphoria wondered if she had already gone too far, and took two steps back. If she could have backed out of the apartment and down into the traffic she would have.

'Come on, child, spit it out.'

'In the street, Mrs Beryl.'

'My sons are meeting my staff in the street? Have you seen them together?'

Euphoria nodded.

'Is money changing hands?'

Euphoria shook her head. She hadn't seen any. But she did think they were taking photographs.

'Of one another?'

'No ma'am.'

'Of this building?'

'No ma'am.'

'Then what on Earth of, child?'

'Of the Fing Ho Chinese Banquet Restaurant, Mrs Beryl.'

The Princess and Shimi exchanged looks.

'They are being good sons,' Shimi ventured.

'How does photographing the Fing Ho Chinese Banquet Restaurant make them good sons? Do you suppose they are planning to take me for a birthday meal? They wouldn't know how old I am. For which I can't entirely blame them. I've never known how old they are.'

'My guess is that they're photographing my place in order to ascertain whether I can keep you in the manner to which you are accustomed.'

'And can you?'

'No, ma'am.'

All things considered, the Princess thinks it's time everyone got to know each other. 'There are members of my family who haven't met for over half a century,' she says. 'Some haven't met at all and others I have never met myself. Introducing you provides me with the perfect excuse to make their acquaintance.'

'What if I don't want to meet any of them?'

For someone who has never experienced such an emotion, the Princess does a wonderful imitation of wounded motherhood. 'But they are my family!'

'That doesn't make them mine.'

'I met your Widows.'

'The Widows don't count.'

Shimi isn't letting her see he's feeling bad about Wanda Wolfsheim. She has been on his conscience. Another person wronged. He'd written apologising for collapsing on her floor before the raffle and she'd written back formally hoping he was well and *being cared for*. There had been no phone calls.

The Princess reads his mind. I am the real cartomancer in this relationship, she has often boasted, and I don't need cards. But she'll humour him. If the Widows don't count, the Widows don't count. 'All the more reason,' she says, 'for you to meet the people who do count for me.'

Shimi peers at her. 'I am flattered that you think they should count for me. But isn't meeting the family usually preparatory to a wedding?'

She peers back at him.

'You don't think I'm proposing to you?'

'I certainly do not. As I recall we have ground rules as to matrimony.'

'We have ground rules as to romance.'

'And it is out of the question to have one without the other?'

'Strange you should ask that. Are *you* thinking of proposing to *me*?'

'I wouldn't know how. I have no experience.'

'Then I hope you are not toying with a susceptible woman's feelings. There is such a thing as breach of promise, you know.'

'At our age?'

'A promise is a promise at any age. And at our age it might be considered particularly cruel. We are unlikely to propose or be proposed to again.'

'Again! For me, remember, it would be the first time.'

'Then you can be the one who wears white.'

He flushes. She knows why. Were his mother's bloomers white?

Another day, another tease. But not, for some reason, this day.

'This subject has become tedious to you,' she says in her kindest voice. 'I knew it would.'

'I fear it's I who have become tedious to you,' he says. 'I don't play as well as you.'

'You libel yourself. Just because your face is long and you hide your watery eyes from people it doesn't mean that you're in earnest. You are as much a comic construct as I am. Nothing you say means what you say it means. You are entirely theatrical. You are your own hyperbole. I am better suited to understand this than anyone.'

'Because you had an earlier encounter with it in Ephraim?'

'Ephraim? Good God, no. Ephraim was a literal-minded joker.

He said "Have fun with me," and so one did. You say "Have no fun with me," and that's an altogether more enticing proposition – at least for a woman like me.'

'Then I'm lucky to have found you.'

'There you go again, not meaning what you say.'

'But I do mean it.'

'It's too late. You've made such an art of gloom that no one will believe there is a lighter, more hopeful you.'

'I am not hopeful. Just appreciative.'

'As am I. But we are both stuck with the parts we learnt to play a long time ago. We are anachronisms – not just because we're old but because we're both actors who cannot accept the literalism of our times. I have sons who are admired for being true to themselves – one with whom people identify, God save us, and another with whom they don't, but at least, they say, they know where they are with him. As though a knave who shows you his true self is preferable to a virtuous man who dissembles! We couldn't be alive, you and I, at a worse time. In an age of authenticity, what business do dissemblers like us have crawling between heaven and earth?'

'Well, we will be gone from here soon.'

'That's what they want to hear us say. We'll be off in a minute – the last relics of the age of irony. As though it's our job to step aside and make life easy for them. Well, I have news for them: as long as we are here we are going to rub their noses in their condescension. One day they'll thank us for it. We keep the back door open for them. We enable the fresh air of the past to blow through.'

'Shall I say that to them when I pass them in the street? *We're hanging on to spite you, and one day you'll thank us for it* . . . Not that they see me when I pass them in the street.'

'Of course they don't see you. To anyone but themselves the young are impervious. That's what believing the past should be wiped away does to their faculties – it makes them blind and deaf. But we still owe them an example, no matter how little they deserve it. We owe them double-dealing, subterfuge, deviancy—'

'Deviancy?'

'Hush – I'm doing this without a thesaurus. Deviancy, yes. And pretence, fiction, sarcasm – the past's great masquerade of insincerity.'

'And what do we owe ourselves?'

Their eyes meet, frivolous and rheumy. Roguish even.

'The game of happiness.'

'We should get married, then.'

'*Should?* Under whose compulsion? The God of Love's?'

She waits to hear what he'll say to that.

3

Since they've been photographing the Fing Ho Chinese Banquet Restaurant, the Princess decides that's where she should take them for their getting-to-know-you-all banquet.

Shimi is surprised she means to go ahead with this. He thought it was conceived spontaneously in response to her sons' meddlesomeness and that she would forget about it the next day.

'Far from it,' she says. 'I want to show you off, introduce you to the hungry generations.'

'What as? Bait?'

'I'll think of something. How do you feel about being described as my *intended*?'

'Depends on your intentions.'

Raymond Ho has proposed his largest round table in a private room and promised a spread to end all spreads. He wonders if Shimi will be performing for the guests. Shimi tells him that the last time he shuffled the deck he ended up unconscious on the floor of someone's private ballroom and is under doctor's orders not to converse with fate again. Besides, he is being introduced to the family of a woman with whom he is 'keeping company' – he is pleased with the expression: there is even something vaguely Chinese about it, he fancies – and is expected to make a good social as well as conversational impression. 'Maybe don't even mention the cards, Raymond.'

Raymond taps his temple and moves on to the question of dietary fads. Shimi has already discussed this with Beryl Dusinbery who says she has no idea what her children and their children eat and doesn't care. They will eat what they are given or they won't. 'I have a passion for sweet-and-sour pork with Singapore noodles,' she says, but admits it is a while since she ate in a Chinese restaurant and accepts that menus might have moved on since. Shimi assures her that with his contacts sweet-and-sour pork shouldn't be out of the question

It is agreed that she and Shimi will be there a good half hour before the others. As at the Widows' Ball, only this time she'll be with him and he won't be taking pills.

'You will sit at my right,' she says, 'otherwise it's immaterial where the rest go. But I have told them to arrive at different times. I don't want the lot descending all at once. That way, too, there is a better chance of my remembering who any of them are.'

She is Joan Crawford tonight, hard as nails in a jet-black feather boa that would have served Mephistopheles as a cloak. The River Styx did not run with blood redder than her lips. She can't trust her hair so wears a small fur Cossack hat at a tilt. 'Don't wear yours,' she warns Shimi. 'We don't want to look twinned.'

'You're making a big effort for this,' Shimi said, when she first appeared before him, 'considering it's only family.'

'There is no *only family*. Those boys of mine have been trying to get power of attorney for the last ten years. I'm reminding them who they're dealing with. "Don't fuck with me, fellas."'

Shimi didn't pick up the film reference but got the gist.

He too is dressed to make a big impression. 'I want you in your Horowitz concert bow but can you try looking less hangdog?' she requested. 'Think Paderewski more.' To which end she loans him a frock coat once worn by a minor pianist whose name escapes her so she claims it to have been Paderewski's own to save explanations. Before they leave the house she runs her fingers through his hair.

'Imagine it's red,' she says. 'Think Polish maestro. Breathe fire. My sons think they're separated by an unbridgeable political gulf but, in truth, like all politicians in this country they're Little Englanders who go to pieces in the presence of Continental genius.'

Whether by chance or cunning, they arrive together. Sandy and Pen. The Princess has prepared Shimi for this meeting by telling him to think he's meeting Laurel and Hardy.

'Which is which?'

'You don't know what Laurel and Hardy look like?'

'Of course I do. What I don't know is which of your sons is Laurel and which is Hardy.'

'The greasy one is Laurel. The morose one—'

'No. Their names. Their parties.'

'You'll work it out.'

Though he knows she has sons beyond pensionable age, Shimi is surprised when he sees them in the flesh. Whichever is Laurel and whichever is Hardy they look older than their mother. He thinks he has seen them before, without knowing who they were, casing the Finchley Road like a pair of bailiffs. Now he must assume he was the reason for their presence. Having spent so much of his life underground, Shimi has a poor understanding of what's been going on in the world above. Being entirely without political preference, it pleases him to think that their divergent systems have come together in suspicion of him. But his ignorance of politics leaves him at sea when it comes to identifying them by ideology.

'I'm Shimi Carmelli,' he says, shaking their hands in turn. 'Your mother has told me all about you but I am unable to work out from your appearance who is the reactionary and who the revolutionary.'

'Well I am not the reactionary,' says Stan Laurel.

'And I am not the revolutionary,' says Oliver Hardy.

'Thank you, that narrows it down,' Shimi says.

'And you,' Sandy says, looking Shimi up and down, but finding it difficult to take his eyes off Shimi's virtuoso dicky bow and Paderewski frock coat, 'what would your politics be?'

'Anarchist,' Shimi says, remembering the Princess's instructions. 'But not a bomb thrower.'

The three men exchange rancid smiles. Not knowing what to say next they are all relieved when the Princess beckons Shimi to her side.

'Do you think we should ask for the windows to be opened?' she whispers. 'The air gets so stuffy with these two in a room.'

'I know you're saying that only to conceal your pride in them,' Shimi whispers back.

She leans in closer and mutters something he cannot make out. Then he realises she is deliberately speaking nonsense in order to exasperate her sons with a display of unbecoming intimacy. Is the old girl blowing in his ear?

Shimi wonders if he ought to reciprocate by blowing in hers. He moves in still closer, nodding, smiling, laughing at the gibberish.

They both get the real joke together: this could be a metaphor for their relationship.

And it's when they get the real joke together that they exasperate the brothers in earnest.

Shimi is momentarily sorry for them. It can't be any fun watching your mother canoodling with a man who isn't your father. How would he have felt? He thinks of the Princess with Ephraim. *That's* how he'd have felt.

He rises again and joins the brothers who take turns to bend and kiss their mother. 'You look radiant,' Sandy says. 'Imperious even,' Pen adds. 'And you both are looking frazzled,' she tells them. 'I hope the offices of state aren't demanding too much of you. Or at least I hope television isn't.' 'I haven't been on television for a fortnight,' Pen says. 'That's a mercy,' the Princess replies. 'A week without seeing you in a vest.'

Li Ling-the-younger is bringing round cocktails. 'My mother's favourite man,' she says touching Shimi's arm.

Shimi wishes she hadn't. The brothers swivel eyes at one another. So this man makes a habit of wooing mothers.

'Mother tells us you are an importer,' Sandy says.

'Was.'

'What did you import?'

'Games.'

'Video games?'

'A little more primitive than that.'

Another mistake, Shimi realises. A wild man, is he?

'And a card player of some sort,' Pen says.

Shimi observes that Pen tilts his head backwards and away when he speaks, like a well-bred dog refusing a poor-quality biscuit.

'No, not a player. For my own amusement, and occasionally at charity events to keep my hand in, I practise the ancient art of cartomancy.'

He won't say any more than that. Let them show their ignorance. Let them ask.

'I bought one of my grandchildren a tarot deck for Christmas,' Pen says, looking at the ceiling. 'Would that be similar?'

'If it's for children, no.'

'Do you have family yourself?' Sandy wonders.

'I have never married,' Shimi replies. He wonders whether to add that he had a brother. Ephraim. They must have met him. But thinks better of it. They might not like the idea of their mother being handed round from brother to brother.

'A bachelor gay, eh?' Sandy laughs, opening a dozen trapdoors.

Shimi shrugs. They will have to do better than that.

'Did you never meet the right woman?' Pen persists.

Damned if I did, Shimi thinks, damned if I didn't. 'I have lived a private life,' he says. 'I have kept myself to myself.'

'It must be difficult, in that case – after so long – to get used to the company of another person.'

'It depends on the other person.'

All three look over at the Princess, who is busying herself with the menu. Shimi hears her asking a waiter if there will be sweet-and-sour pork with Singapore noodles.

'Your mother,' Shimi summons the resolution to say, 'is a highly intelligent, tactful and penetrating woman. She is accomplished in the arts of . . .' He searches for a word. 'Cohabitation' springs to his lips but he swallows it. 'Accommodation,' he decides on finally. Then realises it sounds a little too much like real estate, which will be precisely what they're worried about. 'Adjustment, is what I mean. We understand each other very well. I have immense admiration for her. We place a high value on conversation. It is to us what physical exercise is to youngsters like you. I imagine you are both members of a gym in Westminster. Well, we talk. It keeps the motors turning over. We assist each other with words. More than that, she makes me laugh.'

'Our mother makes you laugh!'

'Yes. Doesn't she you?'

The direct appeal confounds them. Pen withdraws his head. Sandy blows out his cheeks.

'Then it must be my sense of humour,' Shimi concedes. 'Her jokes are hellish, of course. And I can see that growing up with them might have been difficult. I have the advantage of coming to them late.'

'Forgive me, but the disadvantage of your coming to them late,' Pen says, 'is that you might have missed the best of one another.'

'We think we are at the perfect age to enjoy a verbal friendship.'

'It isn't so much the verbal part . . .' Sandy begins.

Shimi opens his eyes wide. You shock me, they say.

Sandy lays a hand on his arm. 'I don't mean that.'

'What I think Sandy means,' Pen says, then isn't sure how quite to put what Sandy means.

Shimi helps them out. 'Who will look after us when we fall ill? More particularly, who will look after me? I am grateful for your concern, but I have the means not to be a liability to your mother . . . or you.'

It is at this point that the second tranche of guests arrive – the children's children, the first, second and thirdborn of Laurel and Hardy, the pampered generation of plentifulness who are no more certain why they're here than their grandmother is as to who they are. It is plain to Shimi, from the way they take him in and recite their names – bending exaggeratedly from the waist, enunciating plainly and wreathing him in watchful smiles – that they are performing a duty for their fathers akin to canvassing deaf voters in an assisted-living facility.

'Shimi Carmelli,' Shimi says, extending a hand to each of them in turn. They take it as though through the bars of a zoo.

I might as well be the last giant panda in captivity to them, Shimi thinks. They have come to watch me breed with their grandmother.

To Shimi they are as zoo creatures themselves, sleek and well-groomed, the men as shiny as alligators, the women exclusive and finely poised like black flamingos. Nastya, who is taking photographs with her mobile phone, allows her mouth to fall open. The Princess fans herself with her boa. 'The poor child is beside herself with excitement,' she says to Shimi. 'She could tell you who's designed every pair of shoes and every handbag. There are people here she's seen on daytime television.'

That they are known to one another is hardly a surprise: they are family. But they strike Shimi, from the way they embrace and peck, as being professionally close too. *How is it going?* they enquire. And there's no need to ask how *what's* going. It's all good news. *Yes, no, really well.* Light bounces from one to another.

The Princess beckons him to her again. 'These are our future,' she says, half-hoping to be overheard. 'Aren't you glad we don't have one?'

'I don't have the words for what I'm seeing,' Shimi says. 'This is another country.'

'No, it's the same country. It's just that you've been away from it too long. You should make peace with it now you're here. Don't bolt again.'

'I've no intention of bolting,' he says.

He loses his hand inside the foliage of her boa and squeezes her shoulder. Sad, the thinness of it. They don't touch one another too often in order to avoid just such thoughts.

'Shall we eat before we make our announcement?' she asks him.

'I didn't know we were making an announcement.'

'Then let's go straight to the food.'

She raps the table with a knife. 'Sit down everybody,' she orders. 'And thank you for not minding that I don't know who you are.'

Whatever is or isn't said over the next three-quarters of an hour Shimi will defeat his hyperthymesia and forget. Because what happens after that is enough, in his estimation, to effect what he has hoped for all his adult life and wipe the whole slate of human memory clean.

'Ah, here he is,' the Princess whispers, as though Shimi has been expecting someone, though Shimi has been expecting no one. Led by Raymond, the late guest, a broadly smiling man in his late middle years, makes his way half-apologetically to the table. He is known to everyone present other than Shimi, except that something about him is known to Shimi too. What is it? The shape of his face? The swarthiness? The grin?

He bends to kiss the Princess, whom he calls Mother, and inclines his head respectfully to Shimi.

'I'm Tahan,' he says.

'This one I know,' the Princess proclaims. 'He is the last of my brood, and the only one worth your time. He is Ephraim's boy. Tahan, meet your Uncle Shimi.'

4

After the twelve months of saying Kaddish for his wife had elapsed, Manolo Carmelli took his sons to the cemetery for the unveiling of the headstone. It was a simple stone, bearing just her name in English and Hebrew, the dates of her birth and death, and the names of the three men she'd left behind. Darling Wife to—Beloved Mother of—

It was a simple ceremony too – a prayer in Hebrew, a few words from Manolo about his love for her, and embraces with members of the family. Shimi and Ephraim went along the line of their mother's sisters to be hugged by each of them in turn. It was like a penance. Had they done wrong? Shimi couldn't speak for Ephraim, but he certainly had. His aunts' tears ran down his face. He didn't attempt to dry them. Let them burn holes in his cheeks.

When they left it was as though their mother had abandoned them for a second time. Shimi had not imagined there could exist so annulled and vacated a place.

Manolo stood with his arms around the shoulders of his sons – yes, even Shimi's – and together they listened to gates closing and voices dying away.

'I would like to sit quietly with you for a while,' he said.

There was a plain wooden bench opposite but he wanted the three of them to sit together at the grave.

'It's cold, I know,' he said. He didn't feel he had to add, 'So imagine what it's like for her.'

If heat rises, Shimi wondered, does cold fall. There are said to be fires in the centre of the earth, but does the temperature drop before you get that far down? And how far down was she?

The boys sat motionless, shoulder to shoulder. Amid the stones they could have been stone themselves. Two more mute offerings on Sonya Carmelli's grave.

No flowers. No relief from stone. No bells. No birds. No illusions of rebirth. Dead meant dead. Shimi thought he would die himself. The company of his father and his brother only increased his loneliness. Who wanted to be reminded that no one could help anyone?

'Are you all right, Dad?' Ephraim asked.

Manolo said nothing for a while. Then he said, 'No, I'm not. I'm not sure there is an all right for me now. But how have you both been? You have been neglected, for which I'm sorry. I didn't think you'd want to see the mess I'm in.'

Shimi thought about saying 'Maybe we could have helped.' But it was Ephraim who actually said it.

Manolo shook his head. 'You two were everything to her. If I'd seen more of you it would have reminded me of what she'd lost. She lived for you. She would have kept you by her side for the duration of the war and another hundred years after that if she'd been able to. She'd have locked you away with her and turned the lights off. "If anything happens to those boys it will kill me," she used to say. But nothing did happen and she died anyway. Where's the fairness in that?'

'Nothing's fair,' Shimi said.

Manolo ignored him. Shimi said what Shimi said.

Ephraim wondered if it had been wrong of him to have spent so much time out of the house. Had he only added to her worries?

'Yes, it added to her worries, but she understood that that was what being a mother entailed. "You know, I sometimes feel I'm out with him, shooting German warplanes down," she used to say. "That's a part of me out there. He's me without my terrors. It's such a privilege, having a child. A frightening privilege, but a privilege. You

266

become more than the person you ever thought you were." She supposed I didn't understand her because I was impatient with that kind of talk. I thought it made the family a chain with too many weak links. Too many places where we could break. But I did understand her. When you have a child you multiply yourself. And if you are the mother of a son you are multiplied ten times over.'

Shimi didn't say – well, he didn't say a thousand things – but in particular he didn't say 'So would I have multiplied her more had I gone running out into the night with a toy rifle over my shoulder, instead of . . .'

But Manolo heard him think it. Another way that having a child increased you: it gave you the power to detect the unexpressed. Like love, it made a psychic of you. Only you couldn't switch it off or transfer it, as you could love. You went on hearing until one of you became a thing of stone. Manolo was referring primarily to his wife – she heard far more of what her sons were feeling and fearing than he did. Something trilled along the blood for her. But he heard some of it. Maybe not enough – and not all of what he heard he liked – but some. He partook of parenthood without being the whole deal. He could shut his ears. He was a father.

But he could hear what Shimi wasn't saying today, holding himself together against the cold, holding back tears, not wanting to give himself away. Manolo liked Ephraim far better than he liked Shimi, but for his poor dear wife's sake he strained to hear Shimi's distress. And, for his poor dear wife's sake, regretted that he hadn't been able to like him more.

'It wasn't just wildness your mother was talking about,' he said with consideration, 'it was an adventure for her simply to wonder what was going on in your heads. "Who are these boys?" she'd ask me. "What a miracle we made them!" She was one of those women who had to have children. No, she wasn't well organised. She lost track of time. She didn't know your timetables off by heart the way some mothers do, didn't always remember to cook you meals on time or wash your clothes. Efficiency was never her style. That was what I loved about her. She was never complete. She needed a sort of mothering — no, a fathering — herself. But she loved the idea of issuing in you, of discovering who she was in you, of becoming someone else even. "I am better for those boys," she used to tell me. "I don't know what you saw in me in the beginning, but you should see far more in me now." And I did. I loved her twice as much for the mother in her.'

They stayed until it grew dark. If they froze, they froze.

Some time after, perhaps because the reverberations of his sons' frozen grief had grown too loud to bear, or because he could no longer live with his own, Manolo disappeared into the night.

Regardless of what had become of him, Shimi and Ephraim went on discussing what he'd told them. Was it true, they wondered, what he said about their mother? She had seemed a half-hearted, almost absent mother to them. Yes, she was a loving, adoring mother even, but only when she remembered to be, when she was able to forget what was troubling her — all those fears, all that fragility, her own sense of her unfitness to be a mother, who could say what it was? The memory of wolves in the Carpathians, maybe. That was not a complaint. They would not dare complain about her in each other's hearing — especially not now they'd seen the icy, unfeeling sepulchre in which she lay. But they didn't recognise their father's fulsome panegyric on motherhood. To them it seemed that children had been the wrong route for her, that she was naturally a more tremulous, isolated person and would have been happier not to be multiplied at all. A person didn't have to extend in every direction. There was such a thing as being sufficient unto oneself. No shame attached to it. So had she lied to her husband to spare his feelings? Or was he lying about what she'd said to spare theirs?

'True or not true, I haven't got the heart to have children myself,' Ephraim said.

'That's now speaking,' Shimi replied. 'I haven't got the heart for anything now either. The difference is – one day *you* will. The memory of her will fade and you'll be yourself again – a lover of life. I know you, Ephraim. I've watched you march out into the world, in love with the very wind in your face. How many times have you pulled me out of bed shouting "Get up, get up! You're missing the day"? And how many times have I told you where to put your day?'

'What does this have to do with anything? I love to be alive for the sake of being alive, not to pass it on to someone else. Do I want to be pulling another person out of bed so they don't miss the day? It's been enough trying to do it with you. And I failed there. Whatever was true for Ma, it isn't true for me that I'd have no life without an extended me to care for. I'm more than enough for me. Besides, do you want to load a kid with the responsibility of living for you?'

'I don't, but you're not me. You have more to go round. You don't shy away from stuff like responsibility. You don't faint.'

'Are you saying you faint so as to avoid responsibility? I've never heard that one before. I thought you fainted because you were super sensitive.'

'I faint because it's hot. I faint from family heat.'

'You want cold? I'll tell you where you can find cold. Go and lie next to her.'

'That's a shit thing to say. You know what I'm talking about.'

'No, I don't. You tell me.'

'Human relations. That sort of hot.'

'Christ, Shim, *human relations*!'

'Monkeys in a zoo, Eph.'

'We're not in a zoo.'

'Cats in a litter then.'

'We're not in a litter either.'

'Yes, we are. Have you ever put your mind to what it would be like to be a Siamese twin? All that heat, Eph. Imagine it. As though it's not tough enough having a younger brother, spying on you every minute.'

'I am not your Siamese twin.'

'Only just, you're not.'

'And I have never spied on you.'

'Haven't you?'

'No, I haven't.'

Leave it, Shimi. 'Well, you might not mean to but you spy just by being there. We all do. It's called family.'

'Then don't have one.'

'I won't.'

'Nor me.'

They shook on it.

And now he is holding Ephraim's son in his arms.

5

Beryl Dusinbery is working on her vows. Euphoria is running in and out of the kitchen with suggestions. She is in high spirits. She knew things were going to work out well for Mrs Beryl from the night of the Widows' Ball when she saw Mr Carmelli being carried into the guest room more dead than alive.

As she has been advised not to interrupt the Princess's thoughts she silently deposits slips onto the desk at which the Princess sits.

'I can't guarantee I'll read any of these, let alone include them,' the Princess says. 'But I want you to know how highly I esteem your efforts.'

Euphoria curtsies, as she's been taught to do when attending the Palace, and says it's an honour just to be allowed to enter submissions.

Every now and then, as a way of breaking from her own labours, the Princess sneaks a look at what Euphoria has deposited.

One she particularly likes is, 'I choose you better than all other men because I tell off my carers less when you are in the house.'

Another, with which Euphoria must surely have been given assistance – she suspects the Queen's hand – reads

> Though all the world ignore us,
> You alone are my thesaurus.

A third, in which the Princess promises to give all her cooking pots and both her goats to Mr Carmelli provided he agrees never to stick pins into dolls made in her likeness, she takes to be a spoof on the Princess's imperialist assumptions. In this she detects the hand of Nastya.

Her own vows are not progressing well. At moments of significance in her life she has always turned to literature, but in the past those moments have been tragic or at the worst tragicomic. She has no light touch in herself and no taste for it in others. Those happier works by South American fantasists and minor English essayists that might have given her inspiration for her vows she is not acquainted with. As a result, a leaden bookishness is marring all she writes. She has transcribed and torn up half the sonnets of Shakespeare, most of *Antony and Cleopatra,* and all of Catherine Earnshaw's speech to Nellie Dean. 'Nellie, I am Shimi Carmelli,' neither scans nor convinces.

From time to time she leaves her desk and walks to the guest room, as it is still called, where she finds Shimi lying fully clothed on the bed chewing a pencil.

She has yet to see him in pyjamas and comments on this every time she thinks pyjamas are what he ought to be in.

'It's an intimacy too far,' he says.

'Will it always be?'

'I'm not sure. I'm not planning my wardrobe too far ahead.'

'And how are you going with your vows?'

'I'm making them in my head.'

'What about on paper?'

'Are you afraid I will forget them?'

'You? No. The day you forget something the earth will forget to turn. But in case anything should happen to you I'd like to know where they are.'

'I've told you. In my head.'

'But in case anything should happen to your head . . .'

'In such an event you won't be needing vows.'

'I take this to mean you are not making progress.'

'I do this kind of thing better in a bathroom,' he confesses.

'This kind of thing?'

'Thinking.'

'Then do it in the bathroom.'

'I can't face negotiating the Finchley Road.'

She shrugs her shoulders. Hadn't she told him it would be so. 'Are you telling me that even a temporary bathroom on this side of the road won't work for thinking in?'

'It's not ideal,' he says.

The Princess had, after all, made her announcement before guests left the Fing Ho Banquet Restaurant.

Shimi was not there. He was walking the streets with Tahan, who would have dearly liked to sit and talk but Shimi couldn't trust himself to look into the eyes of Ephraim's son without making an idiot of himself. He held Tahan's hand as they walked. Had he ever done such a thing with Ephraim, when they were little? Had he ever held hands with anybody? He didn't feel fatherly; he felt what he was: avuncular. Uncle Raffi had showed him how to do that.

For the first half mile they never spoke.

It was Shimi who cracked first. 'This is so—'

'I know,' Tahan said.

Whereupon silence fell again for another half mile.

The Princess was glad that Shimi wasn't there. As she wrote in her diary later there were things she could say without him she would not otherwise have dared . . .

Scared of him, am I? Unlikely. I'm not one of his Widows who think he's Ivan the Terrible because he looks down in the dumps and wears a fur hat. You don't take a man at his own valuation, whatever it is. You Jane, me Tarzan. You Jane, me Jane. Same difference. They don't know who they're meant to be. Shimi the Not-So-Terrible in his mother's drawers judged himself by standards of masculinity worn out even then.

Leave yourself alone, I tell him. Which means I must leave him alone too. I saw his face when I called him my 'intended'. Fear in his eyes. What's she going to do with me now? He wants me to run the show but doesn't know who I'm showing him to or why. All things considered, he held himself together very well.

So there you are, then. I'm not scared of him, I'm scared for him.

Now, with Mr Carmelli and his feelings out of the way, I can say what I want to say without having to take him into account. 'My intended' is how I refer to him in my address to Laurel and Hardy's assembled progeny, whereupon they make sounds like fireworks going off. Could have been an American Primary. I haven't told you what I intend doing with him yet, I go on – which was his joke, but then what's his is mine now – and they stamp and hoot again. All but Stan and Ollie, of course, who can't be happy for me. I don't blame them. I taught them how not to be happy for me.

I know what you're all thinking, I say. 'Another of her mistakes.' But let me ask you this: where would any of you be but for my mistakes? So what if this is one more? I have to go on doing what I do. I can't claim to have learnt anything. It's not wisdom you need at my age, it's luck. And I've had the devil's luck . . .

You will by now, I hope, have had the opportunity to make the acquaintance of what the devil sent me – my unexpected man.

They look around to see where he is. I don't tell them he is out on the night with the last blood relation he has in the whole wide world and never knew he had him until tonight. I don't want to hear one of those collective 'Ahs!' I feign bashfulness for him instead. He hates the lime-light and has never before been anyone's intended. Been waiting for Miss Right all this time. And along I come. So he too is in luck.

They all say 'Ah!' anyway.

Here I went into an uncharacteristic reverie. In Mr Carmelli, let me tell you, I have met a man better than all the others – no offence intended – in that, if for no other reason, he considers himself worse. You will grasp that I don't mean to demean him – far from it – when I say he is the only adult male I've ever met who doesn't doubt he's half the time ridiculous. When I said as much to him – for we are nothing if not candid with each other – he replied that I was the only woman he'd ever met who didn't mind.

Laurel and Hardy came to kiss me afterwards. We hope it all works out well for you this time, Mother, they lied. I let the Chinese cocktails loosen my tongue. 'What would either of you know about this time or the last,' I said. 'You represent a defunct principle.'

'We belong to separate parties,' Pen thought he had to remind me. I could have wept for him. He was as cloth-eared and dull of tongue as his father.

I took him by one of his cloth ears. 'Who's talking politics? You represent a defunct principle of maleness.'

Just don't ask me what the new principle is.

Oh, and to round the evening off in style the Moldovan whore takes a group picture on her mobile phone. I suspect she is still selling photographs to Laurel and Hardy. I admire her business initiative. It shows Eastern Europe is changing.

'Say cheeses,' she says.

I suggest they say Beryl Carmelli for a broader smile.

6

Later that night the Princess had invited Shimi to sit by her bed so they could debrief each other on the evening's events. He had given her time to settle herself in bed, so she was sitting up when he arrived, wearing an innocently embroidered bedjacket tied in black ribbons at her neck. Innocent in the sense that it bore as yet no mention of death. He sat down on the heavy Maharajah chair, his dicky bow untied so that it hung loose like a Mississippi gambler's.

'Quite a night,' they both said together.

The next thing they knew it was morning.

'My God,' the Princess cried when she woke to find Shimi sitting still half asleep in the Maharajah chair with his dicky bow untied, 'we've spent the night together!'

Thereafter, she made a habit of calling him in.

One evening, Shimi returns to the walk he had taken with Tahan. He has been fairly reticent about it so far, pleading emotional exhaustion. The discovery of a nephew he never knew he had has affected him so strongly, he says, that he is yet to collect his impressions. There is no hurry, the Princess assures him, but he has a question.

'What could Tahan have meant,' he asks, 'by describing you as generous?'

'In what context?'

'In the context of your relations.'

'You mean my sons?'

'No, I mean your relations with each other.'

'You didn't think to ask him yourself?'

'I was embarrassed to.'

'Because?'

'For the reason I am always embarrassed to ask questions. I don't want to show the degree of my ignorance.'

'Well you know what they say? If you don't ask . . .'

'Which is why I'm asking you.'

'Why he thought me generous? Do you think me ungenerous?'

'Why he would use such a strange term to describe his mother. Loving, I'd understand. Close. Adoring . . .'

'You needn't go on. I don't think I can bear listening to you searching for words to describe a mother. The reason Tahan didn't sound like a man referring to his mother is that I'm not.'

'You aren't Tahan's mother?'

'What made you think I was?'

'You introduced him as the best of your brood.'

'A figure of speech. I brought him up.'

Shimi falls silent.

'So he is not your child with Ephraim?'

'Oh, you brothers, you brothers! How often must I tell you? I don't remember whether Ephraim and I were ever lovers. Those you sleep with only to sleep with you remember because there's nothing to forget. Where you feel more it is not so simple. You can inhabit a borderline of desire sometimes, and neither go across nor back. Even when your memory is in perfect working order you won't be able to describe exactly how far you ventured in either direction.'

'That's not a condition I recognise.'

'No, I'm sure you don't. That's because when you see a border you retreat from it. But we're talking about me now. And one thing I can be sure about is that I never bore your brother a child.'

'So who did?'

'I don't know.'

(The gypsy, Shimi thinks. Ephraim stole her caravan, then he stole her honour.)

'Didn't he tell you?'

'He must have but I don't remember. Who cares?'

(Definitely the gypsy.)

'Who cares? Maybe the mother cares. Maybe Tahan cares.'

'I know mothers are your subject but why are you concerning yourself with Tahan's? Did he complain to you of feeling orphaned?'

'There was hardly time for that. We had a lot of ground to cover.'

'Such as my generosity. It sounds a strange conversation.'

'Of course it was a strange conversation.

'I hope you aren't displeased you met him?'

'How could I be?'

'But I can see you are displeased with me. Why?'

'Because you didn't tell me he existed earlier.'

'I had to ask him how he felt about meeting you. He was out of the country. Unlike you and me he does good deeds in foreign places. And I wasn't always sure how you'd feel about meeting him.'

'So you weren't planning to drop this bombshell on me from the start?'

'I don't have much of a memory for starts. But no. It crept upon me that I would have to do it. That I couldn't not. You wouldn't have wanted me not?'

'No. I wouldn't. But it's still not clear to me what happened. If he isn't yours – did Ephraim just deposit him on you?'

'In a basket? No. It's a nice thought – the Pharaoh's daughter – I have the cobra headdress – but that wasn't the way it happened. I took him when Ephraim presented him to me, no questions asked. I owed Ephraim many favours. And Tahan was – as Ephraim presented him to me anyway – a motherless child.'

'But you weren't exactly a childless mother.'

Now it is her turn to fall silent.

'Wasn't I?' The pause is interminable. 'So soon – have you forgotten my confidences so soon? You with your amazing memory.'

He reddens furiously, recalling the picture she'd painted of herself as a mere girl, pushing her pram of discontent across those barren moors. You are not a fit mother, her aunt had said, and she'd agreed.

Yes, she'd brought Laurel and Hardy into the world since, but you can't expiate the sin of giving away one child by the simple expedient of having more.

She never never saw the boy again, she'd told him and Shimi, sorrowing for her, had wondered how long never never was. No distance by the measure of his compassion.

'I'm sorry,' he says. 'My mouth runs away with me.'

It's not my mouth that's at fault, he thinks, any more than it's my memory – it's my soul. I have time for no one's mortifications but my own.

She knows what's going through his burning head. She can see into it.

'Look on the bright side,' she says.

'There is no bright side.'

'The blushing boy in you is still alive.'

'I want the boy in me to be dead.'

'You shouldn't. Besides, it would appear that I am still able to shock you. That means you owe me one now.'

'What makes you think I have any shocks in me remaining?'

'There will always be shocks in you remaining . . .'

So, so . . .

So, because it's safer living in the heart of his shames than anywhere else, he tells her about the fragment of humanity in the wheelchair who once – outside a public latrine – begged the most intimate of favours. A fellow wretch. 'I'm desperate, please help me.' The mouth malodorous and clotted. The stench of rotting body. 'It's when I get inside that I can't manage.' *Manage!*

Who turns to Shimi when they can't *manage*? Can't they see what he is?

So what did you do? the Princess asks.

He is surprised she needs to.

'Do you really want to know?'

'Do you really want not to tell me?'

279

'What I really want is for the earth to open—'

'Yes, yes,' she says, 'I've heard all that. You're always wanting the earth to open. It's time you accepted that it never will. Just tell me what you did.'

'I turned my back on him and ran,' he says.

It bears repeating. *I turned my back on him and ran.*

She looks at him long and hard, then beckons him to her. He kneels by her bed, a small boy waiting for his telling-off.

She takes hold of his head. A gentle hand on each temple. She could be holding a crystal ball.

'What are you doing?' he asks.

'I'm stopping the stuff falling out.'

She wonders if with his ears blocked he can hear the music of the spheres.

Neither has any idea how long she holds him for. A minute, an hour, a duration yet to be discovered.

'Now I'll do it for you,' he says, removing her hands a finger at a time.

'Oh, it's too late for me,' she says. 'Most of the stuff's fallen out of me long ago.'

He reminds her of her own words – it's never too late for anything.

Then he places a hand first on one temple, then the other. Like a child holding on to something infinitely precious entrusted to his care.

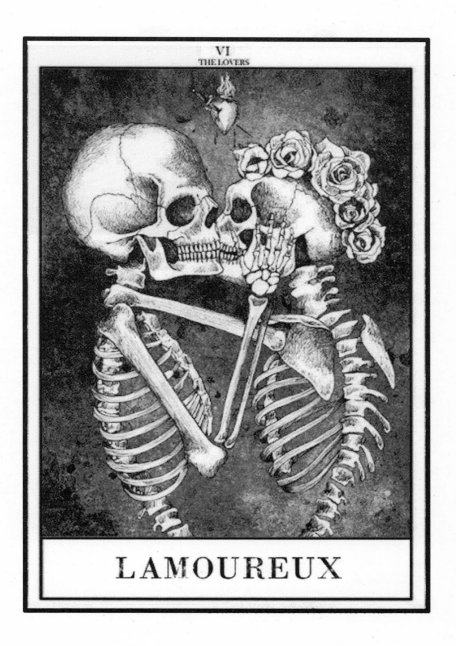